Cherish
ON THE CAPE

USA TODAY BESTSELLING AUTHOR
MK MEREDITH

This book is a work of fiction. Names, characters, places, and incidents are the product of the author's imagination or are used fictitiously. Any resemblance to actual events, locales, or persons, living or dead, is coincidental.

MK Meredith
P.O. Box 1724
Ashburn, VA 20146
Visit my website at www.mkmeredith.com.

Edited by KR Nadelson and Jessica Snyder
Cover design by Kari March Designs

ISBN: 978-0-9990854-5-5
Manufactured in the United States of America
First Edition August 2018

INTRODUCTION

Hello!

I am so thrilled to share my happy ever afters with you, and I hope you love this book! If you haven't yet, enjoy your introduction to the wonderful town of Cape Van Buren with *One Jingle or Two* **FREE** on all e-retailers. Once you fall in love with Alora and Nate (they're irresistible, LOL!), you won't want to leave.

Which makes me so excited to offer you the opportunity to meet Blayne and Jamie! Just sign up to my mailing list, and I'll send *Honor on the Cape* to your email for download to your favorite reading device!

BTW . . . all of my series are inter-connected.

Hugs, loves, & peanut butter!
MK

To my marketing guru and all around cheerleader,
Kerrie Legend.
Your designs are inspired and your passion contagious.
Thank you!

CHAPTER 1

"*P*enis."

Claire Adams choked on her wedding champagne, the fine bubbles racing into her nose with a burn as she stole a furtive glance over her shoulder at the crowd of people. The Fountain of Youth in Van Buren Square had been transformed into a glittering wonderland with gleaming silver candelabras topped with sparkling crystal globes, and the stage and seating areas were currently filled to the brim with the citizens of Cape Van Buren for the wedding of Blayne MacCaffrey and James Astor III.

Finally.

Their wedding was both ten years late and right on time.

The legend surrounding the Fountain of Youth, of explorers searching the northeast coast for its magical healing waters, must be true because nothing else could explain the miracle that brought the pair back together again.

"Maxine! What is wrong with you?" Claire whispered with an intensity she prayed would keep the woman quiet. But what was the saying? On a hope and a prayer? Everybody knew Maxine Van Buren, the previous owner of the Cape and infamous master of nature's finest moonshine, said and did whatever the hell she pleased.

Even at weddings.

Smoothing her silver houndstooth dress, the woman downright snorted.

1

Loud.

With her sleek silver strands swinging just past the edge of her jaw, she flashed a grin.

Seeing the sophisticated woman act like a bar-back always took Claire off guard. Something she was long past due to get over. Claire handed her flute over to a passing waiter in exchange for a mini canning jar of moonshine brewed especially for this night. Maybe she'd handle the easy flow of Maxine's specialty better than the bubbles.

"That's my point, young lady. There's nothing wrong with me. I get a wicked big dose of penis anytime I want, but you've been so celibate, you make the Desert of Maine look like a tropical rainforest."

Claire sniffed, hoping the soft glow of candlelight masked the heat flushing her cheeks. "Shows what you know. That area gets plenty of precipitation." She cringed at the petulant tone in her voice.

Maxine's eyes twinkled. "Oh, so you're all wet then? For Mitch Brennan, I'm guessing."

Just the sound of the man's name made Claire's heart race and palms sweat...in annoyance, of course. He was Mother Nature's ironic joke, looking like the perfect man to take home and introduce to the parents but about as likely to commit as a bull moose—they both courted a harem of willing females, but Mitch's mating season lasted all year long.

"Ohmigod." Grabbing Maxine by the arm, she dragged her toward a cluster of potted palms that were dripping with twinkle lights. Etta James belted the ending to "At Last" in the background while Blayne and Jay swayed together on the dance floor. "Don't you think it's a bit hypocritical to complain about my lack of..." She gritted her teeth to force out the word but lifted her nose instead. "After the talking-to you gave the judge, you're not foolin' anybody. You haven't gotten any since before the gala."

As soon as the words were out of her mouth, she wished on every star in the Maine sky that she could have taken them all back.

But it was clearly too late for that now.

"You must have lost the taste for my moonshine." Maxine slipped the jar from Claire's fingers and downed it. After setting it on a passing tray, she crossed her arms over her bosom and eyed Claire with such a deadly stare she was surprised her legs hadn't run off and abandoned her.

"I'm sorry. I..."

Maxine raised a brow.

"There you are. We've been looking all over for you." One of her best friends, Larkin Van Buren, Maxine's new granddaughter-in-law and the main driving force behind the Archer Conservation Park of Cape Van Buren, broke through the crowd, then placed a kiss on Maxine's cheek.

Whew! Thank God for best friends with *impeccable* timing. Claire was so relieved she wanted to throw her arms around Larkin. But she settled instead for flashing her a warm smile.

Her friend was positively radiant in her emerald strapless pantsuit with the sweetheart neckline and faux fur wrap. Claire eyed her with the slightest sting of envy, then with a small wistful sigh, her gaze drifted to Blayne and Jamie still on the dance floor and in each other's arms. At least her two closest girlfriends got their happy-ever-afters.

Following the tragic car accident that took Larkin's first husband and little boy, Archer, along with Claire's fiancé, it had been impossible to imagine either of them ever seeing "happy" again.

Now here they were. Larkin blissfully married with a new baby girl and badass Blayne gliding about the stage with hearts practically floating around her head.

Claire was ecstatic for them both.

Truly.

But she'd be lying if she said she didn't feel more alone now than ever. It'd be another lie if she pretended anything else was even remotely possible. The last thing she'd ever put herself through was falling in love again. Losing the man of her dreams and her unborn child was enough loss for a lifetime. She could never survive that kind of pain again. Attachments weren't for her.

Ryker Van Buren, Larkin's husband and Maxine's grandson, and his buddy, attorney Mitch Brennan, followed close behind and were deep in conversation, snapping Claire out from under the threatening cloud of despair. They made quite a pair, both well over six feet tall and standing with shoulders about as wide.

Great, just what she needed. She pretended to watch the dance floor, hoping her racing heart would ease.

Mitch rubbed her the wrong way, and the feeling was more than mutual. His arrogant, playboy attitude set her off with a simple glance, and the jerk seemed to relish goading her. It was a miracle when they could get through any communication without throwing barbs, providing endless entertainment for their friends on more than one occasion.

Maxine shot Claire a look of triumph and turned toward their new audience. "Claire here was just telling me about how she isn't in a dry spell at all. In fact, now that Mitch is here, I believe her when she says she's actually quite we—"

"Penis!" Claire blurted out the word much louder than she'd intended.

Both Ryker and Mitch went silent along with Larkin and Maxine, and all four pairs of eyes rotated toward her with the slow motion of shock and awe.

She tilted her head, unable to comprehend what the hell her mouth was doing and wishing it would stop. With a concentrated effort, she refused to look at Mitch, or admire how well his suit jacket stretched over his impossibly broad shoulders or how his thighs looked positively sinful encased in the rich fabric of his slacks. It was so annoying that an arrogant man like him would be so finely built. And that Maxine was right. She *was* in a dry spell.

One she wouldn't risk her heart to break.

Larkin chuckled. "What did we miss?"

"Nothing," Claire stated. "Your friend over here." She jerked her chin toward the older woman. "Is threatening to deny me any moonshine."

"Please. What Claire means to say is she has a hard time saying penis because she hasn't gotten any in years, I'd guess."

Ryker, with his dark hair and intense frown, took a step back with the familiar, panicked look of a grandson who'd seen and heard too much and grabbed Larkin's wrist. "Save me, please."

Larkin's eyes twinkled, but she nodded that happy, indulgent smile of a woman hopelessly in love as she followed her husband to the dance floor.

Mitch drained his champagne glass. "I can help you with that."

"That's what I'm talking about," Maxine exalted, clapping him on the arm.

If eyes could actually pop out of a head, Mitch almost accomplished just that, and his expression was so mortified that Claire struggled between hilarity and offense.

"I didn't mean my penis, er, me. Fuck. Maxine!" He threw her an accusing glare.

Claire looked for an escape from the whole torturous conversation as her feisty friend peppered them with her jubilant laughter.

Could this night get any worse?

Blayne and Jamie were still on the dance floor, weaving in and out of the tall space heaters that looked like lamp posts as one love song ran into another. They'd be no help anytime soon. Her good-for-nothing friends were awful wingwomen now that they were happily coupled. Shit.

Clearing his throat, Mitch continued. "What I mean is, I can help you get back into the dating world. Offer advice, tips, and tricks. Ya know…"

Claire's jaw dropped, then she snapped it closed, refusing to intensify her humiliation. "I'd rather sit through one of Clint Fenwick's lectures on morality than take advice from you, thank you very much." Clint was the self-professed moral compass of Cape Van Buren, keeping his nose in everyone's business—for the sake of the town, of course.

"Which is exactly why you haven't been dating," Mitch said.

Claire put her hands on the ice-blue silk of her dress where it skimmed her hips and faced him straight on, which was a mistake. She had to force her brain to remember her words when looking at him this closely. Damn, was the man sexy as hell. It *totally* wasn't fair.

But what really wasn't fair was probably how much she resented his carefree attitude with relationships. Love was to be cherished, not played with. True love was rare, a gift, and she couldn't stand to see it treated like a party favor.

And that was the thing, she thought, eying his long, solid form with one leisurely sweeping glance.

He didn't love, he played. And she bet he did it damn well with all the practice he'd gotten. "I'm not dating because I don't want to," she returned.

Suddenly, she and Mitch were being propelled to the dance floor.

"Hey!" She tried resisting, but Blayne's joy-filled face stopped her just short of cussing. "It's the singles dance." Looking every bit the glowing bride with her stunning 1920's vintage wedding dress, upswept jet-black hair, and berry-red lips, Blayne kissed the air by Claire's cheeks before stepping to the edge of the dance floor with an expectant look.

Claire, Mitch, and a handful of other singles from Cape Van Buren stood with confused expressions, having been herded onto the dance floor like a bunch of the cattle down at the Somerset Auction.

The blonde bombshell triplets quickly staked their claims, one of whom beelined for Mitch. A look of horror widened his eyes, and he snatched Claire's hips in his large hands, the sudden contact sending a spark of pleasure straight through her limbs.

"What're you doing?" She tried to push him away, but he only drew her closer.

"Saving myself, that's what."

His deep, husky voice so close to her ear sent a shiver along her spine.

Moving into an easy sway, he slid one arm more firmly around her waist. The heat of his body radiated through her silk dress, leaving her restless and wanting. A very bad combination.

"Saving yourself? From a gorgeous blonde bombshell?" She chuckled. "I can never tell them apart, but they are women I'd think you'd run toward not from."

Mitch twirled them around the dance floor. "No way in hell I'm dancing with one of Coach Dawson's daughters. That man scared the crap out of me in high school, and he still scares me now."

Claire tried to listen to what he was saying, but his scent filled her head with images of hot, sexy nights that never ended. Which was dumb, because she would never date the guy even if her heart was available.

And she made no mistake thinking he'd ask her out either. They were like oil and water. So his fear of Coach Dawson must be real if he was choosing to dance with her.

She forced herself to concentrate on the music instead of how her body was on high alert with his closeness. "I figured you'd have made your way through each sister by now."

"Rude much?" he growled, then turned them around the edge of the dance floor once more to Melody Gardot's "Our Love is Easy," his movements fluid and steady.

Claire wanted to laugh. Nothing would be easy with this man—except an orgasm.

And that was a hot promise of fun you could use, my friend.

"Oh, shut up."

"No, you shut up," he gritted out, pulling her closer, making her very aware of his hard, flat abs. "You know, this is what I'm talking about. There's a reason you aren't dating, and it isn't because you're not drop-dead gorgeous. You're about as welcoming as the bees in Ryker's hives."

"What?" she asked, confused. "Wait a minute. Did you just call me rude?"

And drop-dead gorgeous? Now that she hadn't seen coming.

"And for the record, bees are just fine if you know how to handle them," she challenged.

His eyes narrowed to slits as if she had lost her mind. "Oh, I know how to handle anything. I'm dancing with you, aren't I?"

Indignation flared, but before she could form her retort, he continued. "You just told me to shut up. Are you really going to argue?"

"I did not, I..." Wait for a minute. Why the hell couldn't she keep her thoughts straight around this guy? Clearly, it was because he was so damn...annoying.

As the song came to an end, they passed Clint Fenwick standing shoulder-to-shoulder with Schmidty Ames, the owner of the South Cove Lobster House.

"Looks like Brennan's got his eyes set on the widow." This from Clint in a whisper that was anything but quiet.

It took a second for Claire to register he'd meant her, but there was no doubt Mitch understood if the sudden stiffening of his arms was any indication.

Clint was always boisterous with his opinions, but she hadn't realized he could be quite so ignorant with them. Besides, she wasn't technically a widow. Her fiancé died the night before their wedding. Either way, the man was a total ass for what he said. Whether she had her opinions about Mitch or not, to hear the comment from Fenwick at Blayne's wedding was unacceptable. Anger heated her cheeks.

Mitch stopped with the music and turned to face Fenwick.

Claire had to give him credit. He might back away from commitment, but he never did from a challenge.

Which would be more interesting than it had a right to be if she didn't find herself missing the feel of being in his arms. Maybe Maxine was right in taking the moonshine from her because something had seriously gone straight to her head.

7

"*D*o you mind repeating that to me, Mr. Fenwick?" Mitch kept his hands on Claire's tiny waist. For one thing, they fit around her perfectly, for another, if he let her go, he might throttle the man.

Though music still played in the background and the wedding guests were swaying to the romantic melody all around them, it was as if everything had morphed into slow motion for him. This was all he needed. Rumors to accompany the applicant package he was preparing for the city attorney seat.

Being an alleged womanizer was already doing wonders for his professional reputation, adding a public beating to his repertoire would be even better. The sarcasm of his thoughts choked him almost as much as he wanted to choke Fenwick.

"Now, don't go gettin' on, son. Just making conversation over here," Clint said, his arms crossed over the round protrusion of his burgundy vest.

They all stood at the edge of the stage, a dangerous place for a man throwing barbs, though he didn't seem to know it.

Thankfully, the rest of the party continued on around them with too many people and conversations to make out anything of value. The last thing Mitch needed was for the celebration to stop on account of this asshole.

He'd been hearing all about his so-called wild ways for years and was over it back when it had begun. People liked to talk, to judge, and the more negative they could make things seem, the better. Especially people like Clint.

As the man's words set in, Claire's face flushed red.

Clearly, the idea of anyone placing the two of them together mortified her. He had to shove down the rejection, surprised he even cared. Which, of course, he didn't. Not really. Though he usually loved a party, Mitch suddenly found himself exhausted from it all and craved a night with his feet kicked up by the fireplace back at the Cape house, Puzzle the house cat curled into a ball on his lap.

"Apologize to Claire," Mitch gritted out. It was one thing to gossip about his exploits, but to comment about Claire within earshot was insulting, and he wouldn't have it.

"Now, see here." Clint jerked his head to where Schmidty had been standing. "We were just making conversation. It's none of your concern."

The man's look of surprise was almost comical as he found himself standing all alone. Schmidty had melted back into the crowd as soon as the insolent words had left Clint's mouth.

"Is that so?" Mitch asked, taking a step closer.

"Aw, that was great!" Blayne rushed forward with the drunk-on-love look of a woman just married shining from her eyes. Oblivious to the tension, she kissed Mitch on the cheek, laughing as he rubbed it away to get rid of any lipstick left behind.

Jay joined her and clapped Mitch on the shoulder as they moved from the dance floor. "I don't think I realized you had such smooth moves on the dance floor, man. Though I should have guessed with the way you sail through the ladies."

And there it was again. Jay didn't mean anything by it, but the man had been back in town barely five months and had already joined the rest of the town on their opinion. Not one of them had it right.

Mitch rubbed his chin with a chuckle. "Yeah, you should know better by now." The truth of the matter was that he was more honest with any of the women he'd dated than anyone else in town. They knew from "hello" it was all about consensual pleasure, making a memorable moment, and not the beginning of anything long-lasting that would lead to a night like tonight.

One too many times seeing his fun-loving mother all alone, lost in thought and staring out the front bay window when she thought no one was looking after their father had walked out on them, was enough to keep him from ever putting himself in the position to cause the same damage. Where his sister, Mae, avoided relationships for fear of being hurt, he avoided them for fear of hurting someone. It was a family thing.

Janice Brennan was known for her red, bobbing curls, bright laughter, a nose for news and an eye for detail, not to mention the most beautiful gardens in Cape Van Buren.

But most important, she was the best mother a man could ever wish for.

Mitch let Jay's comment go. "Great wedding, man. You look happy."

Jay gave his wife a long, drawn-out once over, leaving Mitch to feel like a peeping Tom. "I am. She scared me there for a minute. But we were meant to be together. No one else works for me."

"Blayne's one of a kind, that's for sure," he agreed.

"It was easy to see no one else would work for her either," Blayne's father,

Noah McCaffrey, said as he joined the growing group. He smiled and listened to his son-in-law's words in the way a father did once he was assured his daughter was happy. He looked more like an indulgent Viking than an Irishman with his great white beard and hair poking out from under his usual paddy cap. "I'm happy you're both so happy, my boy."

Blayne gifted her dad's cheek with a kiss as well. "Aw, thanks, Da."

"What about you?" Jay directed the question back at Mitch, snatching a moonshine from a passing server, taking a sip. "When are you going to let one of the fine ladies of the Cape snag the infamous bachelor?"

Mitch glanced at where Claire and Blayne and now Larkin conspired in their low hum of whispers.

Now why in the hell would his eyes drift to Claire with her pert nose and kiss-me lips at that question? As God was his witness, she was sexy as hell in that damn dress that skimmed over her curves and left her back bare so that no matter where he'd settled his hands when they'd danced he felt the burning imprint of her silky soft skin.

But no way in hell was he going there.

He loved giving the woman a hard time—she often asked for it, with her sharp tongue saved solely for him—but more times than not, he did it to see the fire in her eyes instead of the quiet, aching loneliness that often resided there. And for that reason alone, he'd never consider dating her.

"Hell no. I'll leave that for you and Ryker. Besides, everyone already has me pegged as a terminal bachelor. No reason to let them down."

"They only think it because you taught them to."

Mitch snapped his head up. Had anyone asked, he'd have said the rumor was born from expectation, not the other way around.

His reputation with women really wasn't the problem, but it was the residual effects on his character in general that wreaked havoc for him on the professional front. He loved his work with the Archer Conservation Park of Cape Van Buren. It had instilled in him a greater sense of purpose and accomplishment than anything else he'd ever been involved with.

Which was why he'd jumped at the opportunity when Ryker approached him with a new project. It would help his chances to win the city attorney position, but there was more.

He wanted to feel that way again. That sense of deep satisfaction from making a difference. Being of service was an unexpected but fulfilling calling. He had opportunities elsewhere, Portland as a matter of fact, but the Cape is where he wanted to stay.

But when anyone in town needed help, they'd look right through him and call on someone else.

Someone like Claire.

This beautiful vixen might very well be a thorn in his side, but she was always doing for others. And he admired her for that. Among her various charitable pursuits, she helped the North Cove Mavens, a group of ladies who lived north of the Cape and sparred good-naturedly over superiority with the South Cove Madams. The feud's history was as old as the town itself. He wasn't clear on the specifics, just that it had something to do with two sisters who had lived on opposite sides of the town and a boy.

Typical.

Claire had turned her creativity and love of helping people into a solid business and planned Larkin's baby shower even in light of her own late-term miscarriage after her fiancé's death. She had also planned the wedding they were all enjoying this very minute.

He shook his head as he took in the edgy opulence of her design that fit both Blayne and Jamie to a 'T.'

But Jay's words poked at the back of his mind like a pitchfork against the logs of their high school bonfires, sending hot cinders of ideas floating about in his head. As innocent as they seemed, if you didn't pay attention to those damn white-hot ashes, they could start a fire.

He followed the long line of Claire's legs up past her hips and the impossibly tiny dip of her waist, past the straight line of her spine to the platinum hair topping her head like a damned halo. Her talent and artistic eye were never in question, but her candidacy as a viable dating prospect was.

No way in hell.

She was a woman to be cherished, long-term and steadfast.

He was just fast.

CHAPTER 2

*M*onday morning at the Cape house, Claire closed her eyes, blindly feeling for the smooth surface of the large piece of paper in front of her on the desk. Drunk on self-satisfaction, she grinned.

Blayne and Jay's wedding had been a huge success with multiple event requests coming in from a bar mitzvah to a twenty-fifth-anniversary party. As hard as they may be for her to attend, weddings were great for business. Everyone loved happy-ever-afters, and every detail that she'd put together for Blayne and Jay's big day, down to the red and black miniature roses in the centerpieces, acted as a living business card.

One more milestone for her friends, one more beautiful accomplishment in event planning for her. Blayne was married, Larkin had her new baby, and she had...

Her gaze roamed the front room of the Cape house where she looked forward to holding the art classes for local citizens—especially the kids. The new makeover was a mix of modern and nautical. Earthy tones of driftwood and rope weaved with the bright green of living plants and newly added seashells. It was a decor that invited guests to create their own beauty. Whether through the new bee-keeping club or her very own art program, the Cape was a place to heal and hope and find happiness.

She wanted to find her happy. And she would.

It might be so quiet in the large house that she could hear Puzzle's purr from the attic, but she had her programs at the Center. She had her purpose.

On a small sigh, she focused her concentration and, with a blue crayon and a light grip, drew lines with an easy flow. No premeditated direction, no meaning, just her feelings.

A soothing memory of a running brook filled the room, erasing time, and she lost herself in the ease of the movement. Her fiancé, Jimmy, used to hike with her along the creek in the woods that surrounded his family's home outside of Cape Van Buren. Hand in hand, they'd pick their way through the trees, hopping along the rocks or resting on the banks. The smell of the earth and trees filled her senses, releasing her emotions like a strong breeze on the seeds of a puffed dandelion.

They'd planned and conspired and dreamed, so in love that every single idea they'd had seemed so much more like reality than simply a possibility.

It was where she'd told him about their baby, and she could see the sweet chubby legs of a little girl with a dusting of white hair and eyes bluer than a Maine sky toddling through berry patches, a delighted grin leaving a dimple in each cheek.

It was where he'd asked her to marry him, and they envisioned a wedding of baby's breath and the finest white silk leaving their life canvas blank to be filled with all their hopes and dreams for their little family.

And it was where she'd run to when he'd died in the car accident three years ago...

The familiar sound of water was both heaven and hell for her.

Her hand came to a stop, and she opened her eyes. The silence was deafening, and the absence of earthly scents made her next inhale a disappointment.

On a shaky exhale, she pushed back from her desk and hurriedly opened one of the large, panel, bay windows. Breathing in the comforting scent of the salty ocean breeze, the gentle rhythm of the crashing waves helped drown out the roaring silence left behind, and she leaned into it all for a moment in sweet relief.

It eased her aching senses and calmed her heart.

Grabbing tape from the art table, she secured her paper to the light gray wall, making her wonder how many different pieces of artwork had adorned that wall over the years.

The house used to be the home of Maxine and the Van Buren family before her; then the whole Cape was purchased and almost turned into a housing development by Ryker. But Larkin had a strong tie to the land through her son, Archer, and in the end, she and Ryker had fallen in love, and through that, created a beautiful gift for the whole town.

A place to grow, to heal, to learn.

A place where love knew no bounds and that every citizen in town could call home.

And Claire got to lead the art classes, including those on helping children learn to cope. That was the one closest to her heart.

Since she'd never have any kids of her own, the opportunity to help teach those precious young souls how to handle the ups and downs of life would bring her incredible joy.

She closed her eyes against the pain of her memories, or rather, what would never be.

The sound of her obstetrician's voice telling her that her baby was gone echoed against the prison walls of her memories, and the familiar, suffocating pain of loss compressed her lungs for an intense moment.

Upon its release, she sucked in a breath and blinked until her scribbles came into view.

She eyed them, tilting her head from side to side until she could pull out a few familiar shapes.

A wash of frustration swamped her. How could she expect to teach these children when she couldn't see anything beyond her own pain? All she saw in her drawings were broken baby rattles and car crashes.

She needed to work through this process with someone else to make sure it was ready before the program opened. Since coping skills might touch on sensitive topics in general, Ryker wanted the program vetted for any possible liability. Claire understood, but she also worried.

The program launch was in less than a month, and she wanted it to be a success more than she'd wanted anything since she'd lost everything.

"You aren't going to stand on your head, are you? I might have to call Dr. Stanton if you do."

Claire startled at the sound of Mitch's voice and spun around. "Jesus Christ! You scared me. What are you doing here?" She swore, every time she turned around, his big, broad chest was obstructing her view.

"I have some documents to pore over. It's easier to do in the office here than my loft in town. Too many distractions."

"Ha! Like what, your porn collection?" The immediate rush of heat to her face accompanied her outburst, but she wasn't sure if it was from embarrassment that the sight of him made her think of porn or her natural inclination to give him a hard time. It really wasn't her style...except with him.

She shook her head, feeling like an ass.

Mitch aimed an inquisitive look her way that left her toes curling in her boat shoes. "A collection I clearly need to let you borrow if your wrapped-too-tight, joyful personality is any indication."

His sarcasm washed over her, and she kept silent. She hadn't meant to be rude, but everything with him was a knee-jerk reaction. Letting it go, she asked, "Documents?"

"I'm the Center's attorney, remember?"

"Oh, right." She tapped her head as if she were a dunce. Sometimes, she was pretty sure she was. Then right on cue, a realization dawned. He would be the person Ryker would have analyze her program.

Fucking great.

As he looked about her room, she let her eyes roam over his tall, muscular form. A dark cotton t-shirt was stretched across his broad shoulders, and his chest filled out the front so well she could make out the shapes of his pecs. On a swallow, she forced her eyes back to his, only to find him watching her with a bemused expression on his face.

Crap.

She was still trying to get over the shock of seeing him in her space.

He stepped next to her to take a closer look at her drawing, and as his scent wrapped around her, she stiffened poker-straight.

A little shudder ran through her as he ran a finger along one of the lines left by her crayons. "What's going on here?"

With a shake of her head, she sighed. "Not as much as I'd hoped. I'm working through my process for one of my coping-through-art strategies, but I'm blocked by my own issues."

"Your program. That's right. I need to talk to you about that. But first I have to ask, blocked or enlightened?" He ended the question with a challenge in his tone.

She wrinkled her nose at him. "Blocked."

"I don't think so." His gaze drifted over her face, then back to the paper. "Look here." He pointed toward the middle of the drawing. "See these arcs? They look like a rainbow. And everyone knows a rainbow stands for our hope in tomorrow, that the troubles of today will pass."

She squinted at the lines and stepped closer. A rainbow? Hope?

Confusion clouded her brain. Mitch was the last person she'd ever accuse of being philosophical. But she could see it.

A definite rainbow.

The heat of his body enveloped her, and her own buzzed with awareness. Maybe she felt this way around him because she knew he was a man who lived for pleasure. Something she hadn't experienced much of lately.

She turned her head to find him studying her face, so close, their lips but a few inches apart. Her lungs quit working suddenly, neither taking in nor releasing any air, and the strain of it all burned in her chest.

His mouth was shaped with chiseled edges, full but masculine. And those lips? They looked soft, but she'd bet her next event paycheck they were firm and demanding. She licked her lips.

What she wouldn't give for just one taste...

Mitch cleared his throat, and she sucked in a breath as the sound startled her from her daydreaming and stepped away.

What in the hell was wrong with her lately?

"I have a lot of work to do." She snatched the picture from the wall as she headed back to her work table. She lowered to the chair with her chin in her hand. "This is never going to work unless I can find someone to work through the process first. I refuse to present any half-assed activity to our kids. They deserve better than that."

Mitch gave her a salute. "Good luck with that, sweetheart, and let me know when you do." He threw her a wink, and she imagined it was the same one he threw his dates the next morning when they left his loft.

"It looks like we'll be spending some time together," he went on to say. "And if the irritated look on your face is any indication, you're not any more thrilled about it than I am. But like it or not, I'll be analyzing the steps of your program to watch out for any liability the Cape might face."

"I'll tell you what I told Ryker; this is silly." It wasn't, not really, but fear of losing the program she wanted so strongly made her stand her ground, no matter how shaky. She understood the reasoning behind it; she just didn't want it to be over before it began.

"Let me know when you find your guinea pig. I'll be in the office." His easy strides took him to the door.

And then, just like that, inspiration struck. A spark of intrigue picked up the pace of her heart. It would save time and simplify things. "What about you?"

He slowed, resting a hand on the door frame. "What *about* me, Claire Adams?" His voice was a quiet rumble, and the way he asked the question hinted at so much more than she was able to accommodate.

For some reason, the sound of her name rolling off his tongue sent a wash of goosebumps over her skin. "Let me put you through the paces of my coping strategy."

His eyes widened in surprise.

"For the kids," she added. For a second, she was sure he'd say yes.

"I'm not someone you want to get too close of a look at. I think I'll pass."

She pushed back from the table. "Well, of course, I don't. You're about as deep as a saucer and sleep around like you're in a contest, but I need to make sure this is ready."

"Finally, we agree on something. Because the way I see it, you're *not* ready. Especially if you're going to be standing in judgment toward every kid who walks through those front doors like you do with me."

Indignation heated her face. How dare he? "I do not. You're..."

Yes, she did. Her annoyance was quickly replaced with shame. She had to stop snapping at him all the time.

"I'm what? You seem to have me all figured out, but you're the one you should be looking closer at. You're rude and often a little brat. Not exactly who the kids of Cape Van Buren need as a role model."

And then he opened his mouth, and all she wanted to do was throttle him.

Well, that wasn't the only thing she wanted to do.

But it was the only thing she'd be honest enough to admit.

~

Standing in the checkered foyer of the Cape house, Mitch grinned. He loved watching Claire's skin pinken with anger. At least, the skin left visible from her skinny jeans and oversized knit sweater. He imagined the flush in her cheeks was close to what she looked like right after being well and thoroughly fucked. Not that he'd ever be the lucky man to serve her. She wasn't a love-her-and-leave-her kind of woman.

And that was the *only* kind of female he'd let himself get close to. A woman only interested in a bit of fun.

She opened her pretty mouth to respond, then closed it, pressing her lips together in a tight, straight line. His dick twitched as his body tried to imagine how those lips would feel around him.

Fuck me.

There was something about her that pulled him toward her as strongly as it warned him to stay away. The very reason he had to keep a distance—her vulnerability, her tragic past—were the same things that made him want to wrap his arms around her and make sure nothing ever hurt her again.

What the hell was wrong with him?

It was damned confusing.

He was not a protector or a forever kind of guy, and that was who she needed.

He scratched at the scruff on his chin. Always on the wrong foot with her, he sighed. "Look."

She put a hand up. "No, you're right."

Nothing could have surprised him more than those three words out of her mouth. "Excuse me?"

A small grin pulled at the corners of her mouth, and he felt a weird pop in his chest—as if a seal broke. He probably went too heavy on his chest presses the other day at the gym, he thought, rubbing at the spot below his collarbone.

"I said, you're right."

He leaned against the door frame, trying to figure out what she was up to. "Can I get that in writing?"

She moved past him toward the kitchen. "Shut up." Throwing a glance over her shoulder, she added, "And don't get used to hearing it. This is a one-time occurrence."

He grunted. "We'll see."

In the kitchen, she pulled out a pan of cupcakes from the commercial-sized refrigerator.

Curious and secretly hoping he'd get one, he slid onto one of the black leather stools at the large, white granite island in the middle of the kitchen that mirrored the tin-tiled ceiling above.

Adding a pre-whipped bowl of icing to the table top before him, she pushed a spatula into his hand. "Here, help me ice these, and I'll let you have one."

Confused didn't even begin to explain how he felt as he wrapped his hand around the handle. He was momentarily distracted by Puzzle, who chose that moment to jump into his lap.

He helped the cat settle against him as Claire arranged the items on the table. "Hey, buddy." The cat's purr was soft, and the vibration that hummed against him was comforting.

He wouldn't say it out loud, but it almost seemed she were offering him a truce of sorts. It was a step in the right direction anyway. He was tired of everyone placing bets on who he'd close his next "deal" on, as if his personal life were no different than the deals he made for his clients in commercial real estate.

At the top of his field, he should be flying high, but ever since working on the changes to the Cape with the conservation center, he'd been left feeling restless. He needed more.

He grabbed a cupcake. "Did you make these?"

Claire nodded, her blond hair, pin-straight, brushing past her chin with the movement. When she bent over, her oversized sweater gaped open just enough that the lace edge of her bra showed against the swell of her breasts.

He enjoyed breasts like anyone else, but what really turned him on when it came to Claire was her impossibly tiny waist and the sexy-as-fuck flare of her hips. The combination created the most perfect heart-shaped ass he'd ever seen encased in a pair of jeans.

"I did. Evette shared one of her recipes with me," she said softly. "Baking helps me think, so I made a batch of her lady lemons while ironing out a few details of my program this morning."

So that's why the house had smelled like lemon cookies when he'd come in.

19

Evette Kingsley was the owner and baker at North Cove Confectionery. Her cupcakes would make the sweetest soul turn black for just one more bite.

With a flick of his wrist, he added icing to his spatula and, while spinning the cupcake in one hand, added the white icing to the top.

Claire paused, watching him in surprise. "Ummmm...how do you know how to do that?"

With a shrug, he picked up another cupcake. "Evette and my mom are both North Cove Mavens. I've helped make more cupcakes, tend more gardens, and brew more moonshine than any other man I know. Even Ryker. His time away saved him a bit." He chuckled, warmed by the memory.

That's what happened when a man was raised by a bunch of women. Had his dad stuck around, maybe he'd have developed different skills, but he'd never give up what he had with his mother.

She was a very special woman.

Finishing another cupcake, he eyed it, then placed it back in the pan. He was good at a lot of things, but what really gave him pleasure was the pro bono work he'd been doing for the Cape.

He wanted more, but no one thought of him when they were setting up projects to serve the community.

The hard truth of the matter, if he was honest about it, was he couldn't blame them completely. He was a man of his own making.

Even if it was only to protect those around him.

Claire rounded the island. "Show me how to do that."

He raised a brow at her demand but scooted back from the island and turned toward her. Puzzle lifted his head from his resting place, and she ran a hand from between his ears to his tail, coaxing the cat's eyes closed. Mitch was jealous of a damn cat.

Stepping close with bright-eyed interest, she waited expectantly.

In slow motion, he showed her how he iced the cupcake, then handed his spatula to her. "You try."

She tried to duplicate his movements but ended up with more icing on her fingers than the cake. He had a million different ways to help her with that problem, and ninety percent of them involved his tongue.

Ignoring the direction of his thoughts, he stood, dislodging Puzzle, who shot a look at him that surely wished him straight to hell, and reached around her. "Here, like this."

The warm scent of her perfume hit him with a punch. He was expecting something floral like spring but instead was surrounded in a seductive haze of amber. With his hands on hers, he guided the cupcake under the spatula until the icing covered the top in a smooth cap.

But all he could focus on was her back against his chest, and how he could tuck her head just beneath his chin.

His blood rushed in his ears, but he forced himself to focus. She tried again, biting her lip between her teeth in her concentration. Her hands moved under his, and the silk of her skin glided under his palms.

With a squeal of excitement, she almost bounced in his arms. "That's it. Look!"

She spun, holding the cupcake out between them, delight sparkling in her blue eyes. He'd never noticed how clear they were. Little darker blue specs could be seen in a spiral around her pupil like a kaleidoscope.

Using the deep reserves of his self-control, he resisted the urge to congratulate her smiling lips with a kiss.

He cleared his throat and stepped back.

"You need to date." His words jumped from his mouth without explanation, and he clamped his jaw closed to stop any more from following. But as the idea formed, the more he warmed to it.

Her smile twisted into a grimace. "Excuse me?"

A snappy and irritated Claire was fun to tease and sexy as hell, but a happy and bubbly Claire was far too irresistible.

He had to get her dating—one more layer to keep her out of reach.

"I have a proposition for you."

Besides, it would all work toward his new and improved reputation. A man to turn to for help, an upstanding citizen of Cape Van Buren. He'd get Claire out of her hermitage while helping her prepare her program, and if all went according to plan, it would enable him to dive deep into more pro bono work around Cape Van Buren.

"Let me get you up to speed on dating again, and I'll be your guinea pig for your Coping through Art program."

She blinked twice.

"I do not need help on getting up to speed with dating. I don't want to date. It's as simple as that."

"You're afraid to."

She popped her hands to her hips. "I am not afraid of anything." But her eyes shifted high left, before returning to his face.

He grabbed one of the iced cupcakes and took a large bite, studying her while he chewed, enjoying the explosion of tart lemon in his mouth. "Prove it."

Snatching the cupcake from his hand, she took a bite herself.

"Hey!" He tried to take it back, but she hopped away with a little skip.

Sometimes, she was the cutest damn woman he'd ever met. "You're afraid. Whether it's of the commitment or the process, I'm not sure yet. But dating doesn't mean you have to marry the person."

She snorted. "You would know."

He narrowed his eyes at her. "You're right. I would."

CHAPTER 3

*C*laire wrung her hands together at her waist, trying to disperse the nervous energy that did nothing but produce sweaty palms and a sour stomach.

You can do this. You can do this.

Slowing in front of the Flat Iron Coffeehouse, she peered through the large front window of the cafe. Sitting on the corner of Garden Parkway SW and Van Buren Blvd, it was directly across from the North Cover Confectionery and had a brilliant view of both the town center and the Atlantic off the tip of the Cape.

There he was. Just as he'd said. Jeans and a blue sweater. Clean-cut, not bad looking but nothing compared to Mitch Brennan's gorgeously chiseled features and powerfully muscled physique. Crap.

Why the hell was she thinking about Mitch? It was his fault she was even in this mess to begin with. He had to challenge her about not knowing how to date.

Well, the hell she didn't. Her problem wasn't dating. It was a whole lot more complicated than enjoying a coffee and conversation.

Squaring her shoulders, she smoothed down the fabric of her dress, took a deep, bolstering breath, then pulled open the door of the shop. With purpose in her stride, she walked toward the man sitting at the coffee bar. He glanced up with a look of interest as his eyes traveled the length of her.

As she got closer, she made eye contact, smiled, then walked right past him toward the bathrooms at the back of the shop.

What the hell would they even do? She hated small talk, there was no way she was going to tell him about herself, and besides, she'd gotten old over the past few years. Being an almost widow was not the best for her complexion.

Eyeing herself in the mirror of the coffeehouse bathroom mirror, she stuck her tongue out in a show of disgust. She swore the roadmap of Cape Van Buren was all over her face at this point, at the corners of her eyes and the lines beside her mouth.

She dug her nails into her palms. What the hell was wrong with her? She did not shave her damn legs to just run scared of a simple coffee date.

I am not scared.

You're scared.

"Oh, shut up."

"Excuse me?" A lady Claire recognized from over at the courthouse stared at her from the reflection in the bathroom mirror. She'd exited one of the bathroom stalls and now stood with a backdrop of coffee bean plants behind her.

Claire waved her hand. "No, sorry." She chuckled. "I was just talking to myself."

I have got to stop doing that.

The woman gave an indulgent smile that was more pity than understanding as she did a quick rinse of her hands before leaving the bathroom.

Claire grimaced, washed her own hands with soap just to feel cleaner, then dialed Larkin. "Hey! I need you to come over to the Coffeehouse."

"What's up?" Larkin's said, her voice breathless.

"I made a date—"

"Whoooo!" Larkin's excitement felt like it pierced her eardrum.

She yanked the phone away for a second, then once it was safe, brought it back to her ear. "Anyway, I bailed. And now I'm stuck in the bathroom."

"You are *not*."

"I am."

"Claire, just go have coffee with the guy. Who is it?"

With a shake of her head, she studied her lip-gloss in the mirror, fixing one edge where it was smeared. "One of the partners down at the boathouse. Evette had introduced me."

"You're going to have to go back out there. I just put Max down for her nap and Ryker is over at the Center working with Mitch."

"Damn Mitch. This is all his fault."

"How is this Mitch's fault?" Larkin asked, a curious note to her voice.

Crap.

"Hey, I gotta go. Kisses to baby Max for me." The three-month-old was a beautiful torture. Her scent and the feel of her in Claire's arms every time she nestled that precious baby close reminded her of everything she'd lost, but she wouldn't give it up for the world. She was one of Max's aunties now. And that was a responsibility she wouldn't flake out on.

Claire ignored whatever Larkin was saying and disconnected the call. Her friend was no help, but that was par for the course with a new mama. Blayne was in New Zealand with Jay on their honeymoon, and there was no way in hell she'd call Maxine.

She was on her own. And standing in the bathroom of the Flat Iron Coffeehouse, surrounded by cappuccino art, she felt that fact more acutely than ever before.

And didn't like it one bit.

Tucking her clutch under her arm, she kept her eyes down and made a beeline through the cafe to the front door.

"Claire?"

She heard the masculine voice, but she didn't pause for a second. Once outside, she walked toward the Cape, the heels of her boots echoing a getaway song along the sidewalk bricks past Dine on the Vine, over South Cove Ave and through the gates to the Cape that read, *The Archer Conservation Park of Cape Van Buren, the answer to life's puzzle is love.* And as they did every time she saw it, her eyes filled, but she kept walking.

It was one of those fall days where the air was cool, but the sun was warm. She breathed in the salty breeze that floated in off the Atlantic as if it was a lifeline to freedom. Mortification rolled through her from running away like a coward, but she let it reach her fingertips, then dropped it to the pebbles at her feet.

Maybe Mitch had a point. She'd been out of the game long enough that she couldn't remember how to start back up.

Knowledge was her best friend at this point. She knew she didn't want anything long term. No one was going to settle so deep in her heart that losing them would hurt her ever again.

Arm's length and casual was her new middle name. Well, maybe that was too long for a middle name, but it was certainly her new stance on relationships. It was that or nothing at all, and nothing at all was taking its toll.

Because damn, she wanted to be held, to feel a man's hands sweep up her naked sides and cup her full, aching breasts in his palms. She wanted his warm lips and the rock-solid weight of his chest pressing into her. She wanted to feel Mitch's scruff rub against the sensitive peaks of her...

Whoa.

No way.

She blinked in surprise, catching her toe on a rock in the driveway, and almost falling on her face.

Not Mitch. Where the hell did that come from? Everything associated with sex did not have to lead her to that man for God's sake.

But she did need his help. If she couldn't get over herself and cope with her past enough to have a cup of coffee with a guy, how the hell could she expect to be able to teach children to muster the courage to move beyond the things that may hold them back?

Making her Coping through Art program successful was one of the most important things she'd ever do. If she couldn't be all in, then she shouldn't be there at all. The town deserved better than that.

Taking the front steps of the Cape house two at a time, she threw open the door and charged into the office to find Mitch.

"I'm in."

～

*M*itch could only stare.

Claire's hair was windblown, her cheeks flushed pink, her cleavage straining against the crisscrossing tie at the front of her dress that kept her breasts locked and loaded.

He'd been wrong before.

This was how she'd look like after being well and properly fucked. And nothing could have shocked him more than the surge of raw, irrational jealousy at the thought.

"I'm in," she repeated. Marching up to him, she threw her clutch on the desk between them and continued. "You agree to work through my project—"

"Claire, wait—"

"No, I need to get this out."

"Hold on." He pointed to the front window of the Cape house office, but she barreled on in Claire fashion, pacing a two-foot swath in front of him. Her dress was wrapped at the waist, so narrow he swore his hands would fit around it, then flowed straight down to her knees, drawing his gaze to the tall, black, sinfully sexy boots. She looked hot as hell.

"And you'll give me pointers on how to get back into the dating game. I'm tired of going to bed alone every night."

He couldn't argue. No reason in the world a woman like her should be going to bed alone unless she preferred to.

A throat cleared behind her, and she spun around.

Ryker, standing by the front bay window, raised his water bottle in salute. "Cheers."

Claire slowly turned back to Mitch with daggers in her eyes.

He laughed with a shrug. "I tried to tell you."

Hands balled into fists at her sides and her already flushed cheeks turning an adorable shade of scarlet, she closed her eyes for a second. "Not hard enough."

Ryker squeezed her shoulder. "I've got to get home before little Max wakes up from her nap. I'll tell Larkin to call you."

"Oh, I'm sure you will." Her tone was regretful and made Mitch want to full on croon—which was bullshit.

Ryker's bark of laughter followed him to the front door. "Mitch, let me know what you find out with the easement. You never know what information will inspire a new idea."

The front door closed, leaving a silence behind that was as heavy as Mitch's curiosity. Hitching his leg up on the desk, he settled onto the corner and narrowed his eyes.

"What happened?"

Claire played with a thread hanging from the tie securing the top of her dress. "Nothing. Which is the problem." The look on her face was that of a child having to eat broccoli, but he suspected *he* was the broccoli.

He remained silent as she made her way around the room that mirrored the one her art classes would be held in, though this one had a large business desk, leather tufted chairs, and a seating place by the front window for more casual meetings. Bookshelves ran ceiling-to-floor along the far wall and behind the desk, filled with everything from local history to romance novels.

Claire casually poked at a stack of papers, then ran her fingers over the printer, until she made her way back to his desk. She pulled in a breath, once again pushing up the swell of her breasts in a way that made his fingers itch to cup them.

Shoving his hands into his jean pockets, he waited still.

"I had a coffee date at Flat Iron."

He kept his expression easy. This was what he'd been pushing her to do all along. She needed to unwind. The woman worked at an intensity level that couldn't be good for her heart, or his hide at the rate they were going. She bit his head off every time they talked.

He hadn't figured out what it was about him that always rubbed her the wrong way, but instead of avoiding her over the past months, he'd found himself coming up with reasons to be around her. She energized him in a way no one else had in a long time. Or maybe ever. Which was a thought he wasn't nearly ready to explore.

Maybe he was a masochist.

That would explain a lot, actually.

"A date? Good. Then what's the problem?"

She laughed with a hopeless shake of her head, the razor edge of her pin-straight platinum hair swinging past her jawline. "I ran. I ignored the guy and left...even when he called out my name."

"Why?" Mitch felt for the guy. Almost. But seeing Claire walk away was even sexier than watching her approach. So the poor bastard would survive.

With a groan, she shrugged. "I don't know. I..."

"Yes, you do."

She swung away to pace.

Straightening from the desk, he stepped in front of her, halting her frantic steps. "Let's try something."

Eyeing him with suspicion, she said, "No way."

"Look, we both know I'm not the guy for you. So that makes me safe, right? Just work with me for a second."

"Fine. Whatever," she huffed. "Let's just get this over with, okay?"

"That's the Claire I know." Then, shifting gears, he gazed into her eyes. "Hi, I'm Mitch."

She studied him for a beat then burst out laughing, covering her mouth with her hand.

He let his head fall back. "Yeah, you are awful at this."

Holding her stomach, she grabbed at his arm. "Wait. Wait. It's just that I know who you are. I'd pin a guy like you from a mile away and never give you the chance to talk to me."

He clenched his jaw tight. It shouldn't matter. He'd avoid her too. Way more baggage than his casual, no-strings-attached lifestyle could carry. But, fuck, it still stung.

"Pretend," he gritted out. "If you can handle a conversation with me, then you can with any other jackass out there."

"Oh, great. So your advice is for me to date a jackass? I might as well stick with you then. At least you're safe, like you said."

His sharp laugh bounced off the walls. The way she was always tied up in his thoughts, there was really nothing safe about him at all. If she only knew how badly he'd love to be the one to help her blow off some steam, she'd hightail her pert little ass home faster than the Cape squirrels to their trees when Puzzle was let out.

"Safe. Exactly. So pay attention."

She cleared her throat and focused on him. "Does this mean you'll do it? You'll work through my art program and in return I'll let you give me pointers on how to date without getting emotionally involved?"

The last thing he wanted was her digging any further into his psyche than she already had, but he also needed to help her get back on her feet. Not only in the hopes of having her calm the hell down but because after everything she'd been through, she deserved to live a full life.

He couldn't stand the idea of her all alone, staring out a window on a cold, dark night, like he had seen his own mother do. Besides, if she started dating some fine, upstanding citizen of Cape Van Buren, it would make him keep his distance and look damn good for his reputation to boot. Mitch the Matchmaker.

Had a nice ring to it.

If he could help Claire Adams, maybe people would start seeing the value he actually had to offer this town. This was his home, his people, but they never really saw him.

Not really.

They only saw his dating and drinking and nice clothes. He loved to indulge, but instead of it being seen as a choice, it was judged as a lifestyle of immorality.

They didn't recognize that he was the one who fought for the tenants in the housing complex on the edge of town, or that he fought for tenant rights of different real estate holdings to make sure safety measures were up to date.

Not to mention the whole legal aspect of the easement that made the Archer Conservation Park of Cape Van Buren even possible, including all the law and policy for the non-profit.

He'd been busy.

Well, he'd just get busier. It felt damn good. And he was a man who loved when things felt good.

Giving her one of his best smiles, he said, "Hi, I'm Mitch."

Her lip twitched, but she remained serene. She dipped her chin. "Claire."

His eyes drifted to her mouth—full lips with a very precise cupid's bow. "So, Claire. What do you like to do for fun?" He stepped closer, his voice dropped low, suggestive even.

Her eyes flared, dropping to his lips, then back in panic. "Shit!" She backed away. "I can't do this. I'm not fun." She patted her chest for emphasis. "I'm old and boring and—"

"You're barely twenty-eight. Take it easy." Leaving his hands at his sides, he watched the expressions washing over her face. "Tell me what's going through your mind."

"No one's touched me since Jimmy. Would he hate me for moving on? Will it wash away his memory? Is it disloyal to want to be held again? And what about..."

"Of course, it wouldn't be disloyal," Mitch assured her, his chest clenching at the look of pure sadness on her face.

"He was a *good* man."

The words were like a slap in the face. "And I'm not?"

She stared as if shocked by her own words. "I'm sorry, I didn't mean—"

"Yeah. Ya did." He stepped back behind the desk, a sick rolling in his gut. "That's enough for today." Grabbing his cell, he swiped through to check his messages. Anything to keep him from saying more than he meant to.

Claire reached out, then let her hand drop back to her side. "Okay. You're right. I'll...I'll see you tomorrow."

As she pulled open the front door, he called out. "Let's make something really clear."

"Yes?" She paused.

"I have never lied to any of the women I've dated. And I certainly haven't slept with all of them, though the town likes to think so. But more than that, I have always treated the women I've been fortunate enough to enjoy with respect."

"Sorry." Her whisper barely reached his ears, and he refused to look back her way.

No way in hell did he want her seeing more than she needed to.

He'd help her get out of her shell and perfect her program for the kids and keep his business clear of any town gossips. Then, once he worked through this last project for Ryker, his portfolio would be ready to throw in for the open City Attorney position.

He could remember the first time he'd ever been introduced to the right side of the law and visited the court house as a kid. His mom had sent him off with a family friend who'd happened to work there. Now he had a feeling, she'd done it on purpose.

Claire and the rest of the town could judge all they wanted.

As the City Attorney, he'd be able to do a lot for this town, and the last thing he'd think about was the opinion of this pretty, blue-eyed spitfire who made him feel way too damn much.

CHAPTER 4

*C*laire tossed back a large swallow of Maxine's moonshine, hoping it would warm her bones, as she took stock of all the work they had to do winterizing the North Cove Gardens. The savory scents from North Cove Bistro rode on the light breeze, making her stomach grumble in wanting.

Geographically, she was a South Cove Madam, but when Larkin had set her sights on being friends, Claire hadn't stood a chance. She'd been indoctrinated to the North Cove Mavens before she'd realized what had happened.

And found her home.

Unlike most of her friends, she wasn't originally from Cape Van Buren. She'd moved here to be with Jimmy after finishing college with her Master of Fine Arts. She was an artist deep down. Everything she did was better if she could make it beautiful. One reason she enjoyed her event planning so much.

She'd officially opened her own business just after Larkin's baby shower, at the very strong urging of her friends, but when the opportunity to use her art and help the kids of Cape Van Buren arose, she leaped at the chance. Event planning paid her bills and fueled her creativity, but working at the Center fulfilled her in a way nothing else ever had.

One more sip from the moonshine, then it was time to work. This batch, made from Evette's blueberries and Janice's edible flowers, went down smooth and easy like fresh fruit in whipped cream. Wicked good.

The North Cove Mavens had all arranged their Thursday to combine forces to prune the flowering bushes and wrap some of the more vulnerable perennials. A few pieces from the summer's garden festival still held center stage. It had been another huge hit with the town, but to the Mavens' great consternation, they'd had to share this year's win in a tie with the South Cove Madams.

Maxine fought for a tiebreaker, but with her and Judge Carter on the outs, he refused to even make eye contact with her much less listen to her appeal.

Claire wiped her mouth with the back of her hand, then handed Larkin the jar. "I can't believe Blayne is getting out of this. We should just wait until she comes back."

"And share the moonshine? No way. More for us." Larkin took a sip herself. "It's so good to be drinking again. I think the hardest thing about carrying baby Max was missing out on all the wine and moonshine."

Claire forced a grin. She'd give anything to carry her baby to term. And she'd give up even more. Even Maxine's moonshine.

"Are you okay?" Larkin paused with her pruning shears poised to cut a dying stem from one of the large rose bushes. Her eyes shot wide, and she dropped the scissors to the ground. With a horrified expression on her face, she wrapped an arm around Claire. "I'm so sorry. That was incredibly insensitive of me. I didn't mean anything by it."

Claire shook her head. "You're fine. Stop. I know what you meant."

And she did. There were parts of being pregnant that she hadn't liked. Which, now having her lost her baby, made her feel like karma had a hand in what had happened next. Jimmy had died at the hospital the day he'd gotten in the accident with Larkin's first husband and little boy, Archer.

Claire had been heartbroken, unable to sleep, could barely eat. Panic attacks had kept her on edge for weeks. She'd never imagined that she could bear any more grief than losing the man she loved. Until she woke up to a horrendous pain in her stomach and blood all over her sheets, washing away every last dream she'd hoped to grasp on to.

At just under eight months, her baby had been stillborn. In a panic, she'd grabbed at the sheets, as if holding onto the telltale sign of death could somehow keep life from slipping through her fingers.

A silent wail of despair filled her head with the memory.

She bent to inspect a set of small bushes to give herself a chance to blink back tears before Larkin could see them. Her friend's comment had been fueled by the innocence of happiness. Nothing more, nothing less. There was no reason for her lovely friend to feel guilty for basking in her own joy. She'd had enough sorrow herself.

That said, it was hard for Claire to watch her friends move forward with the life she'd been promised. She was sincerely thrilled for them but sad for herself. She was alone, by choice, and it was something she needed to come to terms with.

Larkin was the bravest woman she'd ever met. Her friend had found her way through the loss of her sweet boy, had trusted her heart, and prepared to risk it for love.

Claire couldn't imagine doing that. She refused to ever put herself in a position again where she could feel that much pain. She'd heard the saying that it was better to have loved and lost than to never have loved at all.

And she called bullshit.

You didn't know what you were missing if you didn't have it in the first place, and when there was a chance it could be lost, not knowing was way better. Ignorance was bliss and all that.

"Promise you're okay?" Larkin asked.

Pulling from her reserves and channeling Blayne's feisty attitude, Claire jumped up, grin in place, and grabbed the moonshine. "Woman, I'm the one who helped you move on at the cemetery way back when, remember? I've already dealt with my shit. I am fine."

And she was...as long as she didn't think about the baby she'd never held in her arms or the man she never would again.

Mitch's face popped into her head. She hadn't meant to hurt his feelings yesterday and had regretted the thoughtless words as soon as they'd popped out. Apparently, she wasn't always very sensitive either.

But she'd also been surprised. He'd never played down what a playboy he was before, and she couldn't understand why it was such a big deal now.

As for Jimmy. He knew how to love a woman. Gentle and quiet. He was always easy. No surprises.

No adventure.

The disloyal thought jerked her from the trap her brain had set as Maxine and Janice joined them.

"Damn *Judge* Carter better stay free and clear of me, I'll tell you that right now." Maxine said the word judge like she questioned its meaning and focused on chopping at a section of one of the bushes that made up the C for the initials of Cape Van Buren.

Janice grabbed the sheers from her friend. "When are you two going to make up already? Your little spat was cute at first, but when it starts affecting the rest of us, enough is enough."

"I agree," Evette added. "I never thought you much of a masochist, but this almost seems to be like pleasure-pain foreplay with the two of you at this point."

Maxine's face went hot. "He embarrassed me in front of half the town."

Janice snorted. "You were selling moonshine while dating a judge. What the hell did you expect him to do?"

Red curls bobbing, Mitch's mother put her hand out for the canning jar, and Claire didn't hesitate. There was no getting between the ladies and their moonshine...or each other.

Maxine eyed Janice with censure. "You sure are enjoying that moonshine you think I should just give away, my friend."

"Oh, I never said that. I just think you should be sneakier than selling it where the judge could find out." Janice laughed. "The extra money goes a long way in my garden and our 'howl at the moon' nights on the Cape.

Larkin titled her head. "Didn't Ryker say you guys had to stop those now that the Cape was opened to the town?"

Three sets of eyes with more spunk and wisdom than the oak trees of Maine had leaves turned toward her with a slow, measured slide.

"Never mind." Larkin raised her hands up to ward them off.

Claire stepped between them all. "Can we get moving? I'm meeting Mitch at the Center at four, and we've barely two hours to get this done."

Janice perked up like a moose on a willow trail. "What's this now?"

Regret and panic caused a pounding at the base of Claire's skull. "Don't *even*. He's helping me get ready for my program for the kids. A bit of an experiment." Then she added with a frown, "And he has final say from a liability standpoint."

"Oh, I'm sure you'd like to experiment on that one," Maxine teased.

Heat flushed through Claire's chest. "Is it always sex with you?"

"That's a dumb question," Evette laughed.

Maxine took back her sheers and worked on shaping the bush in front of her. "A healthy sex life is imperative for a healthy mind and body. How do you think I'm still going so strong?" She slid her hands down her sides with a little shimmy and a wink.

"Ha! Then you better go make up with Judge Carter before it all goes to hell," Evette said.

Janice cackled. "I never thought I'd see the day when we were trying to get *two* North Cove Mavens laid. Normally we try to keep this type of focus on one at a time."

Claire choked midsip of the moonshine. "I do not need or want your help."

"From what I hear, Mitch knows his way around—"

"Stop! Don't say it. He's your son, for God's sake," Claire begged, tipping the jar.

"Whoa, there. Save some for me." Larkin grabbed at it.

Janice was so delighted with her joke, she could barely get her words out. "Please, I make no pretensions about my son and his sex life. He's a grown man. I'd be disturbed if he wasn't getting some. Like we are with you." She pointed at Claire. "Hell, you can barely say penis."

"Ohmigod. Not this again. I can say it just fine."

All three women stared and waited.

"I haven't been dating because I don't want anything serious, not because I'm some sort of prude or afraid of sex."

Janice's gaze eased from teasing to disappointed. "Why wouldn't you want anything serious?"

How could she ever make them understand?

She looked out over the garden grounds at all the beauty they created and nurtured, beauty that fed the souls of anyone who walked through the splendor, inspiring them to create something special themselves. The brick pathways led the way, the rope fences gave them boundaries and direction.

Just like her friends.

They all charged at life with such strength. Well, she was strong, too. Strong enough to know what she wanted and didn't want in life. "I've had true love once. That was enough for me. End of story." She grabbed the jar back from Larkin. "Let's get to work."

∼

*M*itch glanced over his resume one more time.

Just about ready to go. Once he finished this last project for Ryker, he'd have a pretty solid submission for the City Attorney position.

He leaned back in his chair. The Cape house office mirrored the programs room across the foyer, making it way too easy to imagine Claire there. They looked a lot different than the bold navy and eggplant colors that used to cover the walls. It all had suited Maxine, but the new look worked, too, and offered a new start, a new purpose.

Both spaces were painted gray with lots of white and earth tones. The decor brought much of the outdoor seaside feel inside with subtle hints of the coast in the knotted pine wood shelves, nautical rope-edged throw pillows, and the random assortment of seashells that could be found throughout the house. It suited just about anyone who stepped through the Center's doors.

As it should be. A home away from home for every one of them.

He closed out the files just as a knock sounded at the front door. Who the hell could that be? It was an open center. Anyone from town could walk on in until they closed at eight p.m.

Pulling the door open, he jumped to catch falling boxes from Claire's arms. "Take these please." She breezed right on past him while he juggled two boxes and a roll of paper. The scent of earth and the familiar sweet smell of moonshine followed in her wake.

She spun around with her arms out. "Let's get started."

There was something different about her this afternoon.

The last thing he'd expected was a carefree Claire after their last conversation. He'd already prepared his I'm-an-ass speech.

But there was a definite glow in her eye and a blush in her cheeks. He wanted to cup her face and kiss her senseless.

What the fuck?

What the hell about he-wasn't-the-man-for-her did *he* not understand?!

With a mental shake, he moved toward the program room and set the supplies on her desk. "What's all this?"

She stepped up beside him and nudged his hip playfully with hers. "This..." She took the roll of paper and unfurled it across the work table. "Is the first step of your lesson."

He took in her sunshiny blond hair held back by a bandana, her jeans and work boots. The t-shirt she wore was stretched across her breasts in the way that made every man grateful for the invention of Spandex. It said "Celebrate in Color" with a rainbow of handprints all across the front, and he swore when he read it, he could hear her voice.

This woman continued to mystify him. She had strong values. A brilliant mind. Not to mention a far too saucy mouth that he wanted to do wicked things to. There was so much he didn't know about her. She was everywhere and nowhere at the same time.

"Where were you?"

She scowled. "Weeding and pruning. Had I known being a North Cove Maven meant I'd have to pull weeds, I might have thought twice."

Ahhhh, that was it. His mother had mentioned something about preparing the North Gardens for winter. The South Cove Madams took care of the gardens at the south end. She was still pretty sore about the results of the festival, so he'd been steering clear lately.

In a flurry, Claire set out colored pencils and pulled up a dreamy, meditative tune on her phone. "Here. Sit." She grabbed his shoulders, pushing him into a chair.

But instead of releasing him, she kneaded into his muscles with a sigh, following the curve of his shoulder to his biceps, sending all sorts of signals to his dick that were in no way accurate.

"Are you okay?" he asked. Not that he minded, but this was so not like her.

She froze and blinked rapidly. "What? Of course." On a snort, she let him go, then pulled up a chair. He missed the heat of her hands immediately, the ghost-print feeling left behind still humming along his skin.

Wait a second. "Look at me."

Claire did as she was told. He could get lost in the deep crystal blue of her eyes if he were allowed. She grinned, taking him aback.

That wasn't really like her at all. At least not with him around.

With a tap to his nose, she said, "You're so pretty."

He grabbed her finger. Pretty? What. The. Fuck. "You're drunk. Moonshine?"

"The finest kind." She saluted.

"Yeah, I know." Too bad she hadn't brought any with her to their lesson. It would make it a hell of a lot easier to work through her coping skills program.

She tugged at her finger. He resisted for a beat, then released her.

Studying his face, she sighed. "It feels good to be a little numb instead of just empty."

His chest tightened with worry. "How did you get here? Tell me you didn't drive."

"I didn't drive."

"Claire," he growled.

On a giggle, she said, "Larkin dropped me off. I told her you could take me home."

Relief surged through him until she closed her eyes and bent toward him. Breathing in through her nose, she sighed again. "You always smell so damn good."

Warning bells sounded in his head and warred with the desire to taste the lips curved so sweetly before him. She opened her eyes and held his gaze, her mouth hovering just inches from his. It would take no effort at all to lean in and take a sip.

He was parched.

His body tightened, and he shifted in the chair to make room for the over-eager reaction in his pants. God damn it.

As her focus drifted to his lips, she licked hers. His blood pounded in his ears. He needed to get a hold of his damn self and fast.

Clearing his throat, he grabbed a colored pencil, accidentally snapping it in half.

Claire jumped, then grabbed the two pieces from him. "Be careful. I am working with a budget here."

And there she was. Bossy, sassy Claire.

"Okay." She handed him another pencil. "What I want you to do is close your eyes then draw all around on this paper."

He tilted his head. "That's it?"

"For now."

Settling in his chair, he closed his eyes. The feather-light silk of her skin drifted over his knuckles as she guided his hand to the paper. Soft, fluid music floated about his head and mixed with her rich, intoxicating scent in a powerful combination. There was something incredibly seductive about the experience that had no place in what they were doing.

Scenes of sliding skin and soft moans of pleasure clouded his brain. What was he supposed to do again?

"Just move with me," she said.

"Oh, I'll move with you alright."

"Mitch, if you're not going to take this seriously, the deal is off."

He snapped his eyes open and pushed away from the table. Air, that's what he needed, and a little space. Distance.

Abandoning the task and Claire, he walked through the foyer and toward the porch off the back of the kitchen.

"Where are you going?" The disappointment in her voice was clear, but he had to take a second and get his damn body and mind back under control. He must be a glutton for punishment because no other explanation could help him understand why he wanted someone who so clearly did not want him.

No. Scratch that. He did not want. Did. Not. She was simply an enigma. A problem that needed to be solved.

A problem who followed hot on his heels.

He skirted around the large table and stepped to the railing along the west side of the outdoor living space that faced the town.

The sun was low in the sky, hanging just over the trees that edged the far border of Cape Van Buren. A cool breeze had picked up, carrying the scent of sea salt spray with it, and seagulls called from overhead. He loved the Cape. Especially now that the dark cloud caused by Ryker's abusive father years ago had been lifted.

The Cape was a peninsula of richly-wooded earth wrapped in a great rocky shore along the coast of Maine. The Atlantic to the east and the town of Cape Van Buren to the west. It was home.

A home he wanted to help protect.

Claire joined him, sucking in a breath herself. It was impossible to resist out on the Cape. So fresh and clean without the pollution of man. He followed suit, filling his lungs.

"I felt like an ass."

It wasn't a complete lie; he had been uncomfortable with her instructions. Draw with his eyes closed? He could barely make a straight line with them open.

His talents lay in social strategy, finding patterns and gaps, then filling them. Not beauty. He was never much good at that.

But if he were honest with himself, working with her was going to be harder than he thought. Claire Adams was a woman who required a light touch and a committed future. And they both knew he was not the man for either.

"Look, it takes a little time to trust in the process. I'm not here to judge your artistic ability or anything we may uncover. You have to let go of perfection in order to expose the mess."

That's what he was afraid of.

Her words made him restless, and he scratched at his chest. "You'll need to set expectations with your young students, help them see that ahead of time. But with kids, I think they'll trust you more naturally from the start than adults will. It's when we've been touched by life that we find it difficult to trust in what we find around us."

She studied his face. "Why don't you let people see this side of you?"

He ran his hand along the railing. "What are you talking about? I'm myself all the time."

"You're *on* all the time. Fun-loving, thrill-seeking Mitch Brennan. But lately, I've seen a deeper, thoughtful side of you that I don't think many know is there."

"Well, they would if they bothered to look."

She laughed. "You and I both know people are lazy. If you expect them to notice what you aren't showing, you're going to be deeply disappointed."

"But you notice, is that it?" The fact he wanted her to was the problem.

"I'm beginning to. What're we going to do with that?"

His heart drummed in his chest in a solid rhythm he swore he could hear as well as feel. What was she getting at? He could never risk hurting her. Only an ass would consider such a thing, and he was working really hard at not being one. But he was too much like his dad.

"On paper, I mean?" Her clarification filled his gut with the sour twist of being a fool. Of course. Her *art* program.

"Well, how about we use your ability to *see* people to actually handle going on a date." He couldn't help the sarcasm. Spending time with her wrapped him tighter than the rigging on Ryker's sailboat. Trying to get her to loosen up was going to snap him in half.

Her brows shot up. "Did I say something wrong?"

"You? Never. Why would you think that?" He stepped back into the kitchen. "Look, I need to finish up some work for Ryker."

She followed behind him. "You're as moody as Blayne when she doesn't get enough time on the rink, you know that?" She sounded offended, but he was too tired of fighting himself to really care.

"And you're exhausting."

Grabbing one of the cupcakes she'd made using Evette's recipe from the fridge, she took a healthy bite, chewing like her life depended on it.

She was a stress eater. And he found it adorable.

Fuck. And just like that, his irritation rolled away.

What in the hell was he going to do with this woman?

"Give me that." Snatching it from her hand, he took a bite of his own.

One way or another they were both going to get what they wanted.

CHAPTER 5

*C*laire eyed the stage in abject horror.

"You want me to do what again?" Her voice was a furious whisper, gaining them more than a few looks from around the comedy club. Tucked back behind Bellamy's grocers on the south side of town was The Cape Comedy and Nightclub. Entering was like stepping back in time, but the entertainment was the latest and greatest, and the place was packed almost every night of the week.

On Friday afternoons just at the start of happy hour, they held a speak-easy hour. Anything from poetry and music to readings from literary and genre fiction. It was an opportunity to hear and be heard, see and be seen, and Claire wanted no part in hell of it.

"Read this." Mitch handed her a sheet of paper.

Snatching it from his hand, she scanned the two short paragraphs.

"No freaking way."

He had to be kidding. How in the hell was this supposed to help her navigate her way in the dating world?

"Yes, you are. I go through your program. You go through mine."

"There's no point to this but complete humiliation for me," she gritted out.

"Yeah?" He crossed his arms over his chest. "How do you figure?"

Waving the paper under his nose, she said, "Every word on this page is about sex."

43

"And it's something you'd like to do again someday with someone other than yourself." His lips quirked. "Or...am I wrong on that front?"

"Don't be an ass." Heat washed over her chest. "What I may... or may not do in the privacy of my own home is none of your business."

"Well, I'm just glad you didn't try to tell me you don't masturbate, and considering your prickly nature, you could use more of that."

Sputtering like Judge Carter when he caught Maxine selling her moonshine, she argued. "You're a pig, you know that?"

"Aww, come on. It's nothing to be ashamed of, sweetheart." He leaned in, whispered conspiratorially. "Newsflash...we all do it."

What was with him tonight? She couldn't believe he was needling her like this. Scratch that. He was the one man in town who would most certainly get off on getting a rise out of her.

Rolling her eyes, she said, "Back to this. What's this about?"

"It's called poetry, but more, it's a chance to challenge yourself, to banish your fear of judgment, of being noticed."

"I am not afraid of being noticed. Just look at this dress."

His eyes skimmed over her black, clingy sweater dress with a v-neckline deep enough to show off half the swell of her breasts. Afraid. What a crock.

The appreciation in his heated gaze was unmistakable, and her flush depended.

"I never said anything about your looks. You don't hide yourself under clothing or by minimizing your beauty. You don't need help in that department at all." He followed his words with a low, admiring whistle.

She slapped at his arm. "Knock it off."

"But as soon as you start up a conversation, you fly into defense mode or, if your ditching of that poor guy the other day is any indication, you just run."

"I do not."

"How long are you going to keep lying to yourself?" he asked in a slightly patronizing voice that made her want to smack him for real.

She wanted to argue, to tell him he was full of shit, but as she thought back over the past few months alone, she couldn't come up with one example where he was wrong.

Crap.

She glanced over the paper again. "And how is reading this going to help?"

Gentling his stance, he tucked one side of her hair behind her ear, lingering with the ends between his fingers. "You know how when we were kids learning how to ride a bike, the idea of our parents letting go was way scarier than when they actually did?"

She studied his face, lost in his surprisingly soft gaze, and nodded.

"This is that. I think you're out of practice voicing who you are, talking about yourself, your wants, your needs. This is like ripping a Band-Aid off or letting go of your bike. I'm throwing you up there, Claire. If you can read through that poem in front of this crowd and survive, you'll lose your fear of putting yourself out there."

Her heart pounded in her chest, leaving her dizzy and nauseated. Looking over the crowd, she counted a few people she knew. Shelly Anne, the owner of Flat Iron Coffeehouse with her waist-length bohemian braid, Dr. Stanton and his artist son Max, and Evette's niece, Alora, who was running Blayne's store, Eclectic Finds, now that she and Jay would be going back and forth from the U.S. to Ireland. The rest was a blur of familiar but unknown faces.

Sucking in a breath, she cracked her neck from side to side. She could do this.

"Relax. You're not going into a boxing ring." Mitch chuckled.

She made a face. *Says you.*

It wasn't that she was afraid to be noticed or judged, but after Jimmy died, she couldn't think of another man. Her heart had gone with him and their baby. Over time, as the heavy blanket of sadness lifted slightly, she couldn't help the feeling of being disloyal, then that turned into a fear of being...

Crap.

Judged.

But also nervous, uncomfortable, unsure of what to say or how to say it.

Ugh, she was a mess. She could just imagine how pathetic she seemed to this handsome, confident man. Especially now that he could so easily see through her.

Wrapping her arms around her waist, she glanced at Mitch and took in his sleek, black button-up that stretched across his broad chest. The dark color was a great contrast for the intensity of his blue eyes. His hair was short and styled with a hint of product, and his cheeks had the shadow of a groomed five o'clock shadow. He looked every part of the player he was known to be, so how in the hell had he been so insightful?

"Next up at the mic, let's give a Cape Comedy Club welcome to Claire Adams!" The audience broke into their signature two-fingered clap as she froze at the sound of her name.

Butterflies swarmed, and her palms turned sweaty. She grabbed at Mitch's arm.

"You can do this, Claire. It's time."

It's time?

Yes, it really was time. But she'd waited too long. Almost four years had passed since her life had changed so unequivocally. Four years of not being a wife, not being a mother, not fulfilling her dreams. And now the town looked at her with that sad, pitying look that said she must be lonely but just can't seem to move on.

Why did everything have to change? She'd been so happy once upon a time, planning her life. Then all she could do was try and find happiness in planning everyone else's.

She dug her nails into her palms and sucked in a breath as she took the stairs up the stage. Her hand shook as she glanced at the page, then out over the heads that made up the audience. They were just words, just people. Her people really.

Jimmy's teasing grin popped into her head, the way he used to kiss her neck just under her ear. She'd been a pseudo-widow for so long; she didn't know how to be anything else.

She stepped up to the mic, then past it and down the stairs on the other side.

A murmur rose in the crowd, but she kept her head down and made her way out the front door.

As if being chased by a serial killer, she burst out onto the sidewalk of Cape Van Buren Blvd and gulped in a huge breath of air.

Mitch strolled out behind her. "You ran."

The disappointment in his voice pulled her shoulder blades together, and she shook off the regret. She had nothing to feel bad about. "No." She shook her head. "No, I *decided* not to play your silly game."

Sticking his hands in his front pockets, he nodded. "Okay, so helping you fight a fear is silly but scribbling on paper isn't?"

"There is a whole collection of studies that support the work I'm doing with you." She poked his chest, amazed at how it could seem so solid. Snatching her hand away, she made her way to the crosswalk and toward the South Cove Gardens.

"Jimmy would want you to move on, Claire."

She swung around, fire flashing through her veins. "You don't know anything about him."

"You're right. I don't," he said softly. "But I know you. And any man who loved you would not want you to fold inward. If your fiancé was as amazing as you make him sound, he wouldn't either."

And just like that, her anger dissipated. Now all she felt was that all too familiar wave of helplessness. "I don't know who I am anymore." Her hoarse whisper carried on the night breeze, and she wished she'd brought a coat. A nighttime stroll in the gardens hadn't been on her original agenda.

Mitch pulled her close, his heat providing an immediate buffer to the cold, his clean, masculine scent settling around her, making her want to breathe him in.

"Maybe you don't. But don't you want to find out?" he asked.

Did she?

Would she like what she learned? Because right now, what she did know was that she didn't want Mitch to let go. She wanted to sink in, and just for one night, allow herself to feel, *really feel*, without worrying about the consequences. And that thought alone was proof she was losing her mind. To even risk it was ludicrous.

The first time had robbed her of a love and a life.

She didn't have anything else to lose but herself.

~

*M*itch stared into troubled blue eyes that warred with invisible demons behind the scenes. He wanted to make Claire see that they were of her own making.

No man who loved Claire would ever want her to suffer. He'd want her to go after life with all the spit and vinegar she had in her until it turned into something sweet.

"I don't know if I want to find out."

Her body burrowed into his side as they followed the lamp-lit brick path that weaved through the gardens and around the pond. She fit against him just right, falling into step with him at an easy pace. A small shiver shook her frame, so he pulled her in closer. "Yes, you do."

"You don't know that." Her voice was hard...and tired. The second part was what he focused on. It helped to ease his growing awareness to the heat of her body seeping into his, her fresh scent filling his head, and the damn urgent need to kiss the uncertainty from her lips

"But I do." He glanced around the garden, the nautical ropes and aging, splintered wood posts, old ship anchors used as art pieces in the middle of flower beds and seagull sculptures that pointed the way from one area to the next.

The South Cove Madams made sure the park was an experience visitors would want to revisit again and again.

He swore he could literally hear Shelly Anne's voice in his head, he'd heard the favored description so many times. Though beautiful, the set-up was also methodical, pushing people from one area to the next, and before they knew it, they had a solid history of the town through its foliage without realizing they were being taught.

Claire was like that. Making experiences, teaching, sharing. With every event she'd planned, she gave her friends moments they'd remember, offering her own generosity and follow-through without even trying. He'd been watching her since she and Larkin Van Buren had forged their tentative friendship over a year ago.

And he worried that she would give so much of herself she'd eventually end up feeling empty instead of full.

"You're a doer, Claire. A giver. You give without thinking about what you want in return. That'll only last so long before you resent those you love."

Would she slap him if she knew what *he* wanted to give her?

He blinked back to focus, gritting his teeth against his need.

"I'd never." Her snort was adorable, but he could tell she worried about it, too.

He led them to a line of food carts that stood under heat lamps at an apex in the path, purchasing four hot cocoas, two fried cinnamon pastries, and a powdered funnel cake.

"What are you doing?" She grabbed two of the cups with a bewildered look on her face. "We cannot eat all of this."

Fuck. Her look of judgment was so damn cute. She was so restrained he wanted to make her lose her mind in pleasure until she let go.

"Why?" He led her to an iron bench that had the Cape Van Buren logo pressed into the back with the silhouette of the seagulls flying in the sky around the lighthouse. Sliding to one side, he gestured for her to join him.

"It isn't healthy, for one. Everyone knows you get one pastry, not three. And there's only two of us, why would you get four drinks?"

He shook his head. "You're missing the point. Setting up an experience for someone else makes sense to you, but to take part in it yourself knocks you on your ass."

"It does not."

He raised a brow.

She pointed at the drinks. "This is nonsense."

Picking one up, he lifted the lid and breathed it in. "Dark chocolate chipotle. Have you ever tried it?"

She peeked over the rim with interest. "No."

"How about the Peanut Butter Cocoa Dream, or the Bacon and Maple Madcap?"

"No and no."

"Why?" He took a sip of the chipotle hot cocoa. "Do you not like hot cocoa?" He wanted her to try, to taste, enjoy a little pleasure.

"I do, but..."

He pushed the fourth flavor into her hand. "Try this one."

She sniffed it. "Smells good. Like the red hots, we used to eat when we were kids. What's this one called?"

"Better Than Sex." He winked.

"Of course, it is." She rolled her eyes, but tested the temperature, then took a sip. "Oooooh, that is good. Spicy but without the burn."

"Dip this in it." He handed her a cinnamon twist pastry.

She threw him a little side-eye but did as she was told.

He set each cup along the seat between them, removing all the lids. "Dip the twist in each one, then tell me which combo you like best."

Dunking the pastry into another cup, she sighed. "This is decadent."

"But that's just it. Is it, really? Decadence implies an out of reach luxury. This whole experience that cost under twenty bucks is simply hot cocoa and pastries and is easily accessible to anyone. Yet, I bet you've never tried it." He followed suit, taking a bit of his pastry and dipping it in the Peanut Butter Cocoa Dream. The flavors hit him all at once, filling his mouth, warming his body—or it could be the way she wrapped her lips around her damn pastry stick.

He shifted on the bench, trying to focus on what was in his mouth, not what he wanted in hers.

The combination he'd chosen reminded him of the cinnamon and peanut butter toast his mom used to make him as a kid. Hell, last week. Janice was always spoiling him and Mae. She was the one who'd started him on his path of experimentation. Foods, drinks, art, travel. She always pushed him and his sister to live life and not count on anyone else to do it for them.

He wanted to do the same for Claire. The problem was, he didn't know why. Maybe she was part of his journey to becoming an essential member of the town.

"No, you're right." She grinned. "But not all of us just take what we want when we want it."

Sliding his gaze along the curve of her hip to her breasts to her lips, he nodded in agreement. "Neither do I." His tone huskier than he'd meant it to be.

Her eyes flew to his, but he composed his face into a neutral look of interest. "So, which is your favorite?" He pulled apart the funnel cake, handing her one half.

She took it without reservation this time, dipping it into the Bacon Maple. "Let me see."

With her cheeks flushed under the glow of the lamplight, her eyes had a twinkle he hadn't seen before. His heart thumped hard in his chest, and he took the warning in stride. She was enjoying herself...with him. Who'd have thunk it?

"I like the funnel cake best with the Maple Bacon and the cinnamon pastry with the peanut butter. Reminds me of your mom's toast." She laughed. "I swear, she treats us all like we're teenagers instead of almost thirty."

"What about your parents?"

"What about them?" she asked.

"Where do they live? What are they like?"

She studied him as if she were waiting for the punchline of a joke. "Are you serious?"

He held her gaze and finished off the chipotle cocoa.

Settling back against the bench, she let out a sigh. "Not much to tell. We're an average family. My dad's in sales; my mom's a teacher. They had me early on, then had an oops named Katie later in their thirties." She dismissed the question with a wave of her hand. "I don't know what you want to hear. My parents are great. My sisters a character. No deep dark secrets to uncover."

"I'd hope not. You have enough to deal with on your own."

With a soft grunt, she finished her pastry. "I've already dealt with it. This dating thing is simply an issue of being out of practice."

"You ran off the stage."

She shrugged with a smirky twist of her lips, and he had to stop himself from kissing her right then and there.

"That wasn't dating. That was simply me refusing to embarrass myself in front of the whole town."

He gathered their trash, depositing it in the Keep CVB Clean receptacle at the base of the lamplight. "The whole town?" His laugh echoed about the empty park. "Fasbender'd be able to retire early if that were the case. He's working harder to entice people into the comedy club than Larkin does the Conservation Park."

He brushed off his hands and took a slow step in invitation for her to join him. "Regardless, you getting over what people are thinking about you is first on the agenda to putting yourself back out there."

The immediate twist in his gut took him by surprise. Just the idea of another man giving her his cinnamon stick made him want to punch the phantom asshole in the throat.

The moon was high in the sky, casting an impressive glow around the quiet garden. The low rumble of the ocean's waves drifted with the breeze from the marina, reminding him of when he and Ryker used to play hide-and-seek around the parks when they were young. They were good at hiding. Ryker's dad had been good motivation.

Claire rolled her eyes. "Good Lord. Sometimes you're so annoying. Fine!" She snatched the paper he'd given her earlier from her bag, then jumped up on the bench, her skirt fluttering, then settling around her knees.

With a rattle of the paper, she cleared her throat.

*"No valley promised a rise with such grace...*wait a second." She studied the paper harder. "This is not what you gave me to read at the club." Her eyes pinned him with accusation but kept drifting back to the page in her hand.

"A more beautiful landscape would never be faced.

Silken mounds of heaven-sent pleasure.

A touch, a taste, forever to treasure.

Her curves, each dip, a heady drug found.

Her needs, her wants, he found himself bound."

With a dreamy look, the lips he tried so hard to ignore curved up at the corners.

"No prison but home in her embrace.

Each cry of passion, racing the pace.

She peaks, he soars, no earthly tether ties.

Their love transcends divinity skies."

She swayed back and forth with the rhythm of the words, her voice softening as she went.

"Two hearts made one through healing and laughter.

A journey of passion turned happy...ever...after."

Tilting her head, she looked at him, letting the hand holding the paper fall to her side. "Who wrote this?"

The inquisitive look in her eyes shouldn't have made his collar feel too tight, or the cool September night feel quite so warm, but the longer she stared, the more restless he grew.

Clearing his throat, he stepped in front of her and snatched the paper. "I did. Of course, I wasn't going to have you read the other one. It was word-for-word from a sex scene from one of the erotic novels the North Cove Mavens left lying around at my mom's house."

Her lips trembled then split with a grin as she burst out laughing. "Erotic novels?"

She hopped to the ground, falling in step next to him as they headed back to his car. "Yeah, they have a book club meeting each month." He shuddered. "You do not want to be within earshot of that one. Every time they read something dirty, they share notes on what worked and what didn't...in real life." He mimicked Maxine's voice.

Nodding, she said, "I've been to one or two. I love the books, but not necessarily hearing Evette tell us how flexible she is."

Mitch dropped his jaw in horror. "I do not want to know anymore."

"That's what you get for tricking me." They reached his vehicle, but she shook her head. "I think I'm going to call it a night."

He paused, using all his control to hide his disappointment, then turned toward her. "I shouldn't be surprised."

They couldn't be together, but he was on fire every moment they were—and he didn't want it to end.

God damn it.

She gave him a sassy grin, then snatched the poem back from his hand. "I'm keeping this. It's the least you can do for teasing me. And don't be surprised. Be proud. I'm cutting the night short, comfortable enough with myself to do so."

"Give it back." It was ridiculous, but a sliver of panic needled its way between his ribs.

"No." She walked backward. "You said I deserve beautiful things."

That stopped him in his tracks. She thought his poem was beautiful? He shouldn't feel quite so stunned or good about that fact, but there it was. He'd just been messing around...

Thinking of her.

With a wink, she headed south on Van Buren Blvd toward her apartment in South Cove Place. "Quit watching me."

"I'd never leave a lady before she was safely home. Besides, your South Cove has such a great view. I like decadence, remember?"

Her giggle floated back to him as she opened the door to her apartment stairs and paused. "Sheesh. Do you ever stop?"

He took in the sight of her under the glow of the moon and lamplight. Her eyes sparkled, and the smile on her face was genuine. That was a start at least. It would be one lucky son-of-a-bitch who got to follow her on up those stairs.

"Never," he replied. And where she was concerned, he never would. She had too much to give to hide it behind fear.

"Goodnight," she whispered.

He returned the sentiment, caressing his thumb along her cheek, lost in the feel of her soft skin.

They stood staring for an eternal moment that was not nearly enough time.

He wanted nothing as badly as he wanted to carry her up the stairs to her apartment and show her how *good* the night could really be.

Pulling in a shaky breath, she disappeared through the door, and the evening suddenly felt too cool, too quiet, like the sun had set without warning.

Rubbing his chest, he headed toward his car. She didn't have anything to be afraid of by opening up, but he couldn't quite say the same for himself.

CHAPTER 6

*C*laire stretched, luxuriating in mountains of velvety soft bed linens and the afterglow of her sexy dream. Large mounds of thick muscle, slick skin, Mitch's face rising above her.

She bolted upright in a gasp. *No. No. No.*

He was the exact opposite of what she was looking for.

And *if* the day ever came—and she seriously doubted it would—that she actually forgot the pain of her past and even considered something serious, the guy she chose would need to be a man ready to settle down, a gentleman, a man who *wanted* to be committed.

Of course, children were off the table. Having a family wasn't in the cards for her. There was no way she'd risk trying to be a mother again—so that threw another wrench in her challenge besides just getting over herself.

"Do you always talk to yourself?"

On a gasp, Claire slapped her hand over her heart and jerked toward the sound so fast that pain shot up the side of her neck. Larkin stood in the doorway, with a cooing baby Max, and wearing the same worried expression Claire had been getting ever since Larkin told her she was pregnant.

She really wished everyone would quit fretting. Work was great, her project promising and potentially the most fulfilling thing she'd ever do. She was more than fine.

Not having any more children was a choice. *Her* choice.

Creating amazing memories with other people's events was another choice. One that she enjoyed doing. And as far as Mitch went, it was his idea that she wasn't any good at dating. Well, with that one he might be right. But it was from a lack of practice, not because she was afraid.

Yes, you are.

"Shut up," she said

"Are you talking to me this time?" Larkin shifted Max higher against her chest with a bemused expression on her face. Good. It was better than the pity/worry combination she'd been sporting lately.

Claire threw the covers off her legs, sliding to the edge of the bed. "What are you doing here?"

"I've been calling all morning, and you never answered. We were supposed to meet the Mavens at the Flat Iron in order to discuss our strategy for the Van Buren Art Exhibit."

Claire rubbed her eyes and pushed up from the bed. Larkin followed her into the kitchen, going on and on about how worried she was, how much they cared, and how it was time she started getting back out there.

Claire let her rattle on as she prepared coffee in a French press. It was a habit she'd gained from working with Ryker at the conservation center. One she happily continued at home. There was nothing better than the warm, nutty essence of that first brewed carafe of coffee in the morning.

"Are you listening to me?" Larkin paused, adjusting the baby higher on her hip.

"Oh, you're still here? You know breaking and entering is a felony, right?"

Bright green eyes rolled in exasperation. "You never answered our calls and didn't show up when you were supposed to. The last thing I'm going to do is wait around until I hear from you. When people do that they end up finding out their friend was kidnapped, rope-bound and thrown in a trunk."

Claire burst out laughing. "Have you been watching those cold case shows again?"

Larkin sighed and stuck out her tongue good-naturedly. "Little Max hasn't been sleeping very well. There's only so much on TV at two in the morning."

"Two in the morning? I'd think that would be the best time to watch TV. I thought you loved a good *Hot and Hung* episode."

Her friend covered her baby's ears with a gasp. "Not in front of the baby! Now, tell me what's going on." Larkin searched her face for an answer.

Claire poured two cups of coffee, then slid one across her small kitchen island, followed by a small crystal pitcher of cream.

Her whole apartment was champagne and silk. Soft tones, luxurious fabrics, and lots of light created by crystal and glass and mirrors. She loved her little home, and when the world got to be too much, it was her favorite place to be.

With a look of appreciation, Larkin added cream until the dark brew was almost the color of almonds and took a sip with the expected look of ecstasy. "You're getting good at this. Shelly Anne may need to worry."

Everyone agreed Shelly Ann Mills made the best coffee along the coast of Maine, though Evette from the North Coast Confectionery like to pretend it was her coffee that brought the tourists to town.

"I heard a rumor that you were working on some dating project with Mitch?" The questioning tone in her friend's voice made Claire want to laugh, but she bit her tongue instead.

"But I know that can't be true since you've denied any attraction toward the man for the past year." She threw Claire an I-never-believed-you-for-a-second look then settled on her stool with an expectant glint in her eye.

Well, she could just keep on waiting—there was no persuading the woman once she got an idea in her head anyway. Claire thought back to her racy dream, and to the night before with Mitch in the park. The hot cocoa and pastries were such a simple thing, though it brought an enormous amount of pleasure. How many times could she have made her life more special with the tiniest effort? How many people missed out just by being lazy or unaware?

She shook her head. He was getting under her skin, and she couldn't allow that for a second.

She slid her hand along the white countertop of her kitchen. The white on white motif with hints of rose gold calmed her, enabling her to keep a serene smile on her face. Larkin was a little bit like Janice, a bloodhound for details and noticing small changes that could mean big things.

"Look, you guys have been looking at me like I'm going to break for the past year. Then Mitch comes around making stupid accusations that I'm afraid to date. I'm simply proving him wrong. But I'm not an idiot; I am out of practice. So who better to give me a few pointers than the town's most eligible bachelor?"

Larkin giggled. "Eligible bachelor implies that he'd ever consider marriage. I love Mitch, but I don't think that boy is ever going to settle down."

The disappointment that swelled in Claire's chest took her by surprise, but she shook it off. In hindsight, it was better to have all their cards on the table. She wasn't looking to get hurt again, and considering anything serious with a guy like Mitch would be the same as willingly stepping into a whipping den.

Besides, he wasn't interested in her, never would be, and that made him the perfect guy to help her out with this particular situation.

Larkin picked up the piece of paper from the table top with a quizzical look. "What's this?"

Claire snatched it from her hand. "Oh, nothing." She folded the paper then slid it into the front pocket of her pajama shorts.

"It didn't look like nothing. It looks like a poem. Did you write it?" she asked. "I'd love to read it." She reached her hand out, wiggling her fingers.

"Since when have I ever come across as being a poet?"

"Here." Claire reached for baby Max, always amazed at her weight for such a little thing. "She's getting big." Claire dipped her head to take in the powder-fresh scent of the sweet girl. Her heart remembered the promise of new life with a painful squeeze. Flashes of that day sped through her mind. The blood, the pain.

She hid her face in the baby's sweet neck.

But worse than the physical pain was the utter loss of everything.

Tears burned behind her lids. "You're gonna have a great life, little sweet." She whispered the promise in the baby's ear with a smile. Trying to hide the shudder in her breath, she handed the baby back to her mom and brightened the smile pulling her lips wide. "Okay, how did the meeting go with Maxine and the ladies?"

Larkin smirked. "You couldn't get out of it that easy. We've rescheduled. The meeting's in an hour."

Claire snapped her fingers. "So close. Just let me change real quick."

She needed to get her baby—and Mitch—out of her mind, but the words of his poem kept drifting through as if riding the ocean breeze, making it a task in futility.

Meeting up with the North Cove Mavens to hash out their next project would do the trick. It was dangerous to lose focus around those women.

laire followed Larkin and the baby into the luxurious atmosphere of the North Cove Bistro.

Located at the north end of Garden Parkway NW, it had a beautiful view of the ponds and gardens—nature's other rainbow.

The inside was a kaleidoscope of crystal, mirrors, and glass everywhere you looked. The effect was one of the inspirations Claire had used for her own home. It was a favorite place for the town to do brunch, especially when it called for a little bit of decadence.

And there was that word again.

She'd never thought about it much before, and now, after spending time with Mitch, it seemed to keep popping up. But what else would you call a place where hollandaise sauce poured freely and mimosas were a staple?

Maxine was dressed to the nines in her tailored eggplant suit, and she sparkled with every flutter of her ring-adorned fingers. The woman could finish scrubbing three bathrooms and run a marathon and *still* looked look more put together than any other woman in Cape Van Buren. She really needed to give lessons.

Evette and Janice sat with her at the table, disapproving looks upon their faces as she and Larkin approached.

"You know, as an honorary North Cove Maven, it is in poor form for you to blow off a meeting."

Claire shook her head with an exaggerated roll of her eyes. Maxine loved to tease as much as baby Max loved to be held. And as with both, love was the main ingredient.

"She was tired from her date last night," Larkin provided.

Startled, Claire snapped up her head and glared at her friend.

"A date?" Janice leaned toward her from across the table, curiosity bobbing her red curls more than the breeze did off the Atlantic. If she wasn't careful, Mitch's mom would be planning their wedding.

"It was not on a date. The exact opposite, actually."

"I don't know." Larkin teased. "You were with a man, alone, and I'm assuming there was food. Sounds like a date to me."

Claire kicked her friend under the table, then whispered fiercely, "What the hell are you doing?" The enjoyment on Larkin's face had Claire seeing red. "I knew I should have stayed away from you at the very beginning." But she couldn't help but smile at the sounds of Larkin's delighted laughter. She remembered the day Larkin had approached her in the kitchen supply store way back before the conservation center was even a thought.

Seeing the woman around town had been a constant reminder of everything she had lost. Larkin's husband had been the other driver participant in the road rage that ended three lives too soon. And the thought of mending fences had just been too hard. But Larkin had been persistent, and in the end, Claire had also been intrigued by Blayne's feisty protective nature. Before she knew it, she had two new best friends.

And now, aside from Larkin's dirty betrayal, she couldn't imagine life without either of them.

With an exuberance usually found in Janice, Evette popped up from her seat, waving frantically.

"What the hell are you doing? You're going to break something going on like that." Maxine looked around, bewildered.

Alora Kingsley approached the table with a friend Claire didn't recognize.

"Hey, honey." Evette kissed her cheek.

"Hey, Auntie Evette." She grinned at Maxine and the rest of the ladies, landing on Larkin and Claire. "Don't worry. I'm on my way back to Eclectic Finds. It's my lunch break."

Larkin and Claire gave each other a look of bewilderment. "Worried?" Larkin grinned. "Blayne is a wicked businesswoman. If she hired you, it's because you're awesome."

The young woman gave a humble and appreciative nod, then laid a hand on her friend's arm. "North Cove Mavens. This is Sage Mathews. She's back in town as the comic artist for *The Van Buren Tribune*."

The smile on Sage's face was sweet and sincere. Claire like her immediately.

"Hi." The young woman waved.

With a gentle touch, Maxine clasped Sage's hand. "We're so sorry to hear about your grandfather, my dear. He was wicked smart and will be terribly missed."

Horace Rosewater ran the local newspaper, *The Van Buren Tribune*, and had recently passed. The fate of the paper remained up in the air, but the sight of

Sage gave everyone hope that it would continue on in the man's absence. Horace had been uniting Cape Van Buren with news of births and birthdays, graduations and promotions for years. The news of his death had hit everyone pretty hard.

"Thank you so much." Sage pressed her lips together in that way people did when they were trying to hold themselves together. "I'm hoping to keep the paper going. There's been talk that worries me."

Evette turned to Maxine. "Can you talk to Teddy?"

"He's about as likely to listen to me right now as he is to start selling moonshine out of the courthouse kitchens." She chuckled, apparently amused at the vision. She tapped one jeweled finger to her chin. "But let me see what I can do."

Sage's shoulders dropped in relief as she took Maxine in a hug. "Thank you. Anything will help. I know it."

The two ladies said their goodbyes, and Claire watched after them, musing how fast five years could go. They looked so young, but she'd been where they were, and it seemed like yesterday.

The unlikely silence at the table dragged her gaze back to her friends, only to find every pair of nosy eyes on her.

"Give it up, honey," Maxine scolded. "There is no way we are letting this drop."

Claire let out an exasperated breath. How in the hell could they pop right back to Mitch so fast? She hated clichés, but they were like a dog with a bone. "You all are ridiculous. It was not a date, it was..." She thought about what she should call it. Anything she said at this point had the potential to set the ladies off in a direction she never wanted them to go. Where was a damn life compass when you needed one?

"...a business meeting."

"Business meetings don't include sensual, beautiful poems."

"Sensual, huh?" Evette raised her thin eyebrows. As she had gotten older, with her dark hair pulled back into a bun and her long, thin form, she resembled Popeye's wife, Olive Oyl, more and more.

"That poem wasn't for me. I mean, it was for me. But for me to read, not for me on an emotional level." She could hear the words coming out of her mouth but couldn't stop the blathering.

All three ladies leaned in for a conspiratorial whisper.

"Sounds like a date to me," Maxine declared.

Janice smiled. "I have to agree. So, who was the lucky lucky fella?"

Larkin snuggled baby Max to her chest. "Oh, you're gonna love this, Janice."

Claire's jaw dropped open. "What did I ever do to you?" she hissed. "I would expect this from Blayne but never you."

"Yeah, but Blayne isn't here, and I have to admit, I love seeing the fire in your eyes lately."

"What am I going to love?" Janice prodded.

Claire folded her hands in front of her, very aware of the din in the restaurant around them, the multiple conversations, the pop of a champagne cork, the soft melody of some bar lounge soundtrack, and wished with all her might that she could disappear in it all. "Fine. Mitch is giving me pointers on how to get back out into the dating game, and in exchange, I recruited him to help me work through my process for the Coping through Art program for the Center. You know, so we can make sure it's actually going to help our kiddos." She was over-explaining, but hoped like hell, with her fingers and toes crossed, that they would focus on the helping the kids part.

Janice blinked once, twice...

And there it was. Hearts floating about her head.

"Janice, don't get any ideas. We're just friends."

"Friends? Now, this is interesting," his mom responded.

Maxine sipped from her mimosa, a keen edge in her all-knowing gaze. "It sure is. A few weeks ago, they were at each other's throats, but maybe that was just foreplay."

Claire closed her eyes, hoping that when she opened them, all her friends would have disappeared.

No luck.

Crap.

"Look, he teased me for being awful at the dating game, and he was right. And I needed a guinea pig for my program. So... oink, oink." Ignoring the probing looks, she turned her attention back to her plate and took a bite of her eggs Benedict, savoring the delicious, savory sauce and the fleeting moment of silence.

"Wait a minute," Janice said in a suspicious tone. "Did you say he wrote a poem? What was it about?"

Warning bells rang in her head louder than the Van Buren Fire Station's during their Pancake Breakfast fund-raising event.

Claire studied the woman's face for any hint of why she was asking. "It seemed to be about a man and woman...you know. Making love." She set her fork down, rushing on. "I don't know when he wrote it, but it was one he gave me to read at the Cape Comedy and Nightclub's open mic. Just to push me out of my comfort zone."

The hearts that had been floating about Janice's head morphed into full-blown wedding bells. "He only writes poems about things he envisions for his future. Kind of like a vision board. He's been writing them since he was a little boy." She nudged Evette. "I can't say I know of one thing that he hasn't made come true."

Claire choked on her mimosa, and Larkin patted her on the back.

"You have the wrong idea, ladies. As I said before, we are *just friends*." Dread wrapped her chest in a tight squeeze. The last thing she needed was the North Cove Mavens making wedding plans.

"That's the best way to start." Maxine raised her glass for a toast.

She saw the hell Larkin and Blayne had been put through...all at their amusement.

And look how they turned out.

Claire swallowed against the panic clawing up her throat. She might deserve the harassment after laughing at their expense when they were dating. But she was different. She wasn't strong or crazy enough to risk her heart again for a happy ever after...the after was too painful.

CHAPTER 7

*W*ednesday morning, Claire patted Mitch's arm in encouragement, and the heat of her touch raced through him like there was a prize to win. "That's it. Perfect," she praised.

It had been days since he'd last seen her, but she'd had an event Sunday, and he'd had clients and court Monday, so midweek was the soonest they'd been able to reconnect.

The fact he was so aware of the time that had passed made his chest constrict. He had one rule. No attachment.

But her eyes danced in delight, oblivious to his disquiet.

If this was the look she gave every student, they would be bound and determined to please her no matter how ridiculous the task might be.

He felt like an idiot, trying to draw with his eyes closed, but apparently, she was all about the scribbles. It left him feeling edgy. Kind of like hiking through the woods during hunting season. But he'd made a deal. And he was a man of his word.

Her fingers lingered on his bicep, and he tightened it before he could stop himself.

Fucking amateur, but his scolding inner voice had no impact whatsoever because as her hand pressed into his muscle, his dick jumped with the thought of her wrapping those long, slender fingers around it instead.

64

Clearing his throat, he shifted in his seat to make room for the inconvenience.

Finally aware of her actions, she stepped away, pretending to busy herself organizing the art supplies on her work table, but there was no mistaking the soft blush coloring her cheeks.

She grabbed two tacks and his paper. "Okay, now I want you to take a moment and study your drawing. What do you see?"

He followed the curves of his swirling lines. What the hell was she expecting? They were indecipherable marks. He'd been scribbling with his eyes closed, for fuck's sake.

Feeling restless, he stood from his chair, then rounded the desk to sit on the edge. He crossed his arms and stared at the damn picture, unsure why he suddenly felt so annoyed. "I don't know what you want me to say. It's scribble."

"It is, and that is exactly what I wanted you to do with that part of the task. But now, I want you to look closely and see what shapes jump out at you." She spoke with a patient cadence and a kindness in her eyes that made him want to say *yes, ma'am.*

And then scoop her up in his arms and show her just what he was capable of doing with his eyes open.

Unfortunately, that wasn't a possibility, so he studied the frustrating picture more closely. The shapes were the curves of her breasts and the dip of her tiny waist, but he couldn't say any of that. She'd hightail it out of the Cape house faster than the rabbits into the woods when he and Ryker cleared brush from the yards.

He flexed his fingers, studying his picture. "I don't know." Angling his head from side to side, he tried to see something other than a mess. For some reason, he wanted to please her, but he just couldn't see a damn thing.

"Look here." She slid a finger along four circular shapes. "This makes me think of your family."

His family? Nope. His family only had three people in it. Four made no sense. A tightening in his gut left him feeling hot and agitated. Shrugging out of his sweatshirt, he tried to look again.

"Do you see it?" she prompted.

Brushing his hands down the front of his "moose juice" t-shirt, he stared harder, then shook his head. "Nope. Sorry."

She tilted hers, studying his face with a thoughtful curiosity in her gaze, then back at the drawing. The Cape house was silent except for the ticking of the large grandfather clock in the foyer that used to belong to Maxine and Stuart Van Buren. She'd left it for Ryker when he'd bought the property, and then he'd donated it to the Center when he and Larkin had moved out to her house tucked in the woods on the north coast of the North Cove. He and Ryker used to race to sit at the base when the monstrosity struck twelve. They could feel each resounding *dong* in their bones.

His mind wandered in every direction but where it was supposed to. He blamed Claire, and the way her top molded so perfectly to her breasts, making his hands itch to do the same, and how the tie of her shirt made her waist seem so impossibly small that he wanted to wrap his hands around it to see if his fingers could touch. He blinked and focused back on his paper.

Once again, she traced along a few more lines. "How about here? It looks like a couple in a joyous reunion."

He laughed. If he saw a couple, they were in the throes of great sex, not a damn reunion. That implied a commitment. And that wasn't something he was willing to try. You couldn't hurt anyone you didn't make promises to.

"Sorry, sweetheart. That looks more like the beginnings of a happy ending, not a happy ever after," he winked at her.

She gave him a disgusted look, then back at the drawing. "Do you ever think of anything except sex?"

He shrugged. "What do you expect? I'm telling you how I see it. Sorry, your program isn't working. But you're giving it a go. That's what's important."

Thank God a look didn't actually have the power of the intent behind it, or he'd be dead. "I'll have you know, my program is working just fine." She marched up and snatched the drawing from the wall.

Shoving him from the edge of the desk, she pointed to the chair. "Sit."

She slid the paper and colored pencils in front of him. "Now color the images we discussed."

He sighed. "Aww...come on. Are you serious?"

She crossed her arms and tapped her toe. The kids were in for a big surprise if they thought they were going to get away with anything just because she had the sweetest smile and kindest eyes on the Atlantic coast.

66

"Fine." He picked up a black pencil, then colored a section of the paper, being sure to stay within the lines. No reason to tick her off anymore.

After a few minutes, he glanced up to find her watching him from her work table. He paused at the worry in her gaze. "What? I'm doing what you asked."

She nodded once. "The poem. When did you write that?"

He shrugged, coloring as he spoke. Truth be told, the action was relaxing once he got past feeling like a jackass for coloring in the first place. "A few days ago."

She stilled. "Have you written any before?"

Setting the pencil down, he tried to anticipate where her questions were going. "Why?"

"Just something your mother said."

"You can't believe everything my mother says, and not because she lies. Because her perspective may be something altogether different than reality."

"Or she's spot on," she challenged. "What else have you written about?"

Graduating from college, becoming an attorney. Hell, he'd written some words about the city attorney position he wanted, too, but something kept him from sharing any of that with her.

"Nothing specific. The weather, a feeling." Hell, he had no idea what to say.

Her shoulders sagged almost in relief.

"Why?" He handed her his drawing.

Taking it, she turned it until she could study the images right side up. "No reason. Just curious." She walked to the table and stood in front of him.

He dipped his chin.

"I never want to be someone who doesn't give credit where credit is due. It's really beautiful." She looked at him like he were a puzzle to be solved instead of his drawing.

"It is?" The gruffness in his voice surprised him, and he tried again. "You liked it?"

She looked everywhere but at him. "It's sensual and full of worship as if the experience was really transcendent."

His fingers found the edge of her jaw, gliding from below her cheek to her chin. Her skin was smooth, creamy like the homemade, whipped, vanilla cream cheese frosting that Evette iced her cupcakes with.

The poem was the result of a dream. One he shouldn't have had, but it'd stuck with him. His body tightened in anticipation at the memory. "Isn't it?" he rasped.

The tips of his finger brushed her lips, and she sucked in a breath. "Sex is great, but this is real life."

Her upper lip was formed in a perfect cupid's bow, supported by a full lower lip that he could spend hours exploring. Something had shifted over the past few weeks. The feistier she'd gotten with him, the more often he'd sought her out. She was an enigma.

And he wanted her. So. Fucking. Bad.

Wanted to feel her wrapped around him, wanted to sink so deep inside her he wouldn't give a fuck if he ever found his way out—and neither would she.

"Real life deserves transcendence. Real life can be hard and painful, throwing challenge after challenge. Making love is one of the few things where transcendence is possible."

Her eyes heated in interest. "Do you really believe that?"

"Don't you?"

His heart pounded in his chest as her familiar scent tugged him closer. He found his lips inches from hers.

She licked hers, the pink tip of her tongue darting out with her breathless nerves. "I never have."

"Then you've been doing it wrong." Having her so close clouded his judgment. He'd been swinging from irritated to restless to full-on raging lust in the short time he'd spent with her, leaving him ready to explode.

Had her fiancé not taken her to those heights? To where she couldn't tell where she stopped and he started? Where her vision went white, and she could barely breathe?

He leaned closer, desperate to taste her, desperate to feel her against him. A chance to ease the restless need he felt in her presence.

"What are you doing?" She placed her fingers against his chest, just before his mouth claimed hers. The look in her eyes showed a hint of fear or worry and then panic, which caught him off guard and slammed him back to reality.

Stepping back with a chuckle, he shoved his hands in his back pockets. "Completing your second lesson. You handled that just fine."

She blinked. "My second lesson?"

"You held your own, a bit of flirtation. You didn't shut down or run away."

His cover-up came fast. Thank God. He swallowed down his disappointment and frustration.

Her fingers burned against his chest with the scalding heat of her rejection. She could never know he'd almost just kissed her. Believing she might have wanted him to.

The look on her face transformed to confusion then irritation.

Clearly, he was the last person she'd ever want to reach transcendence with.

"Well, I'm glad your little experiment worked."

Pretending to be distracted by his drawing, he picked it up and played busy at studying it, then turned it toward her. "I'm sorry yours didn't."

*L*ater that evening, Claire picked through her closet, cussing at Mitch as she went. He'd made a date for her. A freaking date!

Apparently, the kiss she'd thought had been coming earlier, which had made her heart race in panic and celebration at the same time, had been nothing more than a damn lesson.

Sonofabitch.

Crazy didn't even begin to describe what she'd gotten herself into. Every moment she spent with him only made her want more. She could get lost in his scent, his touch, the low rumble of his sexy voice.

Damn it!

Shaking her head, she rummaged through the pile of heels she was considering. Gold strappy heels, nude pumps, pink champagne, faux snake-skin stilettos.

Apparently, the guy was approved by Larkin. There was an inkling of peace with that thought. Claire could at least rest assured that her friend had her back. Mitch, on the other hand, wasn't quite who she pictured as a matchmaker—unless it was for Bender. The dating app that seemed to be more booty call than a coffee date.

She frowned. That might not be quite fair, but he certainly seemed to choose his own dates based on looks and libido.

Cape Van Buren's very own bombshell police officer Cindy Majors popped into her mind.

"Shit," she whispered into the empty room.

That wasn't fair either. Cindy was wicked smart and funny, too.

With a concerted effort, she stepped into her little slice of paradise.

Her closet. It was her favorite place in her apartment. Saving up from a few recent events she'd planned, she'd had a designer come in and create a little fashion haven in the small space. Glass shelves, stacked clothes hangers, a huge floor-to-ceiling mirror, all accented with silver and pink. The soft tones suited her and promoted a feeling of luxury.

Mitch might even say...decadence.

Which made her think of the fun they'd had in the park, which brought her back to her current situation. And she swore.

He'd been so impressed with how she handled his practice flirting that he thought she was ready for an actual date.

Which was total crap.

First, she hadn't handled it well. She'd wanted him to kiss her so badly, she'd almost grabbed him right then and there and demanded he show her what she was missing.

If the bulge in his jeans was any indication, she was missing a damn helluva lot.

How fucked up was that? Children would be making art in that room, for Pete's sake.

She'd thought his gesture had been genuine. She'd thought he'd wanted her.

She was simply a fool...or a simple fool, which was a double whammy.

Scraping hangers from right to left, she scanned through her blouses. Pulling out a soft peach tailored button-up, she held it in front of her, looking in the mirror. On a sigh, she threw it on the bed, then repeated the action with an ivory spaghetti-strap cami and a gray cashmere v-neck sweater.

Damn it. Now she couldn't even dress herself. This whole situation was humiliating.

She looked at the rainbow of soft colors on her bed, trying to see it from another angle. One thing that was not humiliating was her program. Mitch had dismissed the work as though it had failed, but he had exposed so much of himself that she had been afraid to point it out for fear of scaring him away. So she'd kept her observations to herself.

If the dark silhouette of a person standing behind the drawing he'd made of himself, his sister, and mother was any indication, he had a lot of anger or fear or both surrounding whatever had happened when his dad had abandoned them so long ago.

Moving to her writing desk, she pulled open the center drawer to peek at his drawing once again. He kept surprising her with a sensitivity and creativity he never showed when he was about town. Her heart gave a little shudder as if waking up from a long nap.

"Did you find something?" Mitch asked from the doorway.

She slammed the drawer shut and spun around. Hoping to distract him, she arched her arm toward the bed. "What, so now you want to make me over, too? This isn't *Pretty Woman* you know. Or the *Ugly Truth*."

He shook his head, stepping slowly toward her bed. "How you look or what you wear has never been your problem."

She froze, wanting him closer, but afraid to move.

"You're a knockout, Claire." He slid a finger along her collarbone to her shoulder, sending a shiver down her arm. "Any man would be crazy not to want you."

"You're crazy." Her voice was barely a whisper.

"Not that crazy."

She blinked. Did he just admit to wanting her? Confusion and yearning swamped her. Then why was he sending her off with another man?

Because you told him to, dumbass.

She stood next to him, heat flushing her chest at his words. "You really think I'm a knockout?"

Stepping back, he swallowed hard and ogled her from the top of her head to the tips of her pink polish-covered toes. Suddenly her yoga pants and long-sleeved pullover were too warm for the cold Maine day.

He threw her a wink. "The only thing I'd change about your clothes would be leaving them on the floor."

And there he was...Mitch-about-town. Shameless flirt. Unapologetic playboy. And all-around fun guy. Not to be trusted, but always good for a laugh. She could handle that Mitch. She slapped playfully at his arm. "You are ridiculous."

He nodded. "Pick something already, then meet me out in your living room."

The doorbell rang.

"I'm not expecting anyone." She called out as she slipped her arms into the soft peach button-up.

"I got it." She heard him answer in that sexy, masculine drawl that never failed to send goosebumps up and down her arms.

She believed he did have it. And she wanted him to give it to her. So help her God.

Quickly dropping her pants and throwing her shirt in the corner, she dragged the cashmere sweater over her head, then shoved her legs into a pair of dark-washed skinny jeans. Squeals echoed from her living room, and all she could imagine was that he'd invited Larkin.

That made her pause for a second. With a shake of her head, she ran into her bathroom.

A few quick swipes of deodorant, a spritz of perfume, lip gloss, and black liner, then she grabbed the pink stilettos as she made her way out her bedroom door.

Larkin and Blayne squeezed Mitch from both sides resisting his struggles to be released. Claire hid her giggles behind her fingers.

"Tell me you missed me," Blayne demanded, the look of a well-loved woman shining from her crystal gaze.

Finally freeing himself, Mitch stepped away to hide behind Claire. "I missed you about as much as I miss my mother asking me why all of her Victoria Secret magazines always ended up in my bedroom."

"Ha! That is not surprising." Blayne laughed.

Setting her heels on the floor, Claire threw her arms around her spunky friend. "When did you get back? I thought you had another week."

Blayne shook her head. "We'd decided to keep it to a week. We're heading to Ireland next month to scope out sites for another Eclectic Finds in Glengarriff, but we have a lot to do between the store here and Jamie stepping into his father's seat in the family biz." She slid her arm through Larkin's. "It helps I already have Alora Kingsley running the store here for me."

"Isn't that Evette's niece?" Mitch asked.

"Yes, and the one woman in town you haven't defiled yet." Blayne winked to soften the blow.

Mitch simply stuck up his middle finger.

"You two are like brother and sister. We saw Alora yesterday, by the way. With Horace Rosewater's granddaughter. I like her," Larkin said.

Blayne's berry-red lips stretched wide. "Me, too. I haven't worried about my store since the day I hired her."

Larkin pulled open Claire's wine fridge. "I need wine. Max is hanging with her daddy tonight, so I don't have to be responsible."

Choosing a Malbec, she moved through the motions of removing the foil and cork. "Besides, we need to toast Claire finally getting off her perky but celibate little booty."

Nerves skittered across Claire's chest, feeling as if they were pressing down and stealing her breath. "Okay, I'm meeting a guy for a drink, not a booty call."

She accepted the offered glass from Larkin.

"Oh, come on." Blayne fake whined. "Be like Nike and just do it."

Mitch grabbed a glass and set it none too gently in front of Larkin. "Knock it off. I'd kill the guy if he landed a hand on her." His growl made the room go silent.

Claire couldn't help the thrill that ran through her at his irritation. Was he jealous? The thought made her grin even if it shouldn't.

Blayne and Larkin slowly turned their heads toward Mitch.

She'd rather be going on this date with Mitch. He'd become some sort of seriously sexy safety net. The idea of having to get to know some stranger, of letting him in, sharing her past, made her stomach turn.

He threw up his hands. "He's a buddy of mine. Nice guy. But I'm not a damn pimp, for Christ's sake."

Larkin raised her glass. "Well, regardless of when Claire gets laid, I'm proud of you for getting back out there. Cheers."

"For one, I don't need a man to satisfy myself. I have that covered in just about every corner of my apartment."

Mitch raised a brow.

Claire returned a challenging stare. "Open the drawer to your right."

With a confused frown, he grabbed the shiny silver rod of her junk drawer and pulled. Inside was a flashlight, container of safety pins, super glue, and a small vibrator.

He slammed the door shut and stared at her hard. "What the hell is that doing in there?"

Claire took another sip with a smile. There was something quite satisfying about seeing him rattled. Even if it was only a smidge. "I'm surprised you don't find it...oh, I don't know...decadent."

He guffawed. "It's decadent alright, but in the kitchen?"

She shrugged. "You never know when inspiration will hit. Buzz, buzz."

Truth be told, that particular one was mostly used for a trigger point that always acted up in her left trap muscle when she stood too long while baking. But he didn't need to know that.

And hell. She lived alone. If she wanted to hop up and christen her new granite counter tops, she'd damn well do it. He was the one always telling her to make memorable moments.

Well, she couldn't imagine anything quite as memorable as an orgasm in the middle of the day, surrounded by bundt cakes.

Except maybe if it was with him.

Wait. What?

She tossed back the rest of her wine. *No, no, no.*

Blayne raised her glass. "You rock."

Claire refused to look back at Mitch for fear of imagining him without his shirt on again and slipped on her heels. "Okay. I've got to go. I'm meeting him at six."

Mitch cleared his throat and placed his big hands on her shoulders. "It's a Wednesday. No pressure. No one wants to stay out too late on a work night. Drinks and a few appetizers, maybe. Just chat as you did with me the other night and this morning. You'll be great."

But that was the problem. She could chat with Mitch. He was safe. He was...a friend.

She studied his face.

The revelation took her off guard. She didn't know when it had happened. But as unlikely as she'd ever have thought it, he'd become a friend. She trusted him, even enjoyed his company when he wasn't being an ass. And totally enjoyed the sight of his ass.

Her lips curved up.

"Good. I'm glad to see you excited."

He couldn't read people worth a shit though.

Larkin, Blayne, and Mitch surrounded her by the door. "You never did say why you were here," she said.

Larkin smiled. "For you, of course."

"Mitch called us. He knew you'd feel stronger with the support." She made an I-was-as-surprised-as-you face. "Who'd have thunk it? He might actually be pretty smart."

Mitch rubbed the space between his brow with a tight-lipped growl.

Claire's heart shuddered again. He called them for her? Her heart turned over. Twice.

Stepping up to him, she kissed his cheek, the feel of his scruff against her lips sending a shiver of awareness through her chest. "Thank you."

"You got this," Mitch said in a strained voice as she stepped out the door of her apartment. She looked back to see her two best girlfriends grinning at her with misplaced pride, and Mitch looking at her conflicted, as if being forced to share his favorite toy, and he wanted to fight someone.

But she didn't have shit.

The only reason he thought she could handle this was because she talked to him so easily.

And that was the biggest problem of all.

CHAPTER 8

$\mathcal{M}$itch stepped through the sliding doors of the Cape house kitchen onto the covered back porch, then slammed them closed. The cold sea breeze hit with a shock against his bare skin, but he needed the distraction.

He'd tried to go to bed but couldn't fall asleep, so he'd thrown on a pair of athletic pants and paced the foyer.

Then he'd gone downtown like a crazy bastard to crash the date.

Twice.

Stopping himself just short of anyone seeing him.

Motherfucking hell.

Forcing himself to go back to the Cape, he'd rummaged around to see if he could scout out any hidden reserves of Maxine's moonshine.

Score.

It was well past nine, and Claire should be safely home in her apartment, and maybe even in bed by now.

He hadn't heard from her yet, and the waiting was torture.

Maybe she'd taken the guy home after all.

The image of her showing her date how that damn vibrator worked sparked a pain so irrational that he didn't even know himself anymore.

So he shoved that from his head with all the self-control he possessed.

Sipping from the blue canning jar, he released a grumpy sigh.

He pictured her naked, but alone, God damn it, and surrounded by baked goods. The idea tightened his body to a painful level. He scrubbed at the scruff on his face to keep from rubbing one out right there on the porch.

Fuck.

He couldn't even imagine if Maxine caught him. She'd either have his nuts for it or cheer him on in her healthy, sex-forward way of thinking.

That would be worse.

And then that damned vibrator and a naked Claire covered in powdered sugar popped in his head.

"Jesus Christ. I'm fucking turned on by baked goods now."

A low voice caught his attention from the direction of the well, and he squinted through the darkness to get a better look. Something about a penny and a wish. The silhouette of a person could just barely be seen in the darkness.

"Hey! Who's there?" His bellow echoed back from the trees, louder than he'd expected. But he had a lot of energy to take care of. A damn trespasser would do the trick.

The figure froze. "Crap." The voice was barely audible, but he'd recognize it anywhere, and his body sprung away like he'd downed one of Shelly Anne's espressos.

"Claire?"

She approached from the well, her bare feet silent in the grass, and her heels hanging from her fingers.

"You have to be freezing. What the hell are you doing out there?"

Throwing him an accusing glare, she asked, "What the hell are *you* doing here?"

As she reached the steps, he grabbed her arm and propelled her into the kitchen. Without thinking, he wrapped his arms around her and drew her up against his chest. She was chilled to the bone, her small frame shivering as he pulled the door closed behind them. "I'm living here as the caretaker while I figure out where I want to land. Sold my apartment. Looking at houses."

The city attorney needed a home, a symbol of attachment and commitment. His bachelor pad wasn't doing the job. He'd approached Larkin and Ryker about the caretaker position until they had enough time to really comb out the right candidate to take his place.

She was rubbing her cheek back and forth against his chest, her eyes closed, a half smile on her face. Confusion settled on his shoulders. "Are you okay?"

Her smile fell, and she froze. She blinked a few times, then tilted her head back. "You can let me go now." Her fingers patted his chest in an awkward flutter.

The problem was, he didn't want to let her go. She fit against him so perfectly that he felt weightless. "Not yet. You're shivering." He'd tell the lie again if he could hold her for a second longer. "What are you doing here?" he asked in a soft tone.

"I couldn't go through with it." She mumbled against his chest, sounding dejected and sending a wash of goosebumps over his skin.

A huge flood of relief almost knocked him on his ass.

For his own sanity, he walked her to the bench under the window next to the sliding glass doors. Lifting the seat, he grabbed one of the many blankets Maxine had stored there. That woman had a keen sense of what would be needed and when, from blankets in unusual storing places to wet wipes or batteries. An assortment of supplies could be found in every room.

Running around the house with Ryker as a kid was like being a pirate on a treasure hunt. He couldn't count the times she'd threatened them if they kept stealing her stuff, but a hidden flashlight to a ten-year-old was way too cool to pass up.

Pushing his moonshine into her fingers, he said. "Drink some of this. It'll warm you." As she did what she was told, he wrapped a blanket around her shoulders, then noticed her bare toes.

"For fuck's sake, Claire." With his hand at the small of her back, he propelled her forward. "Come on. I lit a fire. Let's get you warmed up before you drive home."

"I walked."

He almost missed a step as he led her toward the master bedroom.

"You walked. Are you fucking crazy?" His eyes skimmed past the wainscotting that followed up the stairs, now white instead of the black it used to be. "Town isn't far, but you were in those damn heals and it's dark, and the driveway is long."

She looked down at her toes. "I took off my shoes."

Shaking his head, he guided her through the bedroom door to one of the plush, high-backed tufted chairs in front of the fireplace he'd lit earlier.

The master bedroom had changed from Maxine's signature eggplant to different shades of gold. It still wasn't his taste but was sure as hell better than the prissy style it used to be.

Claire would probably love it but still resisted from entering.

"Take it easy," he said on a low chuckle, the rumble filling his chest and the room. "We're only in here because the fireplace was already lit to take off the chill. It is ten o'clock at night, you know."

She relaxed immediately and sunk into the chair where Puzzle rested. The cat jumped down with a sinister stare, then, nose in the air, weaved around her ankles.

On a sigh, she stretched her toes toward the fire. "I've always wanted a fireplace in my bedroom. I imagine it's what you'd call decadent."

She knew him too well at this point. Squatting down at her feet, he lifted one into his hand. She tried to tug it away, but he stopped her. "Listen, you just walked from town—*barefoot*—in thirty-degree weather. Can you stop being stubborn for one damn minute and just let me help you?"

Finally acquiescing, she relaxed back into the chair with a dreamy look on her face as he began to knead the small muscles between the bones of her dainty feet. "Surprised these things can even keep you upright." His voice was gruff, and he swallowed to clear it.

She wiggled her toes. "These *things* served me quite well, thank you very much."

He nodded as he thought of all the ways he wanted to serve her. "Are you going to tell me what happened? Why are you here, Claire?"

She drew in a deep, troubled breath, then let it out in a long exhale. "Started out fine. We ordered drinks, casual conversation, but then his fingers were on my wrist, and his knee was pressing against mine. He started asking me about what I wanted in a relationship. I don't know, I just panicked. Dating is such a big commitment. There are other people to consider. In their lives, in my own. What if we really enjoy each other's company, what if we started spending a lot of time together?"

She shifted in her seat but left her foot in his hand. He changed the motion of his fingers to firm, slow circles. A slight shiver shook her frame, and she closed her eyes.

"So what if all of that happens? Doesn't sound like a negative thing to me." Even though he had to force himself not to squeeze her foot too hard, as if holding on tighter would keep her closer.

This time she did pull her foot away. "Says the man who's never had a relationship longer than foreplay and orgasm."

"Fair enough." He dipped his chin. "But has it ever occurred to you that I have my reasons? It amazes me that no one has ever thought to ask. I know, I know you have your reasons, too. But you yourself said that you wanted to get out there. So, what the hell is stopping you?"

"What if I fall in love?"

Her quiet whisper hit him square in the chest. The idea of her falling in love with another man filled him with an unreasonable amount of jealousy and a pain in his chest he could only imagine felt like a damn heart attack. He forced his question out. "Isn't that what you want?"

She moved her head back and forth. "No, I want companionship, I want a man's hands on me, to feel the weight of him, but I don't want to fall in love. That only opens you up for unimaginable pain."

"You don't really believe that. You can't turn away from love in your life because you're afraid."

His inner voice called him every other name for a hypocrite in the book. But it was different for him. He was afraid of ever hurting anyone like his mother had been hurt, not necessarily afraid of being hurt himself. Though if any of the inconvenient sensations he'd been experiencing since taking on this project with Claire were any indication, getting hurt would be a fine thing to avoid as well.

"I am completely serious," she said her voice stronger now. Pulling her feet up, she tucked them under her butt and leaned against one corner of the chair.

She wasn't a tiny woman, not compared to the average ladies he saw around town. She was tall and fit with a petite frame but not so small that she should look as fragile as she did at that moment. "So how did you end the night?" he asked, careful to keep his voice light.

A slight blush covered her cheeks, and she grimaced. "He went to use the restroom, and I was gone before he came back."

"You did not," Mitch said with a chuckle. "I am never gonna hear the end of this." In the end, he didn't care. Suddenly, his buddy no longer seemed like a good fit for her. She deserved someone extraordinary. And though Cape Van Buren had better than most, extraordinary was not easy to come by.

"Not only that, but you know how long it's been since a man has held me? Since I've kissed anyone? I was this close..." She put her pointer finger and thumb almost touching.

"And don't laugh or make any jokes. I've heard them all from you already."

That statement left him feeling more than a little ashamed, but that was one of the reasons he was helping her. This was a good opportunity to try to make it up to her. And in return, it could enable him to turn a new leaf toward being a citizen who was upstanding and respected, known for caring about the people of this town. Clearly, from her statement, he still had a long way to go.

"I'm not making any jokes. Not tonight."

She glanced up at him warily.

"The only thing I can tell you, is the longer you resist, the harder it will be. It's just a matter of letting yourself be open to a bit of pleasure from someone you are attracted to, someone you trust.

"Are you going volunteer?" she asked with a little smirk.

A surge of red-hot lust coursed through him with such force he almost lost his balance, but he shook his head, forcing out the lie. "No, of course not."

She tilted her head to the side, studying his features, then let her eyes wander down his bare torso. He was still kneeling at her feet and suddenly feeling more exposed than he could ever remember.

"Actually..." She scooted to the edge of her seat. "Would you? I do trust you, and I don't find you unattractive."

His bark of laughter echoed around the room. He could hear the bewilderment and a touch of embarrassment in the sound of it and took a hard swallow. "Me? Is this a joke? All we've done is argue since we met."

"Exactly," Claire said, "I need to break out of this rut and how much safer can I get than with you? I mean the risk of either of us falling in love with each other is pretty much nil."

The look on her face was sincere, and he'd damn well never let her know how much those words hurt, even if they were true. He was a safe bet. He didn't want to get entangled in a committed relationship any more than she did. So why in the hell was it so easy to picture seeing her face first thing every morning?

He cleared his throat. "Are you sure about this?"

She shoved up from the chair and shook out her hands. "Quit stalling, or I'm gonna chicken out. It's like ripping off a bandage. Let me get this first kiss out of the way and then maybe I can go out and be a normal adult on a date. Something's gotta give, or I'm going to get a reputation worse than Julia Roberts in *Runaway Bride*."

His chuckle was low and strangled. "I feel like you might have a thing for Julia Roberts. How the hell did you pull that movie out of your ass?"

"She's my fave. Chick flick nights with my mom," she said as she placed his hands on her hips.

Warning bells clanged in his head as he gripped her waist.

Her fingers didn't know where to settle on his shoulders.

"Do you want me to put on a shirt?"

Her eyes devoured his chest as she darted the tip of her pink tongue out to lick her lips, almost undoing his tenuous hold on his self-control. Clamping down on his need to yank her up against him, he gently pulled her closer.

"I'm sure," she said, adding with a bit of sarcasm. "And no, I'm a big girl. I think I can handle Mitch Brennan without his shirt on."

He flashed a cocky grin. "We'll see."

Holding her gaze, he slowly dipped his head to hover his lips just above hers. Tension played tug-of-war between them, and his blood rushed through his veins in eager anticipation. A little closer.

Closer.

His lips tingled with the hint of moisture from her soft breath.

Just as his lips were about to brush hers, she burst out laughing and dropped her forehead to his chest.

He froze. What the hell just happened? With his hands on her shoulders, he slowly eased back to look into her eyes. "Is everything okay?" He wasn't sure if he should be insulted or concerned.

"Oh my gosh! I am so sorry. I don't know why I'm laughing." Her cheeks blushed red, and the mortification in her eyes eased the sting of her laugh.

There was nothing like a woman laughing in his face just before kissing him to remove the discomfort of an erection. As his body cooled, he muttered, "We don't have to do this, Claire."

"No, no, I want to. I don't know what's wrong with me." She shook out her hands. "Okay, okay. Let's try again."

Her fingertips slid across his chest, leaving a trail of sensation behind them. As she wrapped her arms around his neck, he closed the distance between their mouths once more.

Her sharp crack of laughter made him jump, and he released her. Confusion didn't even begin to describe the emotions running rampant through him. The moment was a physical rollercoaster with the drop and climb of a big hill ride.

"So sorry!" she exclaimed, her cheeks a deep red as if she'd just stepped in from too long in the sun. "What is wrong with me? Oh, my God. I'm such a mess." She moved back in. "Just kiss me. Don't make it soft, don't make it sweet."

He drew her up against his chest and, at the last minute, her cackling laugh filled his head. This time he joined her himself. He didn't have to imagine how mortified she was because he could read it all over her face. She really wasn't ready, and that was okay.

The damn kiss was for her, not him, anyway.

"It's okay, Claire."

"God damn it!" She swore. "I can't believe this."

She stared at him a moment as if having a silent argument behind the scenes, then with a sudden steely gleam in her eye, she slid her fingers into his hair and yanked him forward, slamming her lips against his. His dick jumped to life with demand on contact, and his heart joined in, hammering in his chest. She tasted like his favorite kind of sin. Every decadent treat he'd ever tasted, all rolled into one solid punch.

Indulgent, heady, the kind you couldn't think through but could only feel.

With a soft moan, she eased her hold and slid her lips against his, exploring each edge with her own. Her tongue took a tentative sweep of his mouth, and he dove in after her, prepared to drown and not caring if he ever breathed again.

He knew her taste would be sweet, but he never imagined it would create an instant addiction. Though this kiss might allow her to open up to the world, it left him completely and royally fucked.

He held himself in check as she ran her hands over his shoulders, gripping his biceps. It was everything he could do not to push his straining erection hard against her stomach to help ease the urgency there. She swept her tongue along his lower lip, following it with a gentle bite. Then with a whimper, melted in for more.

That soft, helpless sound was his undoing. On a growl of his own, he swept her up into his arms, encouraging her to wrap her legs around his waist. Gripping the back of her head with his hand, he held her still while he took his turn exploring and tasting, wanting to drown in the flavor that was uniquely and deliciously Claire.

She clung to him, kissing him back as passionately as any wet dream he'd ever had. The scent of her enveloped his head, the taste of her filled his mouth, the feel of her in his arms left him wanting more.

More of something he could never really have.

Somewhere deep in his soul, he found the strength to ease back, breaking away from the urgency of the kiss with smaller, gentler pecks until he was able to look into her eyes. She'd already faced so much pain, and the last thing he wanted to do was inflict any more.

This wicked intelligent, generous and soft-hearted woman who had so much love and passion tied up within her heart had found a way past his defenses.

But she deserved more than a memorable moment.

He had to stay her safe bet.

He had to be the one man who would never hurt her.

And it would be the hardest damn thing he'd ever done in his life.

She whispered, "What just happened?"

Forcing his tone to be light and playful cost him dearly. "I think we ripped your Band-Aid off."

CHAPTER 9

I think I can handle Mitch Brennan without his shirt on.

Famous.

Last.

Words.

Claire followed the path that ran the length of the Cape house lawn and disappeared into the woods. It was cool but not cold, the mid-September sun still able to lend warmth to the salty breeze coming in from the Atlantic.

As she stepped into the foliage, a hush fell like a gossamer veil all around her; muffling the cold, stark reality of every day. The woods on the cape were such a magical place that she could forget for a moment that sad things were even possible.

She loved to follow the path set up for trails and tours and collect herself. The first stop was a bench surrounded by hummingbird feeders and one of the many informative posts she had designed that now resided in different areas around the cape. It humbled her to be trusted to give an experience to visitors through her artwork that would stay with them even once they left.

Running her fingers along the words recessed in the plaque, she mirrored the action along her lips.

That kiss.

She couldn't get the thought of it out of her mind or the taste of him off her tongue. She could smell him and taste him and feel him like the kiss were but a moment ago. She never expected to be so strongly affected by someone's touch.

With a chuckle, she shook her head. Mortification didn't even begin to explain how she felt when she'd kept laughing. If she was honest with herself, she wanted that kiss, but every time he dipped his head she remembered that the last man she had kissed was Jimmy and a weird, awkward hilarity rushed through her.

It was ridiculous and sad all at the same time, and she didn't know how to make it stop. But then when he stepped away and offered to forget the whole idea, an urgency—almost desperation—to move on swept through her.

And she'd thrown herself at him.

Her only saving grace was no one had witnessed the whole debacle, and for some reason, she trusted that Mitch would never tell a soul.

Moving along the trail, she took in the large knotted pines and moss-covered boulders. The hive just across the clearing produced a low buzz in the quiet. Ryker had once talked about how they would be settling in for the winter— much like most of Maine.

She gently slid her hand over the rock, loving the spongy velvet of Mother Nature's green carpet against her palm. How many dreams were woven in this place? How many plans were made? How many hearts broken? There was no telling on a land that had been home to generations of families.

"There you are! Why are we meeting out here?" Blayne ducked through the trees from the yard, looking like a nineteen-twenties pin-up model with her black hair wrapped in a red polka-dot ribbon atop her head and her lips a matching shade. But there was no mistaking the Maine-girl deep inside with her L.L. Bean jacket and work boots. Ireland may have made her, but Maine raised her.

With a grin, Claire waved. "I wanted to pull together the rest of our plans for the Cape Van Buren Fall Art Festival. I have a few ideas for centerpieces using some of earth's gifts." She picked up a pine cone, tossing it toward her friend. There was no way in hell she was admitting that she couldn't quite face Mitch this morning and hiding in the woods was better than risking a run-in at the house.

"Who else is joining us?" Blayne caught the pine cone, then studied it with intense curiosity. "I can work with this."

Claire's heart raced in her chest as she answered. "Larkin, Maxine. The usual crew. And I may have invited the judge."

"What? Are you *crazy?*" The look on Blayne's face would have been comical if Claire didn't understand her panic. Inviting the judge had been a risky move. Maxine was not one to be trifled with and, at the same time, never hesitated to share her opinion on anyone else's life, grandmothering anyone who stepped foot in Cape Van Buren.

Ever since the blow up before the gala earlier in the year, she and the judge had not spoken. But theirs was a love match too sweet to die forever. "You know we have to do something." She stepped to Blayne's side. "But what?"

Her friend cursed in Gaelic. "The judge called her out in front of everyone. You know Maxine."

"I know. But..."

"But we both see that she's miserable underneath her fake facade of a carefree lady out on the town. She misses the damn man just as much as he misses her." Blayne played with the cuff on her jacket. "Does Larkin know?"

"No, I was afraid she would feel obligated to tell Maxine."

"Smart girl," Blayne said.

Claire stared at her. If she knew the truth, she'd never call her smart. "I kissed Mitch." She blurted out the confession, then covered her mouth with her hand.

Her friend's crystal-green eyes went wide, staring back as if Claire had a unicorn horn growing from her forehead.

Just then the judge tucked his head through the foliage path with a wary look. "This is all a little mysterious, Miss Adams." Teddy Carter tugged at the hem of his jacket as he joined them. "What's this all about?"

Claire smiled, hoping it came across more welcoming than a warning to run and hide. "We're finishing up the details for the fall art festival, and as the chairman of the events committee, we needed to get your final approval. I thought it was easiest if you just saw our plan."

Teddy raised his brows. "Surely you could have just brought me samples to the courthouse. I'm a busy man, young lady."

Didn't she know it. It took five different excuses to get the judge to meet her out there in the first place. If they didn't get him and Maxine talking again, they would lose their chance to bring them back together forever.

"I understand, Judge Carter, and I appreciate you stepping out. But as you can imagine, I didn't want to start collecting any materials unless you approved. No reason to disturb the cape if we don't have your okay to do so."

He nodded, considering the view around him. "Such a beautiful place out here. I can't tell you how happy I was when Larkin talked Ryker into conserving this beautiful place and turning it all into a community center."

"Sure." A voice interrupted from the path, and he swung around.

Maxine walked up with Larkin by her side. "I imagine in mixed company you'd like to take credit for it all, too. Throw your weight around a little bit, Mr. Judge-on-the-town."

"Now, Maxine..." Claire said softly.

"Did you do this?" Maxine threw daggers with a bulls-eye precision and jerked her thumb toward the man who broke her heart.

"We need to get past this, Maxine. I know you've been miserable."

Maxine straightened her shoulders with her lips set in a very thin line.

Blayne whispered under her breath. "You did not just admit she's miserable in front of the judge. You aren't getting any moonshine for the rest of your life."

Claire elbowed her in the side. "Look, today's meeting is about the fall art festival, not whatever is going on between you two," Claire said with determination. She hoped her matter-of-fact, logical declaration would make them both look past her manipulation. "Anyway, the reason I had you guys come out here is I think this would be a perfect spot for the festival this year.

The judge shook his head. "We've always done it at the Fountain of Youth."

Claire nodded. "We have, but the wind tends to pick up as we get into September and this area is more protected. It's calmer here, slightly warmer. All the trees block the sea breeze. This would be a perfect place, and we could play off the magic in here starting with a really cool archway at the path opening. Kind of transporting the visitors into a world of magic.

"We could have Ryker sell some of the Cape honey over by the bees, which would also serve to protect that area. There is a small clearing with a hole in the tree canopy that offers a lot of light to display different vendors' art."

Blayne piped up. "I know that Ryker and Jamie had a great climbing tree. We could see if the local climbing chapter would want to set up bungees and have an activity area for the kids."

"That's a great idea," Larkin said softly. "I know Archer would have loved something like that."

Maxine nodded, pretending not to glance at Teddy every five seconds. Claire's heart squeezed with love for the woman. Deep down, she was like the rest of them. Falling in love, but afraid of getting hurt.

At least Larkin and Blayne, she quickly amended.

Teddy looked around, nodding. "I like where you're going with this. But we'd have some liability issues."

"That could be sorted out with liability waivers that everyone signs upon entering." Blayne offered. "We could even have a spot online to make it easy from the beginning."

Claire imagined it all coming together, and her heart swelled in her chest, but she wasn't a dummy. She had to find a foolproof way to make sure Maxine forgave her for meddling. "I thought it could be fun to do kind of a mock kissing booth. Everyone could pay to give Maxine a kiss on the cheek in hopes of a sip of her moonshine."

The judge grumbled. "Maxine and her moonshine."

"Yeah," Larkin said. "But it *is* the finest kind."

"Well, I know I love that idea." Maxine challenged, eyeing the judge with a cold, hard stare.

Blayne wiggled her brows. "Now that Claire's inspired by kissing Mitch, of course, there must be a kissing booth."

Claire wanted to kick her traitorous friend in the shin, but it would be too obvious. "This has nothing to do with Mitch."

The judge raised a brow. "Mitch Brennan? I have to say I'm surprised. Do you really think that's a good idea, Claire? You've had a rough time with it, and well, I love the boy, but..."

The judge's tone came across in a fatherly way, but she found it offensive nonetheless. Raising her hand, she stopped him. "Mitch is a lot more than he puts on. He's responsible, he cares. He actually views the world and the Cape in a very different way than you give him credit for. He wants to make a difference. If any of you would let him, he would."

She didn't know that her voice was rising until she quit talking, but she felt the rush of anger heating her cheeks. "Anyway," she went on, ignoring all the stares, "I thought the money raised could go to a monthly drawing where we treat a couple around town to a date night out. We could get sponsors from the different restaurants to help with special deals and discounts. But I think it would be a cool way for the Cape Center to encourage the marriages of Cape Van Buren to continue to grow stronger."

Maxine smiled. "Now that is a lovely idea. You have to admit it, Teddy."

Teddy looked at Maxine like a parched man faced with the ocean. Everything he could ever want but completely unattainable. "Listen, Maxine...I really feel like we need to talk."

She waved her hands. "Is this meeting over Claire? I have to get back to work, and Mitch was looking for you."

Claire's heart squeezed at the forlorn look on Judge Teddy's face.

"Yes. I just wanted you guys to really see my vision."

The judge nodded. "I really do like it."

"Well, if that's all," Maxine said as she made her way toward the opening in the trees. "Teddy," she called over her shoulder, "meet me at the Flat Iron Saturday morning. Eight sharp. Don't be late." And then she was gone.

Ignoring the looks that Blayne and Larkin exchanged, Claire busied herself by collecting a few more pine cones. They were going to have a lot of questions about that kiss later. Maybe if she could just prevent them from getting her alone.

Gah! When did she become such a coward?

They all watched the judge's expression. "Are you okay?" Blayne asked.

"Are you kidding? I'm better than ever, ladies. That is one date I will not be late to." He disappeared through the brush.

Larkin and Blayne turned to Claire. She threw her hands up with a grin. "I know you both have questions, but I have too much work to do."

"You kissed Mitch?" Larkin asked her eyes wide with surprise.

"I don't know that I'd call it a kiss. More like a debacle if I'm honest, followed by a head dive driven by total desperation." She paced, shoving her hands in her front jean pockets. "I was having a hard time getting past the fact that I haven't kissed anyone since Jimmy. It was supposed to be kind of like ripping the Band-Aid off."

Blayne rubbed her hands together. "The hell it was. That was nothing more than lifting the edge. If you wanna rip the real Band-Aid off, then Mitch is the man for the job. Word around town proves that he knows what he's doing."

Claire's jaw dropped. "I am *not* going to have sex with Mitch."

She definitely wanted to have sex with Mitch.

What the hell is wrong with me?!

Larkin tapped her chin. "Why not? You're single, he's single. You two are friends. And he is sexy as hell. Sometimes that's the perfect person."

"The perfect person for what?" Claire asked.

"Look, you're afraid to jump into a relationship that might hurt you, and you've always said that Mitch's not the kind of man you would ever date, so who would be safer than him?"

Claire nodded, understanding her friend's point, but unable to make her vocal chords work in the face of such an idea. She had said that, but the truth of the matter was she'd been seeing Mitch in a much different light lately.

Her friends tucked an arm through each of hers at the elbow as they walked back towards the Cape house lawn. "I say go for it," Larkin said. "Burn off some steam, clear your mind, then maybe you'll be ready to let go of Jimmy once and for all and open yourself up to a new relationship."

And there it was. The cold fingers of fear, sliding up her spine. Even the thought of loving and losing made her break out into a cold sweat. "You guys know if I start dating again it's just a date, just companionship. I'm not looking for anything long-term."

"But I don't understand." Blayne slowed, turning to face her.

"Are you kidding me? It's pretty straightforward. I am not ever going to put myself through that again. A relationship? A commitment? They imply getting married and having a family. No way, no how."

Larkin rubbed her arm. "I always thought you'd be an amazing mother. I see you with Max, I see you with the children in town."

Claire stopped in her tracks. Memories floating at the edge of her conscience. "You both need to stop." Their words hurt more than they'd ever know. Jimmy's smile, his laugh, the sound of her baby's beating heart, all melded together in a cacophony of yesterdays in her head.

She'd never move in the direction her friends had taken, but maybe she at least needed to distance herself from the shadow of the life she'd never had. At least where companionship was concerned.

"Maybe you guys are right. Mitch would be a great distraction, a great way to jump back in." She swallowed past the lump in her throat and stretched her lips into a makeshift grin.

Blayne laughed. "And we all know you're safe from falling in love with Mitch."

"Isn't that the truth," she said lightly despite the thought of his grin when he'd handed her the cinnamon stick pastry, and his bewilderment when he'd found the vibrator in her kitchen, and the genuine look of purpose when he'd talked about wanting to help the community.

Every moment made her question everything she thought she knew about Cape Van Buren's playboy.

CHAPTER 10

*M*itch knocked at Claire's door, holding two bags of groceries from Bellamy's in his arms and an earnest desire to see her smile without fear in his heart.

He needed to go see Dr. Stanton and have his God damn head checked.

She'd been avoiding him the past few days, ever since giving him the sweetest and hottest kiss of his life. The existence of the two wrapped in one kiss hadn't seemed possible, but holy hell, she'd proven it to be true.

He'd never thought something that started out so awkward could end with such force that he wouldn't be able to get it out of his mind. But if he wasn't awake, he dreamed about it, and if he wasn't sleeping, he thought about it.

Fuck and double fuck.

One part of his brain had warned him of the danger, but his logical self brushed it away. It was lust, pure and simple. Claire was a gorgeous woman with a quick mind, a sweet heart, and an ass that wouldn't quit who'd been putting him in his place since they'd met. It was a combination he'd found intoxicating.

Commitment meant expectations, and expectations meant that emotions and feelings were involved. Such delicate things. Hurting someone would be inevitable. There was no way around it.

And he just couldn't risk hurting Claire.

The door swung open to reveal the object of his distraction in a pair of gray shorts that hugged her round, delicious ass and a lighter gray knit sweater that clung to her breasts as if knitted just for them. And he found another combination he couldn't resist.

She looked up-and-down the street in confusion then glanced at the bags in his hands. "What're you doing here?" she asked.

"I've been thinking. You just need practice. So I'm here to make you dinner. We'll enjoy conversation; we'll flirt, we'll drink...all in the safety of your home. There'll be no reason to run because you're already here."

"Your observation skills are amazing."

He ignored her sarcasm, forcing himself to keep a distance. "And if during the evening, anything I say is one of the triggers that worries you, we can identify it and work through it."

He could hear the idiocy fall from his lips, helpless to shut the fuck up.

She raised a brow. "This is very clinical of you."

He gave a strained chuckle. "Shut up. I promised to help."

She stepped aside for him to enter. "I know you did. If you give me a second, I can go change."

He moved into her space, loving the scent of her all around him. His body tightened in awareness. "You don't need to change. That's the beauty of having dinner in your own home."

But she waved her hand up-and-down his frame. "And sit across from you looking as if you just stepped out of *GQ* magazine? I don't think so."

"Oh? You like this look then?" Pleasure rushed through his chest. He hadn't dressed in anything fancy, just a pair of dark-wash jeans and a dark gray button-up shirt. But if she thought he looked good, then who was he to argue?

"If it would make you more comfortable I can always take my shirt off," he teased, and her cheeks blushed.

Good start.

"Shut up before I change my mind."

He laughed as he followed her into the kitchen, enjoying the sight of her long legs pouring out from her shorts.

"About that kiss," he began.

She swung toward him. "Can we please never speak of that moment again? Please? I have never been so mortified in my life."

Disappointment lodged in his throat as big as a boulder, but he forced himself to swallow it down so he could manage an answer. "Of course. I won't bring it up again."

Claire disappeared into her room, giving him a few minutes to compose himself. He opened a bottle of wine and poured a large glass, downing half of it in one swallow. He needed to get ahold of himself and his emotions. His feelings for Claire were fucking with his whole purpose for being there.

Which was to help her break back out into the world, nothing more nothing less.

He straightened his shoulders and gave himself a quick nod. Time to keep his head in the game.

Starting with dinner.

She returned in a mid-thigh, off-the-shoulder, sweater dress and every good intention he'd had slid down his throat with his next sip of wine. He pushed a glass toward her to keep from checking to see if the sweater was as soft as it looked.

"Here."

"What is it?"

"A Pinot from a winery up in the hills. Small batch, organic. It's one of my favorites."

She gave it a twirl and a sniff then a taste, closing her eyes in enjoyment. "This is good." Hopping up onto the counter, she nodded toward the bag, lifting her chin as if trying to peek inside. "So what's for dinner? And don't think that I don't know you're avoiding working on my program. We were supposed to meet at the Center."

"I'm not avoiding anything, Miss Bossypants. We will. But I feel like we need to turn around your experience on Wednesday as quickly as possible."

And avoid any more tasks that might expose him, but he'd keep that to himself. It was uncomfortable, feeling that she could see something about him, something *in* him, from a simple drawing. But there was no mistaking that she must have seen something if her reaction of slamming the drawer closed was any indication the other night. He'd caught a glimpse of his drawing as the drawer had slid shut.

Clearing his throat, he pulled out baby spinach and an avocado along with chicken breasts, basil, tomatoes, and fresh mozzarella. "Chicken caprese and spinach avocado salad."

She clapped her hands together, and his lips quirked up on their own accord.

"That sounds amazing. When did you learn to cook? This is just another of the many things I find surprising about you."

The only other person who knew he cooked besides his mother and his sister, Mae, was Ryker. He and his sister had learned to cook when they were young in order to help their mom out. There were plenty of evenings when she'd work late, and they'd be making dinner themselves. But along with his mother's teachings to fill their lives with passion were the practical lessons of cooking and housekeeping. Though even then, she reinforced the idea of creating moments. There was no reason to eat boxed macaroni and cheese when you could make homemade Gorgonzola pasta, she'd say.

"Mom always told Mae and me that life is about experiences, making memories. So that's what we do."

"So it's once again about decadence?"

"And why not? You know Janice. When have you ever known her to do anything the generic way if she could help it?"

He opened the container of spinach and dumped it in the colander that she'd had resting next to the sink. "I'm assuming it's OK to use?" he asked.

"You're cooking me dinner. What's mine is yours." She raised her glass in a toast.

"Alright. I like the sound of that." He winked, loving the light flush that deepened on her cheeks the longer he stared.

"Let's put on some music and really do this right." She said, breaking the spell and, if he was a betting man, keeping her face hidden on purpose.

Lumineers floated out from her sound system. "Not what I was expecting. But I like it. Casual and provides a nice atmosphere. You're getting the idea." He rolled the avocado her way. "Here, why don't you cube this."

She tossed it from one hand to the other. "I thought you were supposed to make me dinner. Already trying to shirk your duties?"

"Not in the least." He grabbed the avocado out of mid-air before she could catch it with her other one. "I am a man of my word and live by my duty."

"Sure," she snorted. "Until something shiny and pretty comes along, then bye-bye."

She waved her fingers in a small, mocking wave.

Her words were like a slap in the face as an image came, unbidden, of his mom staring out the window at their father while he walked away, suitcase in hand, so many years ago. "You think that's how I operate? You think that if I decided to make a commitment that I'd end up just hurting the woman. Walk out on her?"

"Honestly?" she replied. "I don't see you ever committing to anyone. Whatever your reasons, you seem happiest with new experiences, not old ones. But I can say this. If you ever did, I think you'd ruin her for anybody who'd ever ask her out again."

He placed the tomatoes and mozzarella inside the chicken then layered on the basil leaves. The pressure in his chest made it difficult to breathe.

"All of you think you know me so well." There was a rough edge to his tone, and he didn't care.

"No." She stepped in front of him. "No, you misunderstand." She took the towel out of his hands, setting it on the counter. Grabbing his hands, she said softly, "I think that if you ever decided to commit to a woman, you would love her in a way that another man would never match. And when something took you away, she'd never be the same again."

"Is that what you're afraid of?" His voice was almost unrecognizable to his own ears. The emotion in his chest went from hurt to humble. It was an extraordinary feeling to have someone see something in him that was both beautiful and bittersweet.

"Claire, is that why you're having such a hard time? You're afraid to care for someone because you think no matter what, it won't work out? That they'll leave or die?"

She dropped his hands and moved back to her wine. "Don't mind me," she said. "The wine's going to my head."

"Claire."

With a shrug, she sipped more wine. "That and the fact that the more days that pass and the more distance I put between myself and my past, the further I feel from the little toddler I should be chasing around my apartment."

The anguish in her eyes and the tremble in her lower lip was his undoing, and he stepped toward her. "Claire," he rasped.

"No, please." She put her hand out to stop him. "If you comfort me, if you wrap your arms around me right now, I will break. And I don't want to."

97

He stopped in his tracks, warring with his urgency to make her feel better and the necessity to put her needs above his.

"Please." She drained her glass with a trembling hand.

"She'll always be with you, Claire. Time. Distance. They don't have a say in a mother's love."

She stared at him, holding his intense gaze as if afraid to look anywhere else. "Do you really believe that?"

"More than anything."

With a slight dip of her chin, she drew in a breath and released it in a drawn-out sigh that ended in a slight shudder. Setting down her wine glass, she grabbed a light pink apron off a hook next to the stove. "Hey, while the chicken is baking, I can teach you how to make Evette's cupcakes."

She wanted to move on to another topic, and he let her.

The pain and confusion and self-doubt that flashed across her face left him feeling powerless. And it was a feeling he fucking hated. So, he focused on the self-doubt. She needed to experience a moment where she was in charge and successful. An experience of mastery. He was always telling her to make moments...so he'd give her this one to do with what she'd like.

An image of her naked breasts covered in flour popped into his mind, and his body tightened. "I've never been much of a baker, but I think with the right teacher, I'd be up to just about anything."

She grinned. "I love how you're ready to try something new at the drop of a hat. I love how easy you are."

Her words were innocent, but the effect of those words and the images of just how easy he wanted to be were anything but.

"You have no idea."

~

*C*laire wished Mitch was easy with her.

Ever since he'd stepped through her front door, all she could concentrate on was how the fabric of his shirt was stretched tautly across his chest and biceps, and how he smelled so good, arousing a hunger in her that superseded everything else.

And that realization shook her to her core.

He was so easy to talk to. The time they'd spent together had enabled them to form a friendship of sorts. It was her friendships that had not only kept her afloat after losing Jimmy and the baby but had pushed her back into a rich and full life. Maybe this was the friendship that would allow her to feel the pleasure of being a woman.

And as Blayne had said, if word around town could be trusted, Mitch Brennan was the man to show her.

The more she thought about it, the more certain she was that Blayne was right. Mitch was a friend, and neither of them wanted a commitment, so who would be more perfect to finally break her dry spell?

Mr. Seduction didn't know it yet, but he was about to be seduced.

With her heart pounding in her chest, she pulled out the flour, raw sugar, and eggs, placing them on the counter. She eyed Mitch up-and-down, taking the scenic route from the tip of his sock-covered toes up along his thickly muscled thighs, to a waist she wanted to explore and a chest she wanted to conquer, all the way to the thick strands of hair on top his head.

Finally, she said, "That'll never do." She wiggled her fingers at his torso.

He crossed his arms and looked down with concern. "I don't understand." And the look on his face proved it to be true. She could only imagine what he was thinking at her bait and switch.

This was going to be fun.

"Even the smallest amount of flour is going to show up on that shirt of yours. Go ahead and take it off. No reason to make it dirty, and I don't have another apron." She answered with an innocent lilt in her voice, forcing herself to look for a whisk when what she really wanted to do was watch him squirm.

He hesitated, looking at her as if she may have gone mad. And maybe she had.

"I think I'll be okay."

"Oh, no." She wagged her pointer finger at him. "I'm not going give you another thing to tease me about. I bet that shirt costs a couple hundred dollars alone. Off with it, mister." She tugged it from the waistband of his jeans, her mouth going dry and his eyes going dark.

A shiver of excitement shot straight to her center, and she almost wept with the sensation. She'd long ago thought she might never feel it again when someone else was in the room.

"I don't think a bare chest is necessarily hygienic."

"I won't tell if you won't." She gave him a coy wink. He held her gaze as if trying to read her mind, then finally gave one slow dip of his chin.

His long, masculine fingers unbuttoned his shirt one by one, and her fingers itched to take over for him, but with a casual air, she pulled out a bowl and her pastry mat as if she wasn't strategizing on how to get him naked faster.

Her music switched to Lo Fang and the slow, sultry melody of "The One That I Want" filled the room. If there was ever a sign telling her to go for it, that was it.

It was about time she took what she wanted. Even if she wasn't looking for anything to last the rest of her lifetime, it was time she quit missing out on the here and now.

Her nervous excitement racked through her, and she shivered.

"Are you cold?" His voice was husky but with enough confusion in his voice to make her chuckle, but she held it back.

"Just the opposite." She sprinkled flour across the mat. "You know, one of the things that I love about baking is the pleasure that it brings. Not only to those who eat it but to the baker as well."

He gave her a hard stare, and she could see the wheels turning.

She'd bet the success of the fall festival that he remembered what was in her junk drawer. More like a treasure trove, if anyone asked her.

But he kept his thoughts to himself.

She dipped her finger in the flour and tapped his nose. "You're all about pleasure, aren't you, big guy?"

Mitch grabbed her wrist. "Who the hell are you? And what have you done with Claire?"

The sound that fell from her lips was one of pure delight. It was fun to flirt when the only consequence was a night of pleasure. When there was no chance of pain or loneliness. "I'm a good student, you know. You told me that life is about making memories and experiences, decadence, indulgence. I can't think of anything more indulgent then making pastries with Mitch Brennan."

Extricating herself from his grasp, she ran her fingers along the waistband of his jeans, dipping them into the front and giving the fabric a tug. The warmth of his skin against the back of her fingers made her melt.

"What are you doing, Claire?" His voice was low and hoarse, and the fact that she was the reason sent a thrill running through her body.

"You're safe, right? You don't want a relationship. I don't want a relationship. But we've become friends...and I trust you." She didn't know where the tremble in her voice came from, but she pushed through it.

"Friends?" he echoed. "Safe? I don't think anyone has ever called me safe before and meant it."

"I don't mean safe in a boring way, I mean safe in a...you won't be able to hurt me kind of way."

The muscles clenched along his jaw, and she could only hope that it was because he wanted this, too.

"Are you sure about this?"

She licked her lips, running a finger along the top edge of his jeans, elated when he sucked in a breath.

"Do you remember when we talked about ripping the Band-Aid off?"

The memory of their kiss flared in his eyes, and she could see that he had been affected by it, too. Which caught her off guard. She figured kissing her wouldn't even rate, much less be memorable, and not because she wasn't a good kisser but because he'd had so much experience. It was impossible for a drop of water to stand out in an ocean.

"Well, I feel like all we did was lift the edge. I need to rip it completely off. Then maybe I can let go and live a little. This is my version of cinnamon pastries and a peanut butter hot cocoa."

He flashed a grin that was both wicked and wise, and she swore her panties would have melted right off her body. Had she been wearing any. Grabbing his hands, she set them on her waist just above her ass and stepped close.

His fingers flexed in the flesh of her hips, yanking her even closer. His erection was large and hard and pushed against her midsection in the way that elicited a waterfall of tiny flutters. She prayed that when he kissed her, she wouldn't start laughing again. She'd had enough mortification to last anyone a lifetime.

No more second-guessing or worrying about the consequences. It was pure, reckless pleasure she sought. And with Mitch, she could get lost and just feel.

Without warning, his lips slammed against hers, and a cry of pleasure caught in her throat. She could taste the wine and something spicy. His scent enveloped her as did his embrace. He was hot and hard and apparently wanted her as much as she wanted him. That in itself was a little miracle.

So many memories rushed into Claire's mind, but they were misplaced distractions. This was a moment to move forward, not look back.

Mitch softened his kiss and eased the tension. "I know you said you're sure about this, but I also know that you don't take any of this lightly. I don't want you to regret that it's with me."

She stared into his blue eyes, humbled by the uncertainty she saw there.

She never imagined she'd see the day that Mitch Brennan was unsure of anything.

Grabbing the hem of her sweater dress, she pulled it up and over her head, revealing that she'd had nothing on underneath.

"The fact that you even thought to ask means that you're a better man that I've given you credit for. It's time for me to move on. Jimmy wouldn't want me to be alone forever. This is a big step for me, but one I'm determined to take."

He frowned, but his eyes roved hungrily over her body in shock and awe. Her nipples peaked, and a wash of goosebumps followed. If he could make her feel like that with a gaze alone, she couldn't wait to actually feel his hands on her.

She stepped toward him, taking his wrists and placing his hands on her breasts. Going up on tiptoes, she pressed a kiss to his lips. "Help me make a memory, Mitch. One that sets the tone for many more to come."

He hesitated a moment longer, then on a low grumbled growl, he swept her into his arms, lifting her off her feet and falling into the kiss at the same time.

"I always knew you'd taste this good. A combination of pastries and wine." She wrapped her arms around his broad shoulders, amazed at the heat of his skin. He was big and hard everywhere, and it was a thrill to feel him against her.

"If I'd known that you didn't have anything on under that dress, I doubt I'd have ever finished making dinner."

"Well, it's a good thing you didn't find out because I'm starving."

He kissed her mouth hard, then asked, "You're sure you don't want me to stop?"

"Don't you dare," she said. Feeling brave and bold under the intensity of his heated gaze, she added, "I want you to *serve* me before you serve me."

His fingers slid to her hips and anchored her on the edge of the countertop. Her body moved easily with her bottom powdered by the flour.

"Someone's getting brazen, maybe even a little cocky." He chuckled.

"I don't know what it is; it doesn't scare me with you."

He dropped his head, gently lifting a breast to his lips and swirling his tongue in circles until he reached her nipple, giving it small, pressured flicks. She could feel each nip through every nerve in her body, making her squirm.

She grasped his head and pressed him more firmly against her breast. His hands were everywhere, along her sides, her buttocks, her thighs, then sliding down to cup her calves. He gently spread her legs farther apart as he trailed kisses down the center of her stomach.

"Mitch," she whispered, breathless with pleasure and anticipation.

"I'm ready to serve you, Mistress Claire." He trailed his lips along her sensitive skin at the juncture where her inner thigh met her torso. Her body gave little pulses of pleasure awaiting his touch. Then his slick, hot tongue met her center with feather-light strokes, and she almost fell off the counter.

"Easy now," he said against her body, maintaining pressure on her thighs to keep her in place. He licked and suckled and twirled his tongue, pushing her higher and higher.

She shamelessly dove her fingers into his hair, keeping him from moving away from that spot. She wanted to grab the meaty flesh of his shoulders, rub her palms across his chest, but more than any of those things, she did not want him to stop, so she sacrificed the pleasure she sought for the pleasure she'd dreamed of.

"I've had dreams of this," she confessed, her voice ragged with desire. She could barely think, as with each delicious stroke of his tongue she lost all threads of conscious thought.

"You dreamed of me?" His question was a demand, and he rose. She cried out at the loss of sensation, but then his mouth slammed down on hers, pulling her into a kiss she'd never imagined. She could taste herself on his tongue, and it was a decadent, heady experience.

"Don't fret, sweetheart," he said. "We've only just begun." He gently nipped at her chin then the side of her neck as he made his way back down to her center. He found her clit and swirled his tongue until she thought she'd lose her mind, one hand gripped his head, the other the counter for fear that she'd fall off.

As he continued to worship her flesh with his mouth, he gently stroked one finger inside of her, and her vision went white.

Pressure built, and pleasure swirled in a tight fist then burst, rocking her body and limbs in pulsing waves. Her hips bucked, and she gripped his shoulders to ride out the sensation and prevent herself from accidentally breaking his neck with her legs.

The orgasm hit her stronger ever before, and she could only imagine it was her pent-up energy that had accumulated over the past couple of years. As her body slowly lowered back to earth, she let her legs drop to the sides.

A low groan followed by slow, soft licks from Mitch sent a flutter of contractions throughout her stomach. "Oh my God," she said. "I think I could curl into a ball and go to sleep right this second."

"Oh, know you're not. We're not finished yet." Gliding back up her body, he worked with one hand at his buckle and zipper, shoving his jeans from his hips. She heard the crinkling sound of a foil packet and peeked at him.

One of the hottest things she had ever seen was him gripping himself in one hand as he rolled the condom down his thick, hard length in the other. Her body responded with flutters of anticipation.

"There's no way I can do that again."

"I don't believe that for a second," he countered. She glanced down at herself and saw traces of flour along her breasts and thighs and a smudge on his face. "I don't think I've ever had this much fun baking before."

He eyed her quizzically. "But you said..."

She laughed. "I was just teasing."

"Then what do you use that little massager for?"

"When I'm on my feet for a long time, I have an area between my shoulder blades that bothers me a lot. It helps."

He flashed her a devilish grin and slid open the drawer. Taking out the small vibrator, he turned the knob, his grin broadening as a buzzing noise filled the air. "I bet this little guy can help you feel better than you've ever imagined."

He grabbed her from the counter and spun her around. Then he placed her hands under his on the counter with his big, warm body wrapped around her. He kissed the back of her neck, dragging his tongue from her shoulder to her ear, then giving her lobe a gentle nibble. "It's time for round two, Claire."

"That's impossible. I'm a one and done kind of girl," she said.

His dark chuckle sent a wash of goosebumps along her skin. "We'll just see about that. I do love a good challenge."

The large, round head of his cock rubbed between her legs, sending her stomach on a slow, rippling ride, then escalating to a full-on wave of pleasure as he thrust inside of her.

He continued to kiss the side of her neck, and she pushed back until there was nowhere left to go. His low, guttural groan was music to her ears, and she decided right then and there it was her favorite sound.

"Holy fuck, you feel better than I could have ever imagined." He stroked in and out with slow, controlled movements, his harsh breathing and the trembling of his arms the only signs that he struggled to restrain himself.

He let go of one hand to pick up the small massager. Encouraging her to spread her legs farther, he placed the device in her hand, guiding it between her legs. She resisted for a second, but then curiosity won over any kind of self-consciousness.

There was little to consider after the man had literally been tasting her.

As he stroked, he turned on the vibrator, sending a rippling pleasure throughout her body. Her hips bucked, unable to control which way they moved. Mitch grabbed onto either side, digging his fingers into her flesh, increasing the tempo of his strokes.

She continued to hold the tip of the massager against herself with slow, small circles. "Oh my God," she said. "Oh, my God."

"That's it, Claire, you've got it. Come with me, baby." His strokes increased, and she had to clench all the muscles in her legs to keep standing as his groan of pleasure met her own.

She shoved back against him, trying to take as much of him in as she possibly could, and pleasure exploded once more, seemingly splitting her body in two. The sensation was so great she dropped the vibrator, pressing her fingers against her clit to increase the intensity of her orgasm.

"Mitch!" she screamed his name.

"I'm here, sweetheart. I'm here."

As the intense sensations within her body ebbed, she felt Mitch slump behind her, resting his forehead in the middle of her back. "I had no idea," she breathed.

"Me, neither."

She didn't believe that for a second, but he was a good friend for saying it.

And that's what she had to keep telling her heart, which wanted to open up and cling to the emotions of gratitude and excitement running through her.

He was her friend, not her forever.

The thought should give her great joy but instead left her body still humming with strokes of phantom pleasure and her heart grasping at thin air.

CHAPTER 11

$\mathcal{E}$arly Saturday morning, before the sun crested the Atlantic horizon, before the birds started singing or the bees buzzing, Mitch and Ryker made their way through the woods of the cape with rolls of black tar paper.

Beekeeping was a passion passed from his grandfather when Ryker was a boy, and one he returned to last year when he moved back to the cape. Thankfully, Larkin had envisioned a different way to help Ryker heal from his painful past. One that allowed Mitch's friend to love the cape again and not sell it off in pieces as he'd originally planned.

"What are we doing again? And why the fuck did I agree? It's freezing out here." Mitch shivered, burrowing deeper into his winter jacket.

"Well, if you're cold, put yourself in the bee's shoes."

"Please, you know my reputation well enough to know my shoe size is way bigger than that."

"You're an ass." Ryker led him toward a hive. "We're out here before they start their day to wrap the hives in the black tar paper to help keep them warm and dry over the winter." He inspected the roll of paper, unfurling it and looking over the front and back. "I was out here last week to inspect each hive. They're all at critical mass, no disease, and abundant food stores. It was a great summer."

Mitch shook his head. "You act like I know what the fuck you're talking about."

"You just pretend you don't in order to get out of helping."

Laughing, Mitch nodded. "That may be true." He couldn't count the number of times he'd skipped out of helping Ryker and his grandfather, Stuart, when they were kids, but his fear of getting stung was way stronger than his desire to learn. As an adult, he was glad. It was those times that Ryker had with his grandfather alone that gave him the courage to come back.

Mitch took the front edge of the paper and held it in place while Ryker slowly made his way around the hive. "Listen. I want to tell you before you hear it from somewhere else…"

Ryker raised a brow, then it dropped back into his usual frown of concentration.

"Last night, Claire and I—"

"Claire and you did what?" Ryker grated out, freezing in place and lowering his chin as he gave him a hard stare.

"Knock off the aggressive stance. It wasn't my idea. I was helping her out." But his fucking problem was he couldn't wait to help her out again. He hadn't been able to get her face out of his mind, her flavor out of his mouth, or the silky slide of her smooth skin off his hands since he'd gone home last night.

"Yeah, that's what they all say. Claire's not one of your trophy-bunny lays."

Mitch gave him the finger. "Do you really think any woman that I've dated would appreciate you calling them that? I know you guys like to rib me, like to give me a hard time. Ever stop to consider that any woman I've ever been with knows exactly where I stand and if she decides to be with me has decided that on her own?" He squared off with his friend, legs braced apart, his arms crossed at his chest, letting the tar paper fall to the ground.

"What the hell are you doing? Grab the paper."

"Fuck your paper, Ryker. To play it off like I could so easily manipulate every woman in Cape Van Buren is simply an insult to their intelligence."

His pal relaxed his shoulders. "You might have a point, but this is Claire. She's already had to deal with more in the past few years than most people do in a lifetime."

"You think I don't know that?" he gritted out, grabbing the paper and carefully holding it back in place until his buddy secured the wrap. Switching gears, he asked, "Is this the hive that produced the honey you're going to sell at the fall festival?"

Ryker grunted. "Some. I have an amazing batch from mid-summer that includes all of the hives. Claire actually modified the logo that Jay had made for Cape Van Buren and added a couple of bees around it for our new labels. She really has an eye for aesthetics and design."

They moved to the next hive. "She does," Mitch agreed. "You can see it in her house, you can see it in any of the events she's planned."

At the word house, Ryker tensed. "Oh, come off that man." Mitch shoved the roll of paper at his friend's chest.

"Look, at this point, she's like a sister. She and Blayne, they go with Larkin as a matching set. I can't separate protecting her from them."

Mitch scrubbed a hand through his hair. "You don't have to protect her from anyone, certainly not me. We've formed a sort of friendship."

Ryker's bark of laughter echoed off the trees, and he grimaced watching the hives for any activity. "I've never known you to be just friends with any woman."

"The fuck you don't," Mitch said. "I've been friends with every woman I've ever been with."

Ryker studied him a moment, then dipped his chin in agreement. "Fair enough."

The two continued to wrap the hives in silence, working comfortably as lifetime friends. Mitch needed to get Ryker on board with the kind of man he really was if he had any hopes of landing the city attorney seat. If his best friend didn't trust him, no one would.

"Hey listen, I'm preparing a portfolio for a new opportunity. Considering the work I've done with Cape Van Buren in its entirety, I'd like you to consider writing a recommendation for me."

Ryker gathered his tools while Mitch collected the remaining tar paper.

"New opportunity?"

Mitch hadn't told anyone about it and wasn't too thrilled to even mention it to his buddy, but if he was going tell anyone, Ryker deserved to know more than anyone else. "Yeah, I'm putting my name in the ring for the city attorney."

"Wow," Ryker said as he led Mitch across the lawn and into the honey room of the Cape house. He washed his hands, drying them on a towel, then turned around and leaned back against the sink. "City attorney, huh?"

Mitch waited for the joke, used to the fact he was often the butt of one.

"Honestly?" Ryker stared at him with a thoughtful expression, gave a nod. "Can't say I'm totally surprised. I was wondering when you were going jump in.

Mitch slowly set the paper on a large shelf against the back wall. "What do you mean, you've been waiting?"

"Dude, how long have we known each other? Practically our whole life? I fuck around with you like anyone else because it's easy and you ask for it and you're a good sport. It's almost therapeutic." He splayed his hand over his chest. "But you've been a man of service your whole life. How many times did you put yourself between my dad and me, even though there was no guarantee you wouldn't get hit, too? How many times did you make room in your house for me? Your whole family has taken care of everyone in this town. It was just a matter of time for you to take on a more public service role."

Shock and something else expanded in Mitch's chest. Ryker was not a feelings kind of guy. The spark of possibility replaced the pressure, and he pulled in a breath. "I don't know what to say."

Ryker grunted. "Please. Don't say anything. It was bad enough I had to sit and listen to Jay pouring his heart out when he and Blayne were working through their shit. Promise me you won't do that to me, and you'll have my vote every time."

"You have my word." Mitch moved a stack of washed hive frames against the wall as Ryker pulled out a large tub. He opened its valve, holding a jar under the spigot as thick, dark honey filled the sterile glass. "And Ryker?"

"Yeah?" he grunted.

"Thanks."

Ryker nodded and put his hand out for another jar. They worked in silence for a moment filling a jar, then sealing it closed.

"What are you going to do about Claire?" Ryker always knew him much better than Mitch wanted him to.

"The fuck if I know," Mitch said.

But the idea of never holding her in his arms again was about as likely as Ryker giving up beekeeping.

There was no walking away from such sweet honey.

*C*laire carried a travel tray full of coffee out the door of the Flat Iron coffee shop, sliding her free hand quickly over the top to stabilize the special brew from flying out of her hands as the brisk wind came off the ocean.

"It's chilly today." She said to Larkin and Blayne as they walked toward Van Buren Square.

"Only a few days till autumn." Blayne also protected the tray she carried while Larkin tightened her grip on a bag of pastries.

The three crossed the street, looking like an L.L. Bean advertisement. "Now explain to me again what we're doing here," Claire asked again. She was trying to pay attention, she really was, but each sigh, each groan, each cry from the night before echoed in her head, setting her body on fire.

An embarrassing situation when she was hanging out with her girlfriends. Larkin slid an exasperated look her way. "Seriously? I've gone over this three times already."

Blayne laughed. "We need to get Claire laid and clear up that foggy brain of hers. That may be the only way she pays attention to us ever again."

Clara's chuckle sounded strained, so she attempted to force it out more naturally.

Blayne tilted her head with a curious look.

"Oh! I know now," Claire said. "We're meeting Maxine."

Larkin nodded. "She has her coffee date which with Judge Carter."

"She's headed to a coffee date with the judge, but we're meeting her for coffee first." Blayne lifted her tray.

Claire shot out her hand, then grabbed the top of her cups again. "That's my point! I just don't get it." If they'd explained it more thoroughly earlier, she hadn't been listening; she'd been stuck in a memory loop that included two orgasms, chicken caprese, and knock-off North Cove Confectionery cupcakes. It was the best dinner she'd ever consumed.

"Claire! Have you not been listening to anything we've said?" Larkin grumbled.

"Oh my God, this day is dragging, and we just started. I'm right here." Claire tried to think back to what they might have been talking about.

"Anyway," Larkin said. "Deep down, I think Maxine's nervous. She really cares for Teddy but also needs to save face from the incident at the Cape house."

"It sure was awkward, and Jamie certainly hadn't helped any." Blayne giggled at the memory of Jay's inability to read a room on the day that Judge Carter caught Maxine selling moonshine at the Cape house.

Larkin and Claire snapped their heads around to look at her. Giggling was a very un-Blayne thing to do, but love did strange things to people. "I think it's cute if she's feeling nervous."

"*Cute?*" Larkin shuddered. "There's nothing cute about Maxine being nervous. It only makes her a little mean, and when she's mean, she threatens to take all the moonshine away."

"We give her way too much control with that moonshine of hers." Claire followed the arch of the Fountain of Youth as they approached the town square, loving the history and presence it maintained in the heart of town.

Blayne shrugged. "Well, until you're able to copy her recipe and make it taste the same, the control is in her hands."

There was a pancake festival taking place, and Evette was there with her North Cove Confectionery booth, setting off a waterfall of tingling memories throughout Claire's body.

The woman's pancakes were as delicious as her cupcakes, and Claire couldn't help but think that a cupcake pancake was pretty damn decadent. "Here take this." Claire shoved the coffee into Larkin's arms.

"Where you going?"

"I'll be right back." She made her way over to Evette's stand. "I would love a lemon blueberry sunrise pancake, please." These were the kind of pancakes that didn't need any syrup. One of Evette's workers handed her the goodies, wrapped in parchment paper stamped with the North Cove Confectionery logo.

The pancakes were warm and the aromas amazing, everything Claire'd never let herself eat for breakfast before. A grin stretched her lips wide, and she took a bite as she made her way back over to her friends.

Blayne and Larkin stared at her. "What's going on?" Blayne demanded.

Claire took another bite. "Oh my gosh, these are fantastic. Have you tried them?"

Larkin nodded. "Yes, they're Ryker's favorite, but I don't think I've ever seen you try them before...something about cupcakes for breakfast not being a healthy choice and all that." Her friend waved her hand at the food.

"Well," Claire admitted. "I was wrong."

Blayne stepped over and broke a piece off, shoving it in her mouth with a sigh. "Holy fuck. These are damn good."

Claire nodded with a laugh.

"Are you ladies gonna get over here with our coffee or what?" Maxine teased.

A local jazz band was playing music on the stage. People milled around the park, trying pancake flavors from several vendors. The smell of roasted coffee filled the air, and of course, Shelly Anne had a stand set up with a line a mile long.

Blayne pointed. "And that is why we got the coffee at the coffeehouse."

Larkin nodded. "Every year that line is atrocious, and I never understood it when you could just go right across the street, but that's the point of the pancake festival, now isn't it?"

Claire finished the pancake and brushed off her hands with a deep sense of satisfaction. She couldn't think of a better way to start the morning after the night of the best sex of her life.

Tendrils of guilt tried to worm their way into her mood with an image of Jimmy's smile. She held it for a moment, and then released it. She would never be able to move on completely or all at once, but Jimmy had been a kind man, a good man, and he would want her to live her life to the fullest.

Having the courage to do that would be one way to honor him. "So, what's this about Maxine?" Claire took a coffee from Larkin and helped herself to another pastry. Why the hell not?

Maxine eyed her up-and-down with interest. The kind of interest Claire wanted to avoid. "What's gotten into you?"

Blayne piped up. "We've been wondering the same thing."

Claire shook her head. "No you don't, this morning is all about you."

"Fly Me to the Moon" played in the background just above the din of the crowd as she tried not to fidget under Maxine's wise stare. The woman was as stylish as ever in her long, black puff jacket and large, silver hoop earrings. The straight edge of her salt and pepper hair swung back-and-forth, playing with the earrings.

Maxine pursed her perfectly lined lips.

"Oh, come off it, Maxine," Janice demanded as she joined the group. "We're all here because you're nervous to see the judge. Just admit it."

Seeing Mitch's mom's red curls shot a blush straight to Claire's own hairline, and she wouldn't have been surprised if her own platinum blond had turned a matching shade. She prayed that no one would notice and worked to keep all eyes on Maxine.

Claire grabbed a pastry from Larkin and another coffee, handing both to their feisty grandmother figure. "How can we help?"

Maxine was busy shooting daggers in good fun at Janice and took the offered meal without a glance.

"You miss him, don't you?" Larkin said gently.

Maxine sighed. "Of course, I do. But he was an ass in front of everyone. I know I'm not innocent. God knows I'm a handful, but I can't abide a man who would humiliate me in front of my family. Because that's who you all are to me. My family."

"Honestly, Maxine?" Blayne interrupted. "Not one of us thought anything other than, 'oh shit, Judge Carter's in trouble.' I don't think he or anyone else has the power to humiliate you. You are too loved and respected by everyone in this town for that to happen. But I have to say this, and I don't want you to get mad at me." She gripped her hands at her waist, looking to Larkin then Claire for strength. "There's is a chance he felt humiliated as well."

Maxine raised her arched brows. "How in the world would he have been humiliated? And why would I be mad at you? I never hold a grudge." Larkin and Claire burst out laughing, not even trying to hold back the humor at that statement.

Maxine scowled when they didn't stop right away. Blayne finally put her hand out, palm up. "He's a county judge. Making your moonshine isn't illegal but selling it is. There's a chance it makes him feel like you don't respect him or his position."

"That's ridiculous! Of course, I respect him. He's the judge."

"You know what I think?" Claire said. All four women looked her way. "I think you care for the judge more than you thought you would, and it scares you. It's easier to have him there but mad at you than it is to have him there loving you."

Maxine stared at her, took a bite of her coffee cake, washed it down with a sip of coffee. Narrowing her eyes, she asked, "Have you learned to say penis in public yet?"

Claire threw her hands up in the air. "I'm done. That's all I got." She looked at Larkin and Blayne, jerking her thumb over her shoulder. "She's all yours." But her own words haunted her.

How many Judge Carters was she missing out on because she was afraid? Just one face popped into her head, with his golden glow and that drop-dead sex-me-up grin, but she shook it away. She didn't have to miss out on him. He would be her safe and easy fun.

She rather liked his lessons of indulgence. Taking a sip of her coffee, she turned back around and caught Janice staring at her with a thoughtful expression on her face.

"Did Mitch give you a lesson last night?"

The coffee had no chance to make it all the way down her throat and instead got caught in her windpipe. A cough burst from her chest, followed by another and another. Larkin and Blayne patted her on her back, and the September breeze blew in thick with their curiosity.

"That's it!" Blayne exclaimed.

All the women gaped at Claire but remained silent. The band on stage had kicked up the energy with the upbeat melody of "New York, New York." Time slowed with her panic, and she could feel the salty ocean air fill her lungs while she tried to catch her breath. The tang of the ocean melded with the sweet aroma of baked goods, and she wished they could go back to the moment when she was enjoying her lemon blueberry sunrise pancake.

"That is not *it*," she gritted out.

Larkin snapped her fingers. "Her cheeks are pink, her eyes are bright, and she was filling her face with sugar. Claire got laid!"

Maxine cheered. "That's my girl."

And Blayne joined in.

Janice had a confused look on her face. "Who's the lucky guy?"

All the blood drained from Claire's face, and she quickly turned back to Maxine and blurted out. "My vibrator!"

CHAPTER 12

*M*itch couldn't begin to describe the irritation scratching at his cloudy brain as he opened the front door of the Cape Van Buren house just a crack to see who the hell was waking him up so early the sun itself had barely stirred.

"Why are you here?" The question grated out as if dragging across a cheese grater.

His mother gave him a hard stare, apparently very confident her reason to wake him up at 7:00 in the morning on a Sunday was beyond important enough. She and Maxine stood shoulder-to-shoulder, their arms crossed, tapping their feet, waiting to be let in.

"What did I ever do to the two of you?" He left the door ajar, dragging his ass to the kitchen to make some coffee. "I need to put some clothes on."

"You're as bad as Ryker, walking around half naked, never knowing who's going to be coming through the front door."

"It's seven in the God damn morning on a Sunday, Maxine. The Center doesn't open until eleven. There shouldn't be anyone at my God damn front door."

"Watch your language," Janice scolded.

Maxine laughed. "You tell him, Janice."

Mitch rolled his eyes as he filled the coffee maker with a few extra spoonfuls of coffee. He had a feeling he was gonna need it. As he went through the motions, the two ladies took their seats at the island.

"Why are you here?"

His mother folded her hands in front of her and leaned on the white island top. "We've come to take you to church." She gave him a look. The kind he used to get when he was a kid walking through the front door after doing something he wasn't allowed to do. It had always driven him crazy how she could know before he'd even stepped through the door.

"The hell do you mean, take me to church? No desire to hear Clint Fenwick talk about the sins of Van Buren while he welcomes the parishioners through the door."

"If you didn't sin, you wouldn't care," Maxine stated with a faux air of propriety.

He shot her a look. "You're one to talk."

"But this isn't about me," she said with a smirk.

He scrubbed his face with his hands and set out three cups. Filling one, he asked, "Would either of you ladies like any?"

His mother jabbed a thumb at Maxine. "She got her fill yesterday. I'm sure she's fine but go ahead and pour me a cup."

"This isn't about me," Maxine repeated, shooting her friend a warning look.

"Did you sleep with Claire?" Janice blurted.

His coffee spurted out his nose, and he grabbed the kitchen towel as his lungs worked to remove the hot liquid from their depths. Pain seared through his chest when he tried to pull in a breath.

Both women rounded the island and started beating him on the back. He threw his hands up to wave them away. "Stop."

He forced air in past the humiliation and leftover coffee in his throat. "Mom! I'm not having this conversation with you."

"I told you, Janice," Maxine said. "It's too weird for a mom to ask. Why don't you wait outside."

Mitch looked at Maxine the same way he did when she'd told him and Ryker to strip and hose off before entering her house after they'd decided to mud wrestle in the woods. "I am not talking to you about this either."

Maxine and Janice exchanged looks; something silent passed between them, then both woman women turned, walked back around the island, and sat down.

Maxine folded her hands in front of her on the table. "If you're not going to talk to your mom and you're not going to talk to me, then you're going to talk to both of us."

Mitch raised his brows. "What kind of logic is that? I'm not talking to either of you."

Janice sighed. "Where did I go wrong? Mae never gives me any trouble."

"Shit. It is too early for this." Mitch scrubbed his face with his hands at the kitchen sink, then downed half of his cup of coffee, careful this time which pipe it went down.

"I don't know, hun, do you think you coddled him too much?"

"Maybe," Janice paused. "You know he did breastfeed longer than his sister did."

"And if I recall," Maxine added, "it took him a long time to potty train."

Mitch could not believe what he was hearing and spun back around. "Why are you doing this to me?"

"Oh, stop your whining," Janice scolded. "We know what this is all about."

"Fine. Enlighten me," he grumbled. Clearly, they weren't gonna let this alone, so the sooner they hashed this out, the sooner they'd be gone.

Both women studied him through narrow eyes. "A special lady," Maxine crowed. Fucking great. Tongues were already wagging that the playboy attorney of Van Buren was messing around with the emotionally fragile Claire Adams? So he was cast as the villain, and they were storming in on their white horses to put a stop to his evil ways. He couldn't help the sharp pain of disappointment in his chest. His own mother didn't even believe he was the right man for Claire.

He drained his coffee then filled it with more.

"You know too much of that isn't good for your stomach." Maxine waved her fingers for a cup.

The discomfort from too much espresso in his stomach would be a comforting distraction from the pain caused by this visit.

"Look, I'm not going with you to church, and I'm not talking to you about my sex life."

Janice raised a brow. "You know that tone never worked with me—"

"Seriously, Mom? I'm a thirty-five-year-old man. I can take whatever tone I want."

Maxine slowly pushed up from the island. "Be that as it may, just remember, there are things that you love that can be lost."

Mitch's head felt like it was a punching bag. It was all too much, too soon, too early in the God damn morning. He loved Maxine to death, but sometimes he had no idea what the hell she was talking about.

He just stared at her.

"So you think this visit is all about you," she continued. "I came by to pick up some crates from downstairs. Need your help to get them out to your mother's car."

She let her words sink in until he finally connected the dots with her threat a few moments before.

Fuck my life.

She was always using her damn moonshine to manipulate people into doing what she wanted. And he was too damn weak to stand up to her and risk losing it. With a sigh, he nodded.

"That's what I thought," Maxine said with a wink.

Janice joined Maxine as they walked toward the foyer. "Put a shirt on first, for goodness sake," his mother added. "You're walking around like you're some sort of gigolo."

Mitch didn't know how much more he could take. Gritting his teeth, he grabbed a sweatshirt off the coat hanger in the foyer and dragged it over his head. They made their way downstairs to the basement.

"Hold on tight to the railing, Maxine. You never know when he reaches his limit and decides to just shove us down the stairs and end us once and for all."

"I don't think he'd risk the moonshine. The town would never forgive him."

Both women cackled behind him, and he bit his tongue. It might be time to find a new favorite vice. But damned if it wasn't the finest kind.

Maxine had given the basement a huge overhaul since she had moved out. The once dirt floor cellar was spotless with a cement floor and temperature and humidity controls. Stainless countertops, white walls, lots of glass and mirrors.

It didn't look like the basement of any other Victorian home he'd ever visited with all the light reflected from the small above-ground windows. Distilling equipment gleamed on the countertops, ready to be used, and barrels of aging moonshine sat in a row against one wall.

Pictures of the North Cover Mavens toasting by the bonfire during one of their Howl at the Moon parties hung along the walls.

"Wow, it really looks great down here. I haven't been down here since you renovated."

"Thank you." Maxine waved her hand at him, her jeweled fingers reflecting all the lights. "Making my moonshine isn't illegal, so there's no reason for me to be hiding in some dark and shadowy underground meth house."

"Nope," he agreed. "But selling it is."

Janice shook her head. "You never did know how to stop while you were ahead."

"Come on." Maxine pointed to a wooden crate full of cobalt blue canning jars. "I would like these three crates taken up to the car."

"No problem." Anything to get them out of the house. He lifted a crate, welcoming the weight and the distraction from their visit, and made his way back up the stairs.

"He's handy to have around." His mother's voice followed him up the stairs. "Good with his hands, always making things around the house when he was a boy."

Mitch kept walking. Joining their conversation was more dangerous than going out to the coast during a nor'easter. He set the crate in the trunk of the car, then went back for the other two while the ladies waited.

They continued to whisper and point as he unloaded the second crate. He ignored them, going back to get the third. His best strategy was to stay silent and get them off the cape. Once he got the last crate secured, he closed the trunk.

"Okay, you're all set. Thanks for the visit. Always good to see you." He kissed Maxine's cheek then his mother's, adding a hug.

The ladies got in the car, but Janice rolled the window down. "About Claire..."

He threw his hands up. "I know, you want me to stay away from her. I got the message loud and clear." He was overreacting, but damn if it didn't hurt to hear the same shit from his own mother.

"On the contrary." Maxine leaned across the front seat to talk to him through the passenger window.

Janice nodded. "We don't want you to stay away from Claire. We think you're the best man for her."

And that same nor'easter couldn't have knocked him over any harder than their words did at that moment. Confusion and doubt, elation and fear, tied his tongue.

He shoved his hands into the front pocket of his hoodie. "No, Mom, I'm not."

She waved dismissively. "You're one confused young man, Mitch. But you'll figure it out." Before he could respond, Maxine put the car in gear and pulled away, driving around the fountain and out toward town.

What the fuck just happened?

He stared at the car until it disappeared from sight, startled when Puzzle weaved around his ankles. Picking up the cat, he hugged him against his chest, comforted by the familiar purr.

The sun was shining but hadn't yet warmed the earth in the early hours, and the breeze coming in off the ocean made him shiver.

They weren't there to tell him to stay away from Claire? Were they insane? There was a good man out there for someone as special as Claire.

But it sure as hell wasn't him.

~

*C*laire finished stringing globe lights across a narrow space between two trees in the woods, making a faux starry sky canopy. The past couple of days had been spent in a haze of lustful memories and barrels of wanting. Wanting to feel the weight of Mitch on her body, wanting the taste of him, the smell of him.

Gliding her palms across the dense muscles of his chest had been an exercise in discovery for sure. She and Jimmy had been so young when they'd met. He'd been a runner, thin and sinewy, which was a different experience than Mitch's thickly muscled physique. The difference between a boy and a man, young love and one that was more mature.

That thought stopped her short. Love? No, no. Lust, desire.

But *not* love.

Been there, done that, and crushed by it. Not happening again. But hot sex with a man she considered a friend? Hell yeah.

Her palms itched at the thought, and she brushed them against her navy blue skirt, trying to ease the sensation. She was going to need to get her hands on him again...and soon.

"Hey." Mitch's voice slid up her spine like a silk caress, and she turned to see him walking toward her from the path that led back to the Cape house.

Nerves raced through her body and lodged in her throat. "Hi." Her tone was as breathless as if she'd gone for a jog...or just finished an energetic round of sex.

There it was again.

She couldn't get enough of him just by looking. He seemed bigger, broader, sexier than when he'd left her apartment. Leaving her in a very real state of post-coital bliss, and she didn't know if she would ever look at her kitchen the same way again. Baking was already one of her favorite things to do, but combine that with mind-blowing sex, and now she might become an addict.

A nervous chuckle escaped her lips. "Are you ready to begin?"

Mitch's eyes flashed in much more than agreement.

"I mean...with the exercise?" The words spilled out, but in her mind, all she could think of was his hot, naked flesh pressing against hers surrounded by the evergreen of the forest. She tried to focus and pointed his attention to the space she'd been working on.

"The trees act as a sort of wind barrier, and the space is big enough that the kids will have plenty of room to stretch out and work. Local artists will be displaying their work all along the path. It will all start here with the art therapy classes, face painting, and hide-and-go-seek here for the kids; then it will end with wine tasting and a coffee bar at the far end of the trail before looping back through." She couldn't help but get caught up in the excitement of her plan. "We wanted to make sure there was a strong enough draw to make everybody complete the whole course. It's gonna be amazing."

"It's brilliant." He looked at her as if he wanted her to teach him to bake again.

A shiver raced up her spine.

"Was this all you?"

"It's a team effort. And if I have anything to say about it, the North Cove Mavens and the South Cove Madams will find a way to work together to make this event a success." Her laugh was breathless. She'd blame it on the task before her and not how much she wanted him to kiss her again.

He nodded as he stepped closer. "But the idea was all you, wasn't it, Claire? You have a way of taking care of people in a very unassuming manner."

She smiled. "You're the only one who would think so. I thought Larkin was gonna kill me for hovering about her like I did when she was pregnant."

He ran a finger along her jaw and tucked an errant lock of hair behind one ear, following the length to the end then skimming his fingers back under her jaw. "Your hair is getting long."

The statement distracted her, and she blinked.

"That had to be hard, seeing your friends get married and seeing Larkin pregnant when I'm sure it is still a raw loss for you."

This was the Mitch that no one else saw, and a bit of wonder washed through her. Her friends understood that she was happy for them, and it was difficult at the same time, but she certainly didn't expect such sensitivity or thought from a man.

Even if he was a friend.

Just a friend.

She had to keep reminding herself, not just because she knew he didn't want a relationship, but to protect her own heart as well. She grabbed his wandering fingers and nodded. "It is, but I am so happy for them."

"You have to want the same for yourself again someday, Claire."

She shook her head. "I had my chance."

"I don't believe that at all." His eyes roved over her face. "I can see you with children and a husband who cherishes you. The family you've always deserved."

A heavy weight constricted her lungs, making it difficult to breathe. "You know, it wasn't easy to get past it all, but I made myself face it. I went to the cemetery. I worked through my steps. And now I've moved on. I'm fine, Mitch. But I will not open myself up to that kind of loss again."

"Just because you lost once and you lost hard, doesn't mean you'll lose again." He squeezed her upper arm with a small shake as if desperate to make her understand.

He got her attention, that was for sure. It was time to focus back on him. "Let's explore this," she said, pulling out his drawing. "You yourself always say that you don't want a commitment. What are *you* afraid of?"

He stared at her a moment then dropped his chin to his chest. "I'm not afraid; I'm practical."

"Oh? And I'm not practical?"

"That's not what I meant, and you know it." He moved to sit down at the long picnic table under the canopy of globe lights. He glanced down at the picture she set before him, and emotion scattered across his face like sand blown in the wind. He didn't even realize how much he said without saying anything at all.

"Look." He tapped at the paper. "I know you mean well with this exercise, and I believe it will make a really big impact on the children in this area, but it just doesn't work for me."

"That's fair." She sat across from him at the table. "Not everything works for everyone. We are all unique, and all of our needs are different. But then, tell me about them." She pointed to the three people with the forth, a shadowy silhouette, standing behind them.

"There's nothing to tell. You know my father left when we were young, everyone knows that.

"Yes." She ran her finger over the dark silhouette. "So the shadow of the person is a man? Your father?"

He looked at her with a raised brow. "I just told you it was my dad or a symbol of his absence. In situations like this, when isn't it the man?"

His words sparked compassion in her heart. She was beginning to see the true Mitch.

"So you think men are the only ones who leave their families?"

A muscle ticked in his jaw. "I'm not an idiot, Claire. I know anyone could leave anyone. But for me, for the people I love, it has been a man who has caused the pain. Have you ever heard of Ryker's story?" He asked his voice gaining an edge. "We were eight years old, and his father sought us out in a drunken rage. He couldn't find a bottle of whiskey that he'd misplaced the last time he was drunk. That man wasn't particular about who he hit, but he did enjoy hitting Ryker the most. I don't know that I've ever felt such fear as I did the night I hid in the Cape house attic." He shut his eyes against the memory, and she steeled herself against reaching out to him, soothing him, afraid he'd stop talking.

"Ryker had told me not to go up there, but I was too scared to listen. It was a trap because once you were cornered in the attic, the only way out was through his dad."

Claire couldn't help it and covered his hand with her own. "I can't imagine." Her heart broke for the man who worried about the little boys he and his buddy used to be. She had heard stories, but it was different hearing it from someone you cared about. Because she did care, whether she wanted to or not.

He pointed to the three people in the foreground that she could only assume was him and Mae and their mother. Their bodies in a fairly spread out position, which was curious to her because she knew that they were a loving trio.

"What happened that night? Did you get out? What did your parents do? Your dad was still with you then, right?"

Mitch grunted. "It was the first night I'd ever heard bone smashed against bone. Ryker ran up and threw himself between his father and me at the last moment."

Claire gasped. "I can't imagine."

"I grabbed an old chair and smashed it over his father's head, stunning him just enough for the two of us to get out. Ryker's eye immediately swelled closed, and blood was gushing from a gash on his cheek. Maxine wasn't home, so we sped off to my house. Just as my father was loading his luggage into his car. He spared us one glance then got in his car and drove away."

"Oh, my God." Claire held her hand to her heart. "What kind of man would see a hurt child and just walk away?" She said the words without realizing she'd said them out loud.

Mitch gave her a pointed look. "He wasn't a man. And neither was Ryker's father. They're barely shadows. Shadows that only exist where light can't reach." His voice sounded gravelly and thick, and she rounded the table, unable to stop herself from going to him.

He turned, sliding one leg over the outside of the bench, and she mirrored his position, straddling the seat in front of him. Placing a hand on his cheek, she smiled. "You aren't that man. You'd never be that man."

He swallowed hard. "I guarantee that neither Ryker's father nor my own ever thought they'd be that man either."

She scooted closer, wrapping her arms around him, trying to ease the pain of the memories. This was what fueled the Mitch that he showed to everyone else.

"And there is one way I can guarantee that I never will be that man, guarantee that the stresses of life will never bring that side out in me."

She placed a finger over his lips, trying to hush such words. Trying to soothe him. Tilting her face, she gently pressed her lips to his once, twice, gliding them back and forth. "You're not that kind of man," she whispered against his mouth.

With tentative strokes, she tasted him. He resisted at first, then on a groan, he gave in and yanked her even closer, pulling her legs up and around his waist. The hard length of him pressed between her legs and a thrill of pleasure shot through her.

It was so different with this man. The sensations were heightened, more intoxicating than anything she'd ever felt before. She didn't know if it was lust or the promise of decadence or the gentle way he caressed her cheeks or the feather-light kisses he fluttered across her collarbone. But with him it was special. Profound. Life-altering, even.

She was falling...hard. And everything in her tried to dig in her heels and pull him to her all at the same time.

"I'm sorry the program isn't working with me," he whispered against her mouth. "I really want this to be a success for you."

She kissed him back hard, trying to absorb the pain and disappointment he felt, the pain he kept hidden from when he and Ryker were young boys. She found it both beautiful and sweet that he thought for a second her project wasn't working for him.

But he was wrong.

It was working better than she'd imagined it would.

He'd revealed more to her than he realized. So much that he would probably not be very happy about the insight he had given her. It was amazing how sensitive so many big, strong men really were.

She pressed her body against his, trying to ease the building desire. She pushed her hands between their bodies to unbuckle his belt and release his zipper. His touch and whispered words emboldened her. Taking the length of him out of his jeans, she gripped him firmly, stroking him to the edge of excitement.

His hands were everywhere, tenderly cupping her breasts, giving a gentle squeeze. Dipping his head, he pushed the V of her t-shirt aside until he was able to bare one pert nipple. Without hesitation, he took it in his mouth, flicking his tongue back and forth over her flesh.

Waves of pleasure built with each caress. "I want you."

"Thank God," he growled.

After shoving his jeans and underwear down his hips, she scrunched her long maxi skirt up around her waist, slid her panties to the side, and stroked herself across the tip of his cock.

His fingers dug into her hips as he encouraged her to continue her exploration. She gently lowered, taking him inside her, thrilling at the sensation of being stretched and filled. She set a rhythm to build their pleasure even more.

Mitch found her clit with his thumb and with feather-light caresses pushed her higher.

She dug into his shoulders, using his shoulders as leverage to lift and drop. Faster and faster the pressure built, his hands stoking her fire, her desire unrestrained, and with his name on her lips, she crested over the precipice, drowning her cry in a deep, hard kiss.

"Holy fuck." His voice was barely audible.

She rested her forehead against his. "I know. I don't know what is wrong with me. I was supposed to be focusing on this festival, but when I saw you all I could think about was getting your pants off."

His low chuckle was full of appreciation. "So much for ripping the Band-Aid off, I think we annihilated a whole bandage."

"I thought one time would be enough to push me forward."

"Maybe you just need to get a little bit of exploration out of your system. I don't mind helping you with that." He pressed into her harder, sealing his sexy offer with a kiss.

She smiled against his lips. "You are so generous." She giggled.

"I really am," he returned with a devilish grin. "Maybe after today, you'll be able to move forward." His voice sounded so strong and so sure, and she admired his ability to keep a distance.

Because as she looked into his blue eyes, recognizing the man he truly was, the idea of moving on from him became harder and harder to bear.

CHAPTER 13

*M*itch couldn't get the sensation of Claire out of his system. She was like a lingering virus that didn't respond to any modern medicine—except this virus made him dream of the future, lose sleep, and left him in a persistent state of wanting.

Forcing his voice to remain distant and detached when he told her maybe she was ready to move on was one of the most difficult things he'd ever done. But he wasn't willing to make a commitment, especially to her. And not because he didn't want to see her face every day or have the right to wrap her in his arms every night, but because he'd never forgive himself when he hurt her.

Yet, at the same time, thinking of her moving on with somebody else was unimaginable.

He squeezed his eyes shut against the excruciating image of her with anyone else but him.

How had he let her creep under his skin so easily?

"Mr. Brennan, do you care to elaborate?" Judge Carter asked.

Yanked back to the present, Mitch pinched the bridge of his nose, trying to focus. His initial interview for the city attorney seat was not the time to be distracted with a relationship he wasn't even in. Most of his problem was Claire, but a solid portion was also the idea of having to sit in judgment, to have to depend on the opinions and acceptance of the adults he spent his childhood avoiding. "Yes sir, I apologize."

"Then please explain to the board why you think you are the best candidate for city attorney."

"You need someone in this position who really knows the town, where the town came from, and where it's going. You need someone who's willing to fight and fight hard to make sure that every life in Cape Van Buren is better for having lived here."

"And you think you can do that?" Clint Fenwick asked with a look of disbelief.

Mitch had to hold back his own belief on how Fenwick ever got elected to a city council seat in the first place. He knew the man meant well, but his judgments often lacked compassion and were fueled by his personal moral code rather than the laws set by the council.

Pulling back his shoulders, he pressed on. "I know I am the one to do it. I've lived here my whole life, I've seen the good and the bad—hell, we all know I've been a part of both."

"That's an understatement."

Mitch let the sotto voce statement slip by. "And I've been working diligently the past few years to help turn around what has not been working."

From the council, "Such as?"

"As you know, I helped secure the easement for the Cape, and I continue to work to make sure the conservation center is set up properly to serve the people of our town. It's an organization that will continue to give back for years to come."

"Easy to do when you're best buds with the owner, is it not?" Judge Carter pushed.

"Or some might say even more difficult. Ryker Van Buren knows all of my faults, yet he still knew I was the best man for the job. He wouldn't trust the center in anyone else's hands. For any of you who know Ryker, you know that says a lot right there."

The board members looked at one another in silent consideration and then back to Mitch.

"I've also been working along the outskirts of town with the housing projects to make sure that our special housing units meet all safety requirements, and I've been holding the landlords to their responsibilities."

"That's not an easy feat," George Carter piped up. "We've had a hard time with that for years."

Mitch nodded. "We have. But it's taken more than trying. I've physically put myself in front of them with documentation and support from local law enforcement relentlessly. It's important for everyone in our town to have a safe, clean place to lay their head."

"What do you have to say about putting someone at the head of our city attorney position who isn't necessarily known for being a family man?"

Mitch gritted his teeth but kept a serene, neutral face. "Being a family man means more than having a wife and children. My family extends well beyond the walls of my home and includes everyone in our town, Judge Carter. Doesn't yours? You're my family. Fenwick, even you're my family, and we don't even like each other."

That got a chuckle from the members and an accepting, good-natured scowl from Clint. At least that was something.

"I've always taken care of my sister and my mother. Janice Brennan would never have accepted anything less. Not to mention Maxine Van Buren."

Judge Carter laughed. "You wouldn't dare not to."

Mitch dipped his chin. "That may be true. The rest of my skills, experience, and abilities speak for themselves. You'll find it all in my portfolio." His heart slammed in his chest as he tried to read the expressions on their faces. He couldn't imagine being passed up for this opportunity. This was what he needed to be doing. This was what would give him fulfillment, make him feel like he was truly a part of something bigger than himself, and really allow him to positively touch the lives of each citizen in their town.

"Well..." Judge Carter straightened the stack of papers in front of him. "I think we have all we need for now. We'll be considering a few more candidates, narrowing the selection down to two and then calling those chosen in for another, more detailed interview. Just the fact that you got this far is an achievement in and of itself, Mr. Brennan."

Mitch forced back the disappointment crawling up his throat. That's what people said to soften the blow of the word no. "I'm the right candidate," he reiterated, standing before them and tapping his finger on the table. "If this council truly knows what they're doing, you will see that already."

As he let himself out of the courthouse, he resisted the urge to go to Claire and tell her everything. He had to stand on his own with this. As he forced his feet to take steps away from where they wanted to go, he acknowledged the physical pain it caused and pushed on.

Though the process of getting the position of city attorney seemed to be one of the hardest things he'd ever done, staying away from Claire might well be impossible.

~

*C*laire braced herself and stared at Larkin and Blayne. "I don't care what Maxine says."

Blayne scoffed. "Until she refuses to let you consume any more moonshine." She snapped her fingers.

"No." Claire shook her head. "I'm serious. I am over this ridiculous feud. The Van Buren art festival and the people of this town are more important than any argument between two sisters that happened so long ago people have forgotten what happened at all."

Larkin piped up. "Me, too. I expect all of you out at the Cape to help with our upcoming Coast Week event. No excuses."

Claire looked around the Fountain of Youth stage and nodded. The early afternoon sun shone onto the stage, offering a welcoming glow. The temperatures were beginning to fall, getting ready for October, but remained pretty comfortable most days.

She had refreshments catered from both the Flat Iron coffeehouse and North Cove Confectionery, giving an enticing array of pastries and coffee and tea and scones. The comforting aroma alone had already attracted a few people she had to turn away because they weren't part of their meeting.

Larkin picked up a scone and took a bite, talking while she chewed. "You're very brave. I'll give you that."

"I'm brave?" Claire teased. "You about ran a man out of his home and off his lands." Larkin's telltale blush infused her skin a bright red.

"Yeah, well, facing down Ryker is one thing, facing down Maxine Van Buren is another." Claire threw her hands up in welcome as Shelly Anne Mills ascended the steps to the stage with her wisdom.

"Well, the past few weeks have proven to me that I am little-by-little not caring so much about what other people think."

Blayne whistled. "A lesson taken straight out of Maxine's own book on life. But, wow, look who's gotten her feisty back!"

Claire grabbed the hands of her best friends, so thankful that they had come into her life. "Thanks to this town and you ladies, I have turned my life around. When you guys first approached me, I was still hiding behind a fortress of anger. And that anger was blocking all of my creativity, making me miss out on the things I really love in life."

Larkin smiled. "You're a huge reason I was able to move on, too, and in ensuring that the Center is becoming such a big success."

Blayne sniffed and gave a dismissive wave to her friends. "Enough! What are we doing here, Claire? And you better have a good explanation because here comes Maxine."

Maxine followed the path toward the Fountain of Youth, eyeing one of the South Cove Madams, Patrice, the grandmother of the man who owned Dine on the Vine. With a sniff, she lifted her nose in the air as she passed, making Shelly Ann laugh.

"Woman, you're such a character. Poor Patrice has no chance standing against you."

Larkin laughed. "Who does? But she loves the people of this town more than anyone else, doesn't she?"

Shelly Anne nodded. "That she does. She has a wicked fine heart."

Maxine and Patrice took the stairs in an awkward stop-start motion. Pretty soon Janice and Evette followed along with the comedy club owner's sister, Kit Fasbender, and Althea Manis, one of the two sisters from ETA, Entertainment and Travel Agency.

Maxine tapped her foot, giving Claire a playful glare. "You better have a good explanation for this."

She channeled her inner Mitch and gave all the ladies her most haughty stare. "Oh, I have a good explanation, and that explanation is we have the fall art festival next week and need to pool our resources and work together to make this a huge hit. This town is more important than any ridiculous feud or competition that you ladies have. This one isn't about North versus South, this one is about Cape Van Buren and raising money for our children."

"Has your program been approved yet?" Evette asked.

Claire's chest responded with a trembling squeeze. Mitch wouldn't let her or the town down.

Would he?

"No, not yet, but it's just a matter of time. I'm sure of it," she said.

Maxine picked up a pastry from the Confectionery, earning a big grin from Evette. "Well, better not be too much time—we only have a week left."

"We're all only too aware," Blayne said.

Claire invited everyone to grab a bite to eat and take a seat. "Look, I called you all here today because I think that we can make this the best event ever. It won't end the friendly..." she rolled her eyes "...fun competition that we've always had, but this event is different."

"Different how?" Janice probed.

"Because this one is for the children of Cape Van Buren. This event will launch all the various programs, and this is our chance to really help make a difference in their lives, to fill a void or offer guidance when they may not always get it at home."

Kit from the comedy club spoke up. "No offense, and I sincerely don't mean this to be rude, but you aren't a parent. How do you think it will be looked upon if the kids are getting advice from someone who doesn't have any of their own?"

The familiar pain and loneliness squeezed Claire's chest. All she ever wanted was a child and a family. Well, this was her way to have that. She thought of how best to answer but was saved by Janice and her nose for news.

"I was under the impression the event and your program were coming along just fine." Janice sipped her Flat Iron coffee, avoiding eye contact with Evette.

Claire took a stack of papers and handed them out to each lady. "If you take a look at this, you'll see that we are well on our way. But I want to take this a step further, and it requires the organization and logistics of the South Cove with the creativity and fun of the North Cove to make it happen."

"The South Cove Madams are fun. What are you talking about?" Shelly Anne frowned.

Maxine whistled. "Shelly Anne, you may be the fun exception. I've partied with you a time or two in our youth."

Shelly Anne held her gaze for a moment. "You sure did. Boy, did we have a good time."

"Did? We still do. You've also been there for me during some really rough times, too." Maxine rolled her eyes. "Now look what you've done, getting me all sentimental."

"We're all family in this town. That's what we do." This from Janice.

Claire finished passing out her itemized list of exactly what needed to be done. "So, you guys will do it then? We'll work together, no problems?"

Patrice shook her head. "No way. I've worked with Maxine before—she gets bossy." Her voice was quiet but firm.

Claire wanted to laugh, these ladies were so amazing and a pain in the ass all at the same time.

"That's because I know how to get things done," Maxine replied.

"I've never seen my son jump so high as when Maxine Van Buren asks him to do something," Janice said.

"Well, that's because Mitch's a smart boy."

"Speaking of Mitch," Althea from ETA interjected. "Did I see you and Mitch out in South Cove Park a few weeks ago, Claire?"

All eyes turned to Claire, and she felt her tenuous hold of control slither through her fingers like the sands out on the beach.

Attempting to change the subject, she clapped her hands together in feigned excitement, which deep down was much more like panic and a need for diversion. "Maxine you never told us how your date went with the judge?"

That did the trick. Maxine's fingers fluttered a bit as if unsure where to settle. "Oh, it was fine."

Shelly Anne sipped from her coffee cup. "It was more than fine. I thought I was going to have to make a no PDA announcement in the coffeehouse from the way they were carrying on."

Maxine preened with an air of sophistication. "You had to do nothing of the sort."

Suddenly, out of nowhere, a baby moose tripped up the steps, running straight to Evette. She let out a small cry of shock, as did most of the other ladies, startling the calf and making it rear back on its tiny legs, take a sharp turn, and then run straight into the table.

Pastries went flying, and Shelly Anne's coffee carafe tipped precariously close to the edge. Maxine jumped to catch it at the same moment Shelly Anne did, and the two women tangled into a crumpled heap.

Kit and Janice tried to get out of the way and ended up tipping over their chairs. The papers that Claire had passed out twirled about like confetti from the commotion, and all she could do was laugh.

Blayne and Larkin looked from her to the mess around them and joined in.

As the excitement settled, Claire held her stomach, aching from laughing so hard. "What in the world just happened?"

The baby moose went back to Evette and leaned into her legs. She patted its head, cooing softly to soothe its poor nerves. "I came across this little fella on a hike through the Cape woods the other day. His mamma had died, and I have a bad feeling that he imprinted on me."

Claire's heart swelled with tenderness, and she couldn't resist petting his sweet face. "Oh, my gosh, what a little cutie."

"He's cute now, but in a very short time the cute turns into dangerous." Evette walked around the stage picking up all the papers, the baby moose at her heels.

"Don't worry about that, Miss Evette," Claire said. "I've got it."

"No, no, this is my fault. I didn't mean for it to happen. I left him in the woods, and he followed me home, then I took him back, but he somehow found me. I need to call the animal control," Evette said.

Blayne grimaced. "What will they do? Nobody better hurt this little guy."

"Let's look into it a little bit more before we call anyone," Shelly Anne suggested, and with that, the North and South Cove ladies were on the same page.

Maxine gave Claire a small nudge. "Alright, lady, you sure are growing balls in your old age."

Claire couldn't do anything but laugh. She loved this woman for being such a model of strength and compassion wrapped up in a feisty, fashionable package.

"You can count on us," Maxine continued. "We'll get everything organized and make this festival everything it's never been before."

"Thank you," Claire whispered, a rush of gratitude making it difficult to speak. She swallowed past the emotion, embracing her friend. "I want this to go really well for Larkin and the Archer Conservation Center of Cape Van Buren. I think my program could help a lot of kids here."

She held Janice's gaze, hoping the woman couldn't see into her heart. "We just need to get your son's approval."

Janice put her hands out. "Like that boy ever listens to me."

Just the thought of him, the sound of his name, sent a flutter of sensations running through Claire's body. The more time she spent with him, the more drawn to him she was.

She watched the calf follow Evette around, its heart on its little moose sleeve.

It was a powerful thing when someone fell in love with you. And all the more devastating when you couldn't love them in return because of the pain they might eventually cause.

CHAPTER 14

*M*itch jogged down the Cape house stairs with a mix of mounting stress and increasing excitement. The Cape was teaming with both citizens and tourists to participate in the last day of the Coast Week event.

The celebration of the state's coastal resources occurred every year with groups of volunteer-organized events to clean every inch of the coast from the shores to the tide waters, bagging, and responsibly disposing of trash that had found its way into the marine habitat.

He looked out over the crowd of people trying to find the platinum head he'd grown so fond of seeing. Finally spotting Claire along the shoreline just south of the lighthouse, he made his way toward her. She was going to be pissed, but part of his decision was to protect her as well. She had her event planning business, which was her livelihood. He didn't want to see her lose it in any potential nasty litigation.

A warm sensation filled his chest as he got closer. Her soft voice met his ears, gentle like the waves gliding onto the sand on a calm summer afternoon. He needed to tell her, tell her it was for her own good, and find a way to keep her at arm's length when all he wanted to do was pull her in closer.

There was more than one way to hurt a woman, and for some damn reason, he was doomed to hit on all of them when it came to Claire.

He was no good for her. He knew it, she knew it. Hell, the whole town knew it.

Pulling in a deep breath of ocean air, he shoved his doubt away and grabbed the garbage bag she held out to him as he approached.

"Thanks."

She grinned. "Where've you been? We've all been slaving away for over an hour now." As she continued to pick and prod through the rocks along the edge of the water, she jerked her chin toward the cape between the house and the South Cove beaches.

A collection of trash bags, six feet tall, was being loaded into Charlie Jones's truck. The contractor's bald head gleamed in the afternoon sun but wasn't a hint brighter than his fire engine red beard. Mitch grinned. The man did good work. He'd been working with Ryker back when his buddy thought turning the Cape into a housing community would be a good way to right his past, but when the project changed, Charlie just rolled with the punches and put his boys to work with renovations on the house with a drive to accommodate visitors to the town's new community center.

"I had some work to catch up on."

Wrinkling her nose, she asked. "Are you going to tell me already? It's wicked torture waiting to hear."

He swallowed the need to give her whatever she wanted and forced out a casual chuckle. "You'll find out with everyone else. But don't worry about it. One way or another, you'll provide an art program."

She frowned as she shoved a plastic cup into her trash bag. "But I don't want to just give art lessons. Hell, Max Stanton could do that."

Max was the son of the town physician but used his hands for sculpting not healing.

Taking a stick with a nail poking out one end from a bucket, Mitch carefully navigated the rocks, trying to get close to the water without getting wet. "Look, I understand. You want to make a real difference. I get it. That's the very reason I want the city attorney position."

He stabbed an empty cigarette pack, disgusted that anyone still smoked and even more disgusted that anyone still threw their garbage on the ground instead of in a can. "Unfortunately, my reputation doesn't help me, not here anyway. Thankfully, Portland is another story."

She froze in the middle of tying down a full garbage bag. "Portland? My parents live that way. I feel like I hardly see them anymore."

Gripping the knot she made, he slung the bag over his shoulder, handing his bag over to her. He continued to poke about the rocks for trash as he talked. "Yeah. I have to keep my options open just in case. There's a chance that I won't get exactly what I want either, and if that happens, I need to have a way to still do the work I know I'm meant for." Clearing his throat, he added, "They've a wicked smart city council in Portland, and the city is bigger than Cape Van Buren, giving me the potential to do even more. They seem very open to my ideas and how I think I can help."

"But you can do that here," she said, a frown forming between her brows.

"That's my plan, but Cape Van Buren doesn't see in me what Portland does."

They made their way off the rocks and back onto the lawn, dodging a few locals as they went.

She swung around. "I don't get you."

He shrugged, unable to follow her train of thought, but feeling as though he were being accused of something. "Don't get what?"

"You. You play at being this big womanizing, life of the party kind of guy when really you're a compassionate, generous man who wants to give back to his city. Why don't you show *that* guy to the city council?" She stomped off.

Jogging to catch up with her, he flung the bag he carried onto Contractor Jones's truck, then grabbed her upper arm and swung her around to face him. "I did."

"Really? When? At your interview?" she scoffed.

"Well, yeah."

She gripped her hands into fists. "Why haven't you been showing them that all this time? What a waste. And now what? You're going to leave and go live in...*Portland?*"

"What's wrong with Portland?" He wasn't following at all and with mounting frustration, jammed his pole into the ground.

"Hey! You better watch what you're doing, young man. Your mother will have a fit." Maxine yelled from the back porch of the Cape house, a cobalt blue jar in her hand.

Mitch glanced down and winced. He'd jabbed the pole right through a bed of purple asters. Carefully pulling the pole out from between the stems of the flowers, he sent an apologetic shrug to Maxine.

Turning his attention back to Claire, he asked again. "What's wrong with Portland?"

She stared at him hard, then finally said. "Nothing. Portland's amazing."

They walked around the Cape house to the front porch, where a sign-in sheet and a stack of directions sat under a paperweight on a small table. She turned the sheet, running her finger over the names as if taking count.

Suddenly, a group of children burst through the front door all screaming at once. "Miss Claire, Miss Claire!"

She started in surprise, then straightened from the desk. Her frown reversed into a smile, brightening her whole face, and he couldn't help being stunned by the transformation. Claire had an easy, friendly style with the kids, asking them questions about the start of their school year. She also let them all know she was very pleased to see them at the Cape, helping to take care of the town, and the pleasure on the face of each kid from such praise was a testament to the bond she'd created with them.

He watched the light in her eyes, the genuine happiness on her face. She loved working with these kids. A picture of her, holding a baby, swaying in front of a large window, popped into his head and left him with a yearning that confused the hell out of him.

She didn't belong to him, a future with her was not his to hope for, but at that moment, seeing the compassion on her face, hearing the kindness in her voice, he wanted it more than anything.

"Now, off you go. Today's the last day, so let's find every tiny piece of trash you possibly can." She placed a hand on one of the children's head and ruffled his hair.

"Okay, Miss Claire, we're on it!" They took off down the stairs and toward the flat beach area of the shore just south of the house.

"How do they know you so well?"

"I hold a paintbar at Blayne's store once a month. It's like the wine and painting bars for adults but with chocolate milk. The kids love it."

Standing alongside her, his chest expanded with something unfamiliar, and he struggled to label it. "You're so good with them. You're going to be an amazing mother someday."

She stiffened. "No. No, I'm not. I love kids, don't get me wrong. But I'll never go through that again."

"Claire, you can't back away from a future, from happiness, because of something that happened in your past."

She tilted her head at him. "Of course, I can. We all do." With a sigh, she turned back to the table and straightened the papers as if keeping herself busy until he left, but he refused to walk away.

"You hold the future of my program in your hands, Mitch. It could be gone with a stroke of a pen. To top it off, you may be moving away. All of it is just further proof that growing attachments only sets a person up for pain."

The drive to pull her into his arms, shield her from all the pain and uncertainty in the world, was so strong that he had to shove his hands into the front pockets of his pants to keep from doing so.

The truth was right there, crushing his chest, and his brain immediately strategized on how to fix the problem that now faced him.

"Meet me at the lighthouse tomorrow night at seven," he said.

"Why?"

"Just do it." He gave a two-fingered salute from his temple and went to find Ryker. Maybe his buddy could talk some sense into him.

Fucking hell.

He was falling in love with a woman who didn't want to be loved.

CHAPTER 15

*S*unday evening, Claire pulled her long gray sweater tighter around her shoulders as she waited for someone to open the bright red lighthouse door. She thought she'd dressed appropriately for this time of the year, but the temperature had dipped lower than they'd reported as the sun disappeared over the trees west of town.

She'd spent most of her day working through a few events that were coming up: Cape Van Buren Halloween contest in October, another Just for Kids Paintbar in two weeks, and some finishing touches on the layout for her Coping through Art program that she was determined to implement at the Center.

All she had to do was get Mitch to sign off on it. She couldn't begin to understand why he was hesitating even for a moment. Well, this was her chance to make sure he saw it her way. She was tired of wanting it so bad.

It was time to make it happen.

The door swung open, and Mitch ushered her in, looking as if he'd stepped out of the pages of an L.L. Bean advertisement for sexy Mainers. His distressed jeans encased his thighs in a way that made her want to dig her fingers in and see if they were as hard as they looked, and his navy cable-knit sweater made his broad shoulders even broader.

The women of Portland were going to love him.

She frowned.

"Did something happen?" he asked, a concerned look in his eyes.

"What?" Shit. "No, no...just thinking."

He led her up the stairs to the main living space, teasing as they went. "If I recall correctly, that's difficult for you, isn't it, Adams?"

That snapped her out of it right quick. He was a wicked pain in the ass, but she chuckled anyway. "Oh, please, we all know thinking for you doesn't venture beyond 'shall I wear boxers or briefs.'"

He flashed her a grin, stopped, and pressed her up against the wall of the stairwell, just outside the living room. "We both know the answer to that."

Oh yeah, they did.

Her heart sped up as the heat of him washed over her. Suddenly her gray sweater was all too warm, and she felt as though she'd have a heat stroke if she didn't get it off.

Dipping his head, he slid his lips over hers.

Her toes curled in her socks, and she sighed into the kiss. As he pulled away, she blinked a few times, not realizing she'd closed her eyes, and cleared her throat. "What'd you do that for?"

With a soft caress of his fingers along her cheek, he said, "I realized I hadn't given you a proper hello, and that must be where all the vinegar was coming from."

His words sunk in, and she gave him a playful slap.

"You're ridiculous."

They just stepped through the door. If she were ever susceptible to even humoring the idea of a happy ever after, the scene that lay before her would be the catalyst for such a crazy idea. The soft earth tones of the newly renovated lighthouse were set aglow with a myriad of tapered candles that flickered shadows around the room. Soft music played in the background, and as she recognized the familiar croon of Etta James, a feeling of returning home washed over her.

Her mother used to play Etta all the time when she was preparing the house for something special. She'd have to tell her mom of this night. It had been a while since they'd spoken, and she knew her mother worried about her baby girl. It was because of that worry that she often stayed away far too long.

The savory aroma of fresh-caught salmon made her mouth water. September meant salmon festivals all up and down the coast of Maine. There was no telling where Mitch scored this particular catch, but if it came from the coast of Maine, then it would be the best she'd ever eaten.

"You cooked?" She made her way into the living room, loving the feel of the thickly padded, plush carpet under her feet. So much that she removed her socks, leaving them by the door, her blue-tipped toes dotting the floor.

"Make yourself at home." He chuckled.

"I couldn't resist, this carpet is amazing."

He nodded. "I believe Jade Dawson did most of the designs for the Cape house and here."

She nodded, having heard the same thing. Jade was one of three triplets, Coach Dawson's daughters. Each one more beautiful than the last and it didn't matter what order you saw them in. They were smart as a whip, bold as any businessman, and determined to make their mark on Cape Van Buren.

"Speaking of the Dawson triplets, have you heard anything about the Hide Away and Stay Inn not being around much longer?"

The place had special memories for everyone in town, especially her friends. The kids of Cape Van Buren had spent many amazing summers on that property, most adults as well.

"It would be such a shame," she said.

The look on Mitch's face spoke volumes. With his background, especially in real estate, she was sure he knew more than he was saying, but she also knew there were some things he just wasn't able to share.

Thinking about that only made her worry about next week, but she decided that she needed one night of pure and utter unadulterated enjoyment devoid of any work-related stress. An evening with Mitch Brennan always promised just that.

Shrugging, he poured two glasses of white wine into stemless wine glasses that boasted the Cape's logo, handed one to her, then lightly tapped her glass with his own. "There are a lot of rumors, so let's focus on what we know. The festival is going to be amazing, thanks to you."

She warmed at his praise, shoving away the censure of her own mind, telling her it shouldn't matter.

"Here's to making a difference in Cape Van Buren."

The Coast Week event warmed her heart but also left it grappling for more. Though she enjoyed her time with the children more than anything else, it came at a cost. It hurt to think that she'd never call any child her own, that the one she had was lost, never to be held or cherished and doted upon like her own mother always had with her.

She swallowed past the lump in her throat and repeated his words. "Here's to helping those of Cape Van Buren."

The wine was cool and crisp, relieving her dry, parched throat and relaxing her muscles from the tight hold of emotions that were pressing down on her. "How did you do all this?" she asked.

"Good friends." The sarcasm was thick, but the smile on his face belied any hard feelings.

"I wanted to show you the kind of date you should be having. A date where you spend time with somebody you enjoy, you eat good food, you share some stories about when you were growing up or the first time you kissed a boy with braces."

She laughed, trying to imagine him in braces. He was probably the one teenager who could pull it off and seem even cooler as a brace-face than without. "You never give up, do you?"

The expression on his face was one of determination, and it sent a shiver of awareness down her spine like the very first time just before he kissed her.

"Look, I feel like I've opened up more since you and I started a couple of weeks ago. You've helped me realize that in some ways I was avoiding pleasure when I didn't have to."

His eyes grew dark, and she put her hand up to stop him from moving toward her. "I mean pleasure in the broadest sense of the term. Eating good food, listening to good music, enjoying my friends, heck, just in joining in on the fun of this wonderful town. I'd been missing out a little for fear of what...looking silly?" She stared into her glass. "Or needy? I don't know which is even worse in my mind. You've helped me figure out how to live more fully. And that is no small feat."

"And I'm not done." His voice was low and suggestive like she imagined he'd use with a jury when he needed to be his most persuasive. "Tonight is just about you. No agenda, I'm not trying to get anything out of you, and this will not end up with us naked, though it pains me to even say the words."

She giggled, to hide the immediate deflated feeling she experienced herself.

"You need to be cherished, Claire." His bright eyes bore into her own,

145

demanding she hear him without any more words. The intensity of his gaze thickened the air between them, making it difficult for her to breathe. The ocean waves raged against the rocks, creating an echoed hum that sang through the foundation of the lighthouse.

"Why do you care so much?" she whispered, at that moment wanting him to hold her and at the same time feeling as though if she didn't move away, she might not make it out alive. "You might not even be here this time next year."

His eyes darkened, and he rubbed his hand over his chest. He pulled out a stool for her at the small counter that made a peninsula between the kitchen and the living room. She'd always loved the way he moved. It was fluid and graceful even with his impressive size.

"Me possibly not be here next year is one of the main reasons for tonight."

She slid onto the stool, wrapping her hands around her wine glass. "That's a bit dramatic, isn't it?" she teased. "As if I'll never see my friend Mitch again?"

He narrowed his eyes at her with a small shake of his head. "No, I'm pointing out that you save special things for a moment that you think is special enough, where I am trying to challenge you to look at every moment as uniquely special."

He turned off the stove and pulled out a baking dish, setting it on top of the anchor trivet on the counter. The heat must have seeped through the dishtowel he used because he snatched his hand away, shaking it out with a soft curse.

"Hey, Mitch? Ovens are hot."

"Drink your wine, smart ass, and just think about what I said."

A yearning grew deep inside her as she watched him move around the kitchen. Accepting that every moment was special strengthened her fear. It allowed her to grow closer to those she loved, in turn, increasing the chances of pain when they were taken away.

"I get the whole live in the moment message, but there are some things that are more important than others. We can't indulge all the time, it isn't healthy."

Mitch looked at her out of the corner of his eye with a smirk that always transformed his face from handsome to sexy, and she took a swallow of her wine to prevent herself from asking to skip dinner and jump straight to dessert.

"Who says?" he asked.

She opened her mouth to toss back a retort but had nothing. His blatant refusal to accept the norm excited something deep within her. Life with this man would never be boring.

That was a promise.

He plated a dish of salmon and what looked to be herbed rice. Grabbing a lemon from a bowl, he sliced it into quarters as if he had done this a thousand times before. "Life can be terribly short. If we always wait for a special occasion, there's a chance it might get missed altogether."

He placed a plate in front of her and slid onto the stool, his knee resting against her thigh. A swift rush of awareness swept through her on contact, but she forced herself not to move away, and he didn't either. The heat of him reminded her of how it felt to be in his arms, the delicious weight of his body pressing into hers.

Making her yearn and dream and wish for things to be different as she followed the lines of his profile, the straight edge of his nose, and the strong angle of his jaw.

"Mitch." She said his name softly, not sure what she wanted even as she asked.

He lifted a hand as if he were going to touch her face but let it drop back to the counter and picked up his fork. "*You* are the special occasion, Claire."

She shook her head. Not because she didn't believe him but because she believed he meant every word.

Silence filled the room as he studied her. "Cherished." He slid his fork beneath a tender piece of salmon. His movements were always so gentle.

She'd never noticed that before.

"Cherished?" She whispered, her heart throbbing in her chest.

"It's what you need to be, Claire. Don't settle for anything less."

She pulled in a shaky breath, wanting to reach out to him, but afraid if she did, she'd never let go.

~

*M*itch watched in wonder as Claire's struggle played across her face.

Her sweet smile dipped to a frown, then moved on to a tremble. Her eyes were both bright and wary. She lifted her hand for a moment, then fingers fluttering, set it back in her lap.

He meant every word he said. She needed, no *deserved*, to be cherished—

147

held softly in love *and* with urgent passion. His own arms yearned to reach out and wrap around her familiar frame.

But he took another bite of salmon instead.

They ate in silence except for Claire's moans of gustatory pleasure. The sounds set off all kinds of images in his head, and a very different kind of hunger filled his soul.

"You're an amazing cook. I shouldn't be surprised, but I always seem to be with you." She spoke in a soft tone of awe.

"My mom..."

"Of course. Janice is a superwoman." A giggle escaped her lips followed by a small burp, and she slipped her fingers over her mouth. "I'm so sorry. I can't believe I just did that."

"I'll take it as a compliment. You did say I'm a good cook."

She grinned, and his heart stuttered in his chest. Her beauty was never a question, but the look on her face in a moment of unguarded pleasure was nothing short of stunning.

"You're good at a lot of things."

"Really good." He flashed a wicked grin.

"And you hide behind your excess," she said, punctuating each word with a small stab of her fork in the air.

A restless, itchy sensation pushed him up from his stool. Grabbing his plate, he walked to the sink. "Not sure what you mean there."

"Well, you are frustrated with the lens of your reputation the town views you through, but whenever something might get serious, you make a joke, make a move, do something to hide behind the cavalier persona you've created."

He set his dish in the sink, wincing at the sound of ceramic hitting the stainless steel. "I don't hide."

She shook her head. "It used to drive me crazy, wondering how you got through life seemingly avoiding responsibility...or reality." With a sip of her wine, she joined him at the sink, staring through the window that framed a beautiful view of the Atlantic Ocean stretching as far as the eye could see. "But really, you were hiding."

A tight sensation strung his shoulder blades tight, and he busied himself with rinsing the dishes. He scoffed. "Please, what do I have to hide from?"

Besides the direction of his life, lonely and without purpose, the warmth in her smile, the promise of love.

"From the looks of your drawings...attachment. It's as if you're afraid of allowing yourself to get close."

The image of his father walking away, getting in his car, and driving off floated in a blurry haze in his mind.

But instead of admitting it to her, instead of telling her how he really felt—that he'd fallen for her and it scared the shit out of him—he tossed the towel onto the counter, grabbed the bottle of wine, and wiggled it back and forth. "Apparently, someone has had a little too much to drink."

The concerned glow in her eyes vanished, leaving something more akin to pain, but he resisted the urge to soothe the small wrinkle that formed between her brow.

"That was rude."

"Or maybe you're simply embarrassed that your psychoanalysis of some crayon scribbles is way off."

Claire took a step back as if smacked, then with a determined set to her chin, grabbed her long gray sweater and headed for the door. "Psycho is right."

A crumb of regret irritated the back of his throat. "Look, I get that you're trying to help, but you can't go saying this kind of thing to a kid taking a class at the Center. Parents would be calling in complaints non-stop."

She hesitated a few stairs down, throwing daggers back up at him. "This kind of thing? Are you *kidding* me?"

With a wave of her hand, she continued down the stairs that spiraled the perimeter of the lighthouse, grumbling as she went. If they'd been talking about anyone else, he'd have loved her passion. But they were talking about him. And he'd panicked.

And he didn't like it one bit.

Seeing her storm down the stairs scared him even more. He followed close behind, regretting every ignorant word he'd said.

Fuck.

An urgency to make it right pushed him forward. "Claire, wait."

"I am credits away from my degree in psychology. The only thing between me and a license are a few classes and a test. Just because you can't handle your own damn baggage does not mean that I'm wrong. And for the record..."

She burst through the archway into the main entrance by the front door, yanking on her Bean boots with sharp, jerky tugs. "...any kid I've ever worked with has handled the feedback with a hell of a lot more grace than you just did. The problem here isn't me or my program. It's you and your own issues."

Pulling the heavy door open with a grunt, she swung back around.

He took the opportunity to drag her into his arms, slamming his mouth to hers. The feel of her lips, of her arms sliding up around his neck, and her melting into him, drove home the very real fact that he was done for.

Her taste would remain on his tongue a lifetime, and the feel of her in his arms an eternity. A small moan escaped from between her lips, and every nerve in his body responded with an immediate surge of interest.

But as quickly as she'd melted, she stiffened and pulled back with her lips in a thin line of resignation.

"There's something here between us. You feel it. I know you do," he rasped out around the emotion lodged in his throat.

"It's not what we agreed on," she whispered.

"But it's there, isn't it?"

She nodded in agreement, then snapped her chin up as if catching herself. "I have to go."

"No, you don't."

"You know I do."

"Now who's hiding?"

Ignoring him, she backed through the door. "I hope you get your issues figured out before you make your final decision about my program. It would be a shame for the kids of our town to miss out on strong coping skills because you're too afraid to face your own problems."

Denial sprung to his lips, but she shut the door in his face. And it reverberated in his chest just as it had when his dad slammed the car door closed so many years ago.

This was the very reason he'd known all along he needed to keep his distance from her. He was made for the lust and attraction of relationships, but attachment? One single commitment where he was responsible for the happiness of another?

This was a prime example of how truly bad he was at something like that.

CHAPTER 16

*M*itch looked at his mom, a sensation of complete and utter gratitude overwhelming him. After the way things were left with Claire, he'd worked his ass off not getting anything done. Sleep eluded him, so he tried to work, but he couldn't think worth a shit and stared at legal documents as if it were the first he'd ever seen them.

"Bless you, woman." He grabbed the casserole, pulling in the savory aroma of sausage and cheese as he led the way into the Cape house kitchen.

His time there was coming to an end. He and Ryker had been slowly working through applicants to sit in the caretaker position on a full-time basis. Which meant he had to get his ass in gear and figure out where the hell he was going to live.

Portland or Cape Van Buren?

Having to make such a choice in his life had never crossed his mind before, but after speaking with the mayor in Portland, it might just be an opportunity he couldn't pass up.

But the decision was nowhere near as difficult as the one to give Claire space. Not seeing her every day seemed like an impossible way to live, but he owed her the best of him. And the best was distance.

She'd been right. He had issues. And that was the last thing she needed in her life. More than ever, he had to leave her in peace.

"Since I haven't heard from you in over twenty-four hours, I was afraid you might not be eating. You always loved breakfast for dinner."

"Who doesn't? Brinner is the best meal." He forced his tone to be light and turned the stove on to warm, then placed the dish inside. Straightening, he leaned back against the counter, crossing his arms over his chest. His mother's red curls cascaded about her face as she humored him with her knowing smile. "What's *eating* you?"

"Why did Dad leave?"

Her grin fell, and his immediate regret for being the cause almost made him choke. Shoving from the table, he skirted the island and grabbed his mom's hands. "Never mind. It was a stupid question. Just forget I said anything. I'm an idiot."

"Shh shh shh..." she soothed, squeezing his hands in reassurance. "The question simply took me off guard." She placed her palm against his cheek, looking his face over as if it were her favorite art piece. "Does this have anything to do with the work you've been doing with Claire?"

He dropped to a stool. "How'd you know about that?" Throwing a hand up, he chuckled—the kind of forced noise that hurt coming out. "Never mind. Stupid question. Of course, you do." But he doubted she knew how fucked over in love he was, or how he insulted her program.

He scrubbed a hand over his jaw.

Janice was known for having an eye for details and a nose for news. Everyone joked that Maxine knew everything going on in town, but the truth of the matter was she was fed the information by Janice.

"She said I hide from reality."

The look from his mother was the same one he used to get when he said he'd cleaned his room but he'd really shoved all his dirty clothes under his bed, and everything else was smashed into his closet. She saw through him like he was plastic wrap, and he knew it, but he still tried to pull one over on her every chance he got. And still found himself surprised when it didn't work.

"Look, your dad leaving was hard. Things tend to be shrouded by very murky water when they hit you from out of the blue. But you were hurt by more than him leaving; you were hurt by the pain Ryker was in when he left, the pain you saw me in. I never meant for you to see it, but I began to put two and two together when you began to hang out with me on Friday nights instead of meeting your friends at the park for a pick-up game of football."

She cradled his face in her hands, gently rubbing his cheeks with her thumbs just like she used to when he had trouble settling down for sleep. The action poured a wash of calm over him, and he couldn't help but smile at his Pavlovian response.

Mothers were like emotional ninjas, and his was the master.

"You were always such a happy person that seeing you sad was like a kid seeing Santa cry," he admitted gruffly.

"You've always been a big feeler. Which was why I had to pick myself up by the bootstraps wicked quick after I realized what was happening."

"I'm sorry if I made it harder for you."

She kissed his cheek. "On the contrary, my darling, you helped me wake up. I hadn't noticed your father was unhappy and it almost took me too long to notice you were scared."

"I wasn't scared." The denial spilled from his lips as if his mother was trying to decide whether or not to let him watch a scary movie that he really really wanted to see.

A smirk quirked up her lips. "Sorry, sad, confused, worried. Whatever the case may be. I wasn't paying as close attention to what you and Mae needed as I should have. But Claire. Claire not only pays attention, but she also has incredible insight. I'd listen to what she has to say."

"It doesn't really matter though, does it? I'm not the right man for her."

An interesting light shone from his mother's gaze. One that was different than anything else he'd ever seen before, and it left him restless.

"Well, isn't that interesting." She clicked her tongue against her cheek, a clever and mischievous look in her gaze.

Oh no.

He needed to tell her not to get any ideas, stat, but before he could utter a word, she made her way to the sliding glass doors. "Would you look at that?" She turned back to Mitch.

Speak of the devil...or angel with platinum hair, a probing gaze, and an ass that would make a saintly man weep. Claire was strolling along the South Cove shoreline.

"Go," she said.

Leaving his mother to let herself out, he made his way down the back porch steps and across the lawn to the small patch of beach that ran a short length of the Cape's south side. "You've been avoiding me." It had been two days since they'd spoken. If any of the women he'd dated ever told him it had been too long since they'd talked after only two days, he'd have moved on at the speed of light.

And there he was.

Claire kept her head down, every now and again picking up a small shell from the bubbling surf to examine it closer. A few ended up being gently placed in the basket she carried, while others were put back where she'd found them.

His eyes drifted over her. She was dressed in loose fitting jeans that were rolled up to her knees, and a long-sleeved tee was layered under a hooded sweater that was the same remarkable color as her sky-blue eyes. Her Bean boots and socks lay abandoned next to a towel a few feet away.

"Your feet have to be freezing."

Still no answer.

Mitch pulled in a breath and let out a deep sigh. "Really? The silent treatment?" The sight of her opened something in him that he wasn't too sure had ever seen the light of day before. "Look, you were right. I hide. I don't want to hurt anyone like my dad hurt my mother. Hurt me and Mae. There are no guarantees in life. No wedding, no 'I do,' no ring...hell, no contract can guarantee that either party within a transaction won't end up being hurt."

He paused for her reaction, but she simply picked up another shell, and he gritted his teeth. Why couldn't she understand?

"Claire, I don't want to hurt you. I care. Fuck. I think I love you, but..."

Reaching out for her, he was about to place his hand on her shoulder when she looked up, her eyes widened in shock, and she jumped away with a scream.

"Oh my God!" she yelled, taking a step back but landing on an uneven rock. Her ankle bent awkwardly, and she threw her arms out, shells flying from her basket in her flailing attempt to right herself.

Mitch caught her about her waist but his forward momentum was too much with her backward momentum, and they both met an oncoming wave, landing in a foot of seawater.

With a confused look, Claire searched his face as she pulled earbuds from her ears.

She hadn't heard a word he'd said.

Both relief and disappointment held his tongue. He'd meant it, but as he held her searching gaze with his own, doubt and fear kept him from repeating it.

"I thought you'd gone into town with Ryker and Jay to set up the town hall for tomorrow night's meeting," she said breathless and trembling.

He shook his head, shoving himself up from the water, resisting the backward motion of sand slipping out from beneath his hand.

Once he was on sure footing, he reached for Claire.

She hesitated. "Are you sure you want to help me? Aren't you afraid I'll try and trick you with my psycho mumbo jumbo?"

He spread his fingers wide in a silent demand that she take his hand.

"Newsflash, sweetheart. You tricked me long before the mumbo jumbo."

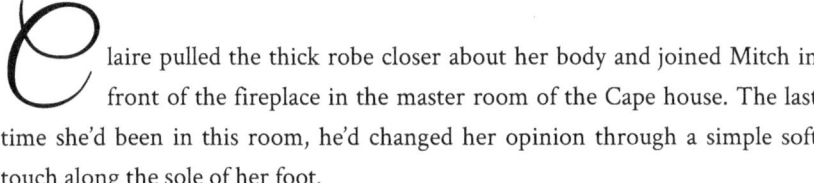

Claire pulled the thick robe closer about her body and joined Mitch in front of the fireplace in the master room of the Cape house. The last time she'd been in this room, he'd changed her opinion through a simple soft touch along the sole of her foot.

"Here, sip on this." He pushed a tumbler of Scotch into her hand, directing her to one of the high-backed tufted chairs.

They sat in silence for a moment, reminding Claire of all the times she and Jimmy had done the same. Simply sitting together, warm and comfortable. Willing to absorb the tranquility of enjoying one another's presence in cozy, companionable silence.

A lovely sensation of acceptance fluttered through her with the thought. She didn't feel guilty or sad that she now shared the moment with Mitch. Just content.

Puzzle jumped up on her lap, already purring, circled on her thighs, then lay down.

Jimmy would have liked Mitch...and Puzzle. She ran her hand down the cat's back.

Well, truth be told, Jimmy wouldn't have been able to stand the Mitch that everyone knew, not the guy that picked up the tab at the local bar, Gin & Tonic, then had his pick of ladies to go home with. But he would have really liked the real Mitch.

The one she'd gotten to know and admire.

But she was still mad at him, so there was that. Part of that anger was because he'd forced her to face the fact that there was something between them. It had been easier to handle when she thought there was no way he'd ever truly feel anything for her. Then he was safe.

Now, he was more dangerous than anyone she'd ever met.

"I'm sorry for what I said about your program." His words were simple, straightforward, and exactly what she'd needed to hear. And the program was so much easier to handle than any feelings between them.

"You were insulting."

"I know. Being an ass is pretty easy for me."

She raised her glass to his and clinked the side gently. "Me, too."

"You hit a nerve I'm not quite ready to conquer, and there is real liability for the Center when it comes to our dealings with children."

She sipped from her glass, hoping the peaty flavor would lend some flexibility to her tongue. "I'm well aware of that. I am an educated woman, Mitch."

"I know. But there are laws..." He trailed off. "What were you doing outside?"

"Damn it! My shells." Flopping back against the chair, she groaned. "They're for an activity for the kids."

"Of course, they are." He sat with his elbows on his thighs, the fire reflecting from his gaze leaving her feeling quite toasty. "You'll make a really great mother someday, Claire Adams."

"You know I'm not having any children. I've already told you."

"I understand fear, it—"

"It's more than that. It's intuition."

His curiosity was genuine and so focused she felt as though he pulled the words from her mouth. She spoke, weaving the setting of a dream, or rather a nightmare, that she'd had time and again since losing her baby.

"I'm in a house. I don't know where, it isn't one I recognize, but I know how to go from room to room as if I'd been there before. There's a storm, lightning, thunder... A baby's cry echoes throughout the house. I know it's a little girl, my baby... I feel her in the depths of my soul. But starting with a nursery of lime green and soft pink, I just catch the shadow of a toddler but can't reach her, can't see her face.

"Every time I have this dream, it goes through each second the exact same way it had in the dream before. I run to the master bedroom next, then the kitchen, knowing the way every time, but each room I enter seems to be just as she moves on, leaving behind an essence of innocence, of love, but completely out of reach... I can't get to her."

She paused in her retelling, her hand holding Puzzle too firmly, as her chest filled with the heavy burden of sadness, like life's anchor, making her unable to go back or move forward.

The cat stretched out of her grasp but didn't get down.

"Even without my unwillingness to ever risk feeling that kind of pain again, this dream is a lesson I can't ignore. A sign that motherhood is simply not for me." The familiar wretched pain seared in her chest and tears stung behind her lids.

Mitch slid his fingers under her own, but instead of just holding her hand, he pulled her out of her chair and onto his lap. Puzzle jumped to the floor with an indignant meow. She welcomed the comfort of his arms banded about her like a great life preserver, keeping her afloat, no fear of going under.

If only...

Giving in to his sweet ministrations, she tucked her nose into the crook of his neck. Breathing in his warm skin, a heady mixture of spicy cologne and his unique male scent, reminded her of the Cape lawn after a hard rain. Earthy, crisp, with a hint of home.

"What if it is though." His voice vibrated against her cheek.

She stiffened, but he held her tight.

"Hear me out. What if the dream isn't about a daughter you aren't meant to have, but the daughter you are meant to have...if you'd only reach for her."

His words struck her with the fear of possibility, of love and loss, and she had no words.

So instead, she drained her glass, then slammed her lips to his.

His mouth remained still beneath hers, but as she rubbed her hands up the solid mounds of his chest to his shoulders, he opened to her with a low, gravelly groan.

"Claire," he growled his warning, but she couldn't heed it. Wouldn't pull back.

She needed something to ease the growing anxiety of getting too close, needing too much, wanting more than she could ever have.

Kissing him was the exact opposite of a solution, but it was one of the few moments lately where she could lose herself in the decadent pleasure of life instead of being afraid of losing what she didn't even have.

With a sudden surge forward, Mitch had her flat on her back in front of the fireplace, and in seconds, her robe splayed open. He straddled her, devouring her naked body with hungry eyes. "I can't get enough. Never enough."

Sliding his mouth over hers, he dove deep, their tongues teasing, tasting. She helped pull his shirt over his head, then waited as he shoved his pants from his hips.

Her body was on fire with every stroke of his rough hands over her skin, cupping her breasts, raking down her sides to grab her ass.

"You are so God damn beautiful," he ground out as he lifted her to him.

Wrapping her legs around his waist, she trapped him against her, rubbing against his cock, fueling the intense need to feel him inside of her again.

"I need you. Now," she begged.

He was too much and all at once. An overwhelming presence that she craved again and again. His scent and taste making her drunk and unable to think beyond the very real need to have him.

Spreading her legs, he adjusted so the head of his cock was poised to give her what she wanted.

"Don't wait."

He gathered her arms above her head.

"Mitch!" She lifted her hips, trying to take him inside.

"Look at me," he demanded in a growl.

Afraid to see too much, but more afraid not to feel all that he had to offer, she met his intense gaze.

"There's no forgetting me, Claire. There's no forgetting us. No matter what."

Denying the pull between them was no longer possible. "Never," she whispered.

And in one fluid stroke forward, he filled her world with a brilliant flash of cresting sensation until she spiraled beyond the reach of reality.

Nothing mattered but the feel of him around her, his voice in her ear, his taste on her tongue. Emotion pushed dangerous words to her lips, but she swallowed them down as his frenzied strokes took them both higher and higher.

"Claire," he ground out.

"I'm with you." And in one deep thrust, it was the most honest they'd been with each other since they'd met.

As their bodies melted back to reality, Mitch cradled her head in his hands and rested his forehead against hers. "What have we done?" He slid to his side, pulling her into his chest and curving his body around hers.

She wasn't sure, but what she did know was that she felt safe in his arms.

Cherished.

Wasn't he the one who said she shouldn't settle for anything less? "Stay here with me. Don't take that job in Portland," she whispered as she dozed off.

CHAPTER 17

*M*itch put up two fingers to the bartender working the cash bar inside the town hall. It looked like every citizen in town was arriving to hear updates on the council positions, including the city attorney seat, and the coming weekend's Cape Van Buren Fall Art Festival being held out on the Cape.

It wasn't a formal meeting, thank God, because he needed a drink more than his next breath.

The town hall was two stories of open space with large beams and a huge anchor-inspired chandelier. It smelled of Old English wood oil and the briny call of the Atlantic.

"Your regular, Mitch?" The tall, willowy brunette grabbed a tumbler and the Ardbeg from the top shelf. Her knit sweater lifted just enough to hint at the smoothness of her skin, and her jet-black waves skimmed the top of her jeans.

She was exactly his type. Beautiful, kind, and available. In fact, they'd had fun once or twice in the past, but not even one spark of interest nudged him to make a move. Just the opposite. Instead, he wanted to...give her advice.

He dipped his chin, biting the inside of his cheek. Cynthia Marshall had been a bartender since they'd all done their twenty-one run, and he couldn't help but wonder why the hell she hadn't gone on to get a formal education, instead choosing to serve drinks. He hated seeing potential go to waste.

God help him. He'd somehow grown old, or worse...

In love with someone else.

With an urgent need to quell the ludicrous thoughts imploding his brain, he grabbed the tumbler and tossed it back, slamming his hands along the bar top and leaning into the pain of the fire burning through his chest.

"Jesus. What'd you do that for?" She reached out to pat his back, but he lifted a hand to stop her and stepped back.

He welcomed the discomfort. It distracted him from all the wanting.

A wanting that only grew exponentially worse since having Claire in front of the fireplace back on the Cape. When she'd asked him to stay, he asked her to repeat herself, unable to believe his own ears. But she'd already fallen asleep.

He'd wanted to shout, yes, he'd stay. He'd wanted to wake her up and make her admit she loved him, then make love to her all over again.

Instead, he'd watched her sleep, soaking in every smooth inch of her face. Memorizing it, the way her brows arched, how her lips turned up at the ends. He'd stroked her silken cheek and smoothed her hair back from her temples.

And all that wanting proved to him more than anything else why he had to leave. As they'd grown closer, she'd never been able to even consider a conversation about what was happening between them. Her pain wouldn't allow her to.

He had his issues, but she also had hers.

She wasn't ready.

So, he was going to accept the city attorney seat offered by Portland. Her whispered request had only magnified the importance of distance. He would work to be there for her every day of his life, but there was no possible way to get through forever without hurting her somehow.

He'd promised her that he was a safe bet.

And he'd fucked it up.

She was so terrified of being hurt, of feeling that kind of pain again, that he refused to risk it.

But there was also no possible way he could handle seeing her sweet smile as she made her way down Van Buren Blvd or breathing in her scent that was all Claire and sunshine and sensuality. And now that she was feeling settled in how she could date without forming an attachment, there was no way in fucking hell he'd be able to see her with some Mainer or worse yet, some flatlander, without punching him in the face.

He knew it was an ignorant thought and he didn't care.

Leaving hurt like hell but staying would be torture.

"You speaking tonight?" Cynthia asked, breaking into his thoughts.

Sliding the glass for another, he waited to answer as she poured two more fingers' worth. Glass in hand, a calm settled over him, and he dipped his chin in confirmation. "Briefly."

She studied him, a curious expression in her gaze. "She's changed you."

There was no way to experience Claire Adams and not be changed, but he wasn't about to respond and invite any kind of speculation.

In a town like Cape Van Buren, gossip only created tornadoes from a spring breeze.

Maxine and Janice appeared out of nowhere, sliding their arms through the crook of his elbow on each side, flanking him like thorns on a rose bush. It might be an unkind thought, but these two never seemed to need anything from him that had his best interest in mind.

"What do you want?"

His mother gave him her wide-eyed look of innocence, and all his spidey-senses sprung to high alert.

"What, a mother can't say hello to her son?" Her red curls were tucked under a paddy cap that Blayne had brought back from Glengarriff.

He stopped, barely aware of the din of conversations around him as he looked at the two women for any sign of what was about to happen. "No. You two have proven time and again that when you band together, bad things are about to happen."

With a scoff, Maxine grabbed a glass of red wine from a tray that was making its way around the town hall like a celebrity crowd surfing at Coachella. "Oh, please. Like what?"

The deluge of memories from the earliest he could remember including jail, the police, moonshine, and the many different mayors hit him all at once, but instead of going into it with Maxine—because no one ever came out on top—he simply crossed his arms over his chest.

"What."

Maxine had the gall to look annoyed. "Well, if you're going to be like that."

"You'd think I didn't raise him right with that tone," Janice added.

A smile quivered at the corners of both women's lips, making all the warning alarms in his head clang at once.

"No. The answer is no." He walked away, weaving through the crowd toward the front of the room. But the ladies were on his tail like a moose after an elder tree.

Evette stepped right in front of him, stopping him in his tracks, and as he turned to go around her, Shelly Anne cut him off. What. The. Fuck. A South Cove Madame helping a North Cove Maven? This had to be a first.

"What the hell is going on?"

Shelly Anne grinned. "We're seeing some of the benefits of working together. Claire had some very good points about her plan for the festival."

His mother circled him, stopping when she stood in front of him once again. "Remember how the festival is raising money for local kids?"

There was no winning if they were pitting him against children in need.

God damn it.

Out of the corner of his eye, platinum locks glistened in the soft evening light.

Claire. He could feel her, a soft thrumming through his blood, a low humming in his mind. He rubbed at his chest.

"Get to it, Mom."

"We want to auction off your services."

All the blood drained from his face, and the world seemed to tilt precariously.

"Ladies, you are terrible. Leave him alone." Claire to the rescue.

He threw her a grateful smile.

With a pat to his shoulder, she tilted her head as if trying to figure out what the confusion was. "Oh, make no mistake. We do want to auction you off for your services."

Every fiber of his body tensed at the sight of her before him. The word *services* falling from Claire's mouth made him think of slick, sexy nights and cries of pleasures.

"What in the hell?"

"Your legal services, silly." Maxine pushed a jar of moonshine into his hands. "We'd never do that to you."

He rolled his eyes in an exaggerated, the-hell-you-wouldn't arc, and grabbed the moonshine before she changed her mind.

"It's for a good cause." Claire's comment was soft and slid up beneath his dress shirt as if her fingers caressed him.

With a nod, he spoke low for her ears only. "We need to talk."

Judge Carter grabbed the microphone as if preparing to call the town to order, but instead covered it with his hands and leaned toward Mitch.

"Are the rumors true?"

Mitch furrowed his brow. "Rumors?"

"That we're losing you to Portland after all?"

The hand that Claire had on his arm fell away to her side, and a look of betrayal crossed her face. She knew he was thinking about it. And hell, it was Portland, Maine, not Portland, Oregon. The commute was barely the length of a good movie.

"Claire." He tried to grab her hand.

"No. Don't touch me."

He could handle her anger, but the pain and something way too close to fear that he saw in her eyes was unbearable.

And there it was, a spring breeze to a tornado.

~

*I*t was everything Claire could do not to let her eyes fill with the tears of loss that burned behind her lids. "You're leaving." This shouldn't be a surprise to her, so why did it hurt so bad?

The look on his face was shaken. She'd give him the benefit of the doubt that this was the news that he'd hoped to talk to her about, but he should have done it yesterday, hell, weeks ago before she grew so fond of him. Before she wanted to be with him.

But all you've ever said is that you never would.

She tried to block out the voice in her head. She *had* said that, but those words had as much to do with the knowledge that he never wanted to settle down as it had with her own fears. The thing was, she'd grown to count on and crave his companionship.

She never dreamed that would have to end because he'd choose to leave.

Living in Portland wasn't another country, but it might as well be when it came to the goings-on of her everyday. Suddenly her future was stark and cold.

She hated September.

"Claire, I had every intention of letting you know what my plan was. I didn't come to this decision lightly. Portland wants me, Mitch Brennan, and everything I have to offer. Cape Van Buren wants an attorney, but they don't know if I'm the right fit. If they don't know by now how much I love this town, there's no convincing them."

He grabbed her hand and refused to let go as she tried to pull away.

"I need to be able to really do some good; it's something that has been driving me for a long time. Since I can't do that here, Portland has made me an offer I can't refuse."

Away from the town, away from the Archer Conservation Park of Cape Van Buren where love was supposed to be the piece that completed any of life's puzzles.

Love.

Pain slashed through her heart. How the hell had she let that happen?

"And my program?" She hated that her voice trembled. Hated that anyone could hear her weakness. They already looked at her as though she'd break if the wind blew too hard. Well, everyone but Larkin and Blayne.

Mitch looked to her best friends, who had joined them within the past few minutes, but they both shrugged and flanked their friend in a united front. They always had her back, and at that moment, a great wave of love washed over her, warring with the loss she felt thinking of Mitch not just moving away.

But choosing it over her. That was the kicker.

"I needed to talk to you about that, too."

A crushing weight of despair stole her breath. "You aren't approving it?"

"I am, but..."

His *but* ruined any hope she'd had.

"This is my life you're screwing with, Mitch." Her whisper sounded anguished to her ears, and she cleared her throat to make it stronger. "What the hell was the point of all of this? You deny me because you couldn't handle the truth about your own damn daddy issues?"

He reeled back as if struck.

She knew it was uncalled for, and immediately regretted the words, but he was taking everything from her, including himself. The one thing she always counted on being safe, being constant. A man she not only called friend but lover and confidant.

And her program, too.

"You talk of wanting to make a difference, well, I do, too. This program, these coping workshops, were my way to make sure the children of Cape Van Buren grew up a little less fucked-up than the rest of us."

Mitch pulled in a breath, his hands in a tight ball at each side.

Didn't he understand how badly he was hurting her, how he was stripping away the things in life she'd created to cope with her own tragic loss?

"It's not no forever, but in order to make the programs as beneficial as you want them to be, you need more leverage. You need to finish your degree, so these classes can constitute as actual art therapy. I think that is the best direction for the Cape Center."

Throwing her unfinished degree back in her face, making her remember why she'd stopped—the sound of no heartbeat in her fiancé as he lay on the coroner's table, the sound of no heartbeat from her baby as she herself lay on the examination table—was the last drop of water that turned a wave into a tsunami.

She was done.

"How could you?" She hated the tremble in her voice but couldn't hold it back.

"Claire, I—" he choked out.

Shrugging away from her friends, she took a step back.

It might not be fair, but at that moment, looking at all the faces she'd grown to love, she needed to protect herself and not worry so much about them as she had been all this time. Alluding to the day she'd met Larkin and Blayne in the park, she said. "Sometimes I wish I could go back. Go back and take another path."

"You don't mean that." Anguish shone from Mitch's eyes, but it didn't matter.

"But I do."

Because then none of it would have led her to befriend the man she'd fallen so hopelessly in love with.

The look on Larkin and Blayne's faces left her feeling ashamed.

In her own pain, she'd just hurt the only two people who really loved her.

CHAPTER 18

Claire lifted her head, swearing up a storm so strong that the lobstermen would be embarrassed.

Confused by the loud, jarring noise coming from her front door, she pushed up from the couch, moaning at the pounding in her head and pulling her hair out of the dried drool against her cheek.

With a frown, she took in the empty bottles of wine on their sides next to the numerous empty cupcake wrappers on her coffee table and what looked to be a flower explosion in her kitchen. There were dirty bowls caked with dried batter on the counter, used spatulas, and open containers of sugar and flour.

She held a hand to her head and groaned, trying to make her way to the front door with hopes of getting the incessant banging to stop. She unlocked the door and pulled it open just a crack, looking through with one eye open. No sooner had the door moved when Maxine and her mother were pushing their way through and past her into the apartment.

"Mom? When did you get to town? What are you guys doing?" She turned around too fast, and her stomach protested with a sickly lurch. All she could do was wrap her arms around herself and pray for an early end.

That's what she got for drowning her misery in wine and a half dozen knock-off North Cove Confectionery cupcakes that she had baked last night after the town hall meeting.

"Mom?" Her mother shrugged off the question as she placed dirty bowls and spatulas into the sink and turned on the water. "Don't clean."

Her mother chuckled. "Don't clean? Is that your new strategy in life?"

Maxine walked over to the coffee table and the embarrassing evidence of Claire's misery with a few judgmental clucks. "You're quite the party animal, my dear."

Claire could argue and fight and resist, but history had already shown her that if Maxine had an agenda, she would see it through. And before she knew it, the two women had her out of her house and walking down the basement stairs of the Cape house.

She stood in the middle of the brew room, facing down huge pressure cookers and barrels of moonshine. "I'm all for getting my hands on barrels of more of your moonshine," Claire said. "If my broken heart makes you release your tight-fisted grip on it, then maybe I'll ask Mitch to break my heart all over again."

Her mother rolled her eyes. "Quit being so dramatic."

"Mom!" Claire couldn't believe her ears. She shot Maxine an accusatory glare. The woman was a bad influence.

Maxine ignored her and handed each of them an apron as she donned one herself, tying it behind her back. "Making my moonshine isn't just because it's the finest kind. It's always been very cathartic. When I had to face the reality of losing my son and seeing him as no more than the angry, violent shell of a man that he used to be, when the universe thought it was time to take the love of my life..."

An image of Stuart Van Buren, Maxine's late husband, hung proudly on one basement wall over the barrels of moonshine, and she studied it a moment in silence. Blowing a kiss to the man in the photo, she continued, "Making my moonshine gave me an outlet. Each step, the timing, the care, it helped me see that life was a similar process. You do your best to put together the most delicious combinations, sometimes they work, sometimes they don't, but the process of trying is living."

She raised her hand to stop Claire from interrupting. "Really living."

Claire ran her fingers along one stainless steel counter. "I'm living. I'm not Larkin, who was hiding away. As a matter of fact, I can confidently say I helped her break out of that particular shell."

Her mother gave her a doting smile and ran her hand over her hair. "You did help Larkin, but you were lying to yourself. You kept living as far as starting your event planning business and continuing with some of your art. But you never went back and finished your degree, and you avoided relationships as if they were a death sentence."

Emotion clogged Claire's throat, the image of Jimmy's broken body in the coroner's office leaving her legs weak and her heart bruised. She sunk to one of the stools. "I can't do it again, Mom. It was one reason I went along with Mitch and the crazy idea of dating without becoming attached."

"Crazy is right." Maxine chuckled. "But not in the way you think. For one thing, Mitch is as good as they come. Not a lot of people know it, but that's only because they're lazy...and jealous." She pushed one of the pressure cookers into Claire's arms.

Claire knew only too well how much judgment she'd reserved for the man for simply being happy and carefree.

"Fill this about halfway with distilled water. Tessa, you can begin washing and prepping these berries while I prepare the petals." Maxine turned on the low hum of Pandora from her phone.

The women moved through the steps of each task in a quiet harmony of their own.

"Let me ask you this." Maxine popped a berry in her mouth. "If you lost your mother, what would that mean for you?"

Claire paused at the awful question and looked at Maxine as if she'd finally gone crazy. "I would be devastated. What the hell, Maxine?"

Maxine looked at Tessa with a get-a-load-of-this-one shake of her head. "And me? What would losing me mean to you?"

Claire narrowed her eyes. "Well, at the moment that might be my new mission."

Maxine flashed her a mischievous grin. "I do like to see that spark in your eye, but seriously..."

Claire set the half-filled pot on the large stove with a sigh. "I would feel like a part of me were missing. What are you getting at?"

Her mother called her by her childhood nickname. "Monkey, don't you see? You can't hide from attachment, and you can't avoid pain by keeping love out of your life. What are you going to do? Not be close to me and your father? Turn your back on Larkin and Blayne, like I heard you stupidly implied at the town hall meeting last night?"

She ran a loving hand over Claire's hair, and she leaned into it. "Closing yourself in a bubble doesn't protect you from love, sweetheart. It simply starves you from everything good in life, and you end up hurt anyway. You already have so much to lose simply by being a part of this amazing community with your friends and your family. I don't see you ever giving that up."

Claire swallowed hard and shook her head. How many times had her dad tried to get her to move home? So many she couldn't count. And every time, she'd told him that as much as she loved them, Cape Van Buren was where her heart was.

"Of course not."

Her mother grabbed one hand. "Then why are you trying so hard to turn away from the man you love? From the future you know you want?" She swallowed and cleared her throat. "Jimmy was a special young man, moving on doesn't change that. And the sweet angel that looks over you? She wasn't your only chance at motherhood. I can feel it."

Claire shook her head. "I can't. I feel like…"

"What, monkey? What is it?"

Every shard of her broken dreams seemed to tear at her all at once, and her voice cracked. "I feel like if I move on that, I'll lose her forever."

Her mother wrapped her in her arms. "That's not how it works, my sweet girl. She's with you in every breath you take, every laugh, every moment of joy. In every sunrise and crashing wave. I bet you see her in everything you do."

"How did you know?" Claire whispered, comforted that her mother understood so clearly. The ache in her chest forced its way in tears down her cheeks.

"Because it's how I feel about you. It's how Larkin feels about Archer. It isn't the loss of your baby that makes you feel that way. She's a part of you. You are her mother. And you'll feel the same about any other children you bring to this world."

Claire rested her head against her mother's chest for a moment, comforted by the gentle rhythm of her heartbeat. "I love you, Mom."

Her mother pressed her lips to the top of her head.

"You, too, Maxine."

Maxine nodded. "And I you. Now, go find your best friends and make things right. Your mother and I will finish up here."

Claire grimaced. "Are they really upset with me?"

Her mother raised a brow. "I heard about it all the way in Portland. How would you feel?"

Shame clogged her throat, and she simply dipped her chin.

"Here, take these, I hear they can go a long way with an apology." Maxine handed her a couple jars of moonshine.

Claire took the generous gifts, but she wasn't sure if Maxine's moonshine could even get her out of this mess.

～

"*W*hat is this about?" Blayne demanded as she and Larkin approached Claire at the cemetery.

Her friend was dressed to kill in a fitted pencil skirt and polka-dot top, her hair in its usual vintage updo, and a look that warned of a mood Claire didn't want to test. Larkin was more casual in jeans and a sweater, missing her usual smile.

Blayne stood as if ready to pounce.

"I'm sorry." Claire faced them, ready to face her consequence of being an awful ass.

Larkin looked away and then back, her eyes wavering. "Really?"

"That was a pretty crappy thing to say." Blayne didn't ease her stance at all, though her voice had a slight tremor to it.

Claire nodded. "It was. It's not the first time I've ever said something shitty, right?" Giving them a silly grin, she shoved her hair back from her face, hoping they'd find the humor in something that wasn't funny.

Larkin's shoulders dropped, and Blayne's protective stance relaxed. "We know you were hurting." Blaine reached out her hand, and Claire didn't hesitate to take it, relieved for the connection. One she trusted with all her heart.

Larkin looked around. "Why are we here? You already dealt with all of this. In fact, you're the one who made me face my demons with my dead ex-husband." She made a face at Blayne. "Claire had me yell like a crazy woman at John for what he did."

Claire scuffed her foot into the cold ground. "It was a little different. You had a very real reason to be mad at your ex-husband, and it left you feeling guilty. I didn't have to yell at Jimmy, nor did I feel resentment for anything that happened with the accident. Not in the same way. I said goodbye, I cried."

She sucked in a breath, happy to fill her lungs against the suffocation of her pain. "It looked like I was moving forward with my life, with my new business, but I was avoiding everything I was and truly wanted. I'm so afraid of ever feeling that kind of pain again."

And it finally hit home to her that pushing Mitch away and deciding not to have him in her life hurt every bit as much as if something had happened to him. In the end, the result would be the same. Her, alone, without the man she had grown to love.

She should have told him.

The idiocy behind her actions pushed a strangled laugh from her throat. "I don't know how to fix this."

Her friends slid their arm through hers. "We can help, but I want to meet your baby," Larkin said.

"So do I," Blayne whispered.

Their ready acceptance and acknowledgment of her child conceived by a great love eased a measure of the heavy weight she'd been carrying in her heart for a long time.

Losing love was an experience filled with immense pain, but being loved was one of such incredible joy.

She wished she'd realized it sooner.

CHAPTER 19

*M*itch scrubbed the teak deck of Ryker's boat, putting every fiber of every muscle he possessed into it, and instead of ignoring the burn, he welcomed it.

Anything was better than the searing pressure in his chest every time his mind flashed back to Claire's stricken expression when she found out he was leaving for Portland.

It hadn't been an easy decision. Leaving her was like holding his breath, a desperate and urgent sensation with no chance to survive.

But she was terrified of anything serious, any connection.

Any pain.

At the very least, he could give her peace.

He could do that for her, needed to. He dipped the brush into the soapy water, spreading it out a foot around him, and then settled in to scrub again. The ocean breeze was cool, and the seagulls called to one another overhead. Any other day he would be in paradise.

A sharp jab at his shoulder had him looking up, and he found Ryker standing above him, holding out a beer. "A little cold to be scrubbing my deck, isn't it? Besides, what bet did you lose? Did you try and arm wrestle Martha again? You know no one can beat that beast."

Martha, or Sebastian Marth, the mayor of Cape Van Buren, was a huge man with an even bigger heart. He hated small talk and never lost an arm-wrestling match.

Mitch sat back on his ass and took the beer. With gratitude, he tipped his head back, letting it flow down his throat in hopes it would numb him from the inside out.

"I need to keep busy. You take us out so often, I figured it was the least I could do."

Ryker sat down, resting his elbows on his knees. "No, that's not what you're doing. I've been right where you are, or have you forgotten? You're hiding."

Mitch said a few choice words, finished off his beer, then pushed back on his hands and knees to scrub. "The fuck I am. I'm leaving for Portland tomorrow, and I'm just trying to stay busy today and avoid my mom and Maxine."

Ryker chuckled, tipping back his beer. "Yeah, grandmother has a way with words, doesn't she?"

Mitch grunted as he scrubbed.

"Dude, what the fuck are you doing going to Portland?"

"I'm going to finally be a bigger part of a community. Cape Van Buren doesn't want me. I'll face the music of my past mistakes, but it's time I start doing something more."

"And you have to go all the way to Portland for that? If you want to make a change, if you want this town to see you as something more than the party-going womanizer they think you are, then stay and show them what you're truly made of."

"That's all I've been trying to do."

"How so?"

Mitch blew out a breath. "You know the old housing north of town? The new policy changes, the renovations?"

"Of course. It was big news. It's something that needed to happen a long time ago."

Mitch's shoulders burned while he scrubbed, waiting for his buddy to catch on.

Ryker slapped a thigh. "That was you? Motherfucker, why haven't you said anything?"

Mitch dipped the brush, swirling it around in the soapy water, then found another few feet to scrub. There was great satisfaction in hard work. Forcing away the dinge and revealing the clean teak beneath.

"The board knows." He snorted. "And that's not all. I've been working for the rights of tenants and low-income housing for years. I jumped at the chance to work with you in the conservation center because of what it would do for this town. I went for the city attorney seat because I want to do more. But it's not enough. So, I'm off to Portland."

Every word he said was true, but his heart wasn't in Portland, the people he loved weren't in Portland, the view that he wanted to wake up to every day wasn't in Portland.

He had too much to give to let it go to waste. It was time to take control.

And run away from Claire and everything you're afraid of.

No, protecting her.

But he recognized the lie. He was protecting himself.

"Fuck." He swore and scrubbed harder.

"You've done all of that, you've worked that hard, and you're just going to run?" Ryker shoved his shoulder. "Sounds like a coward's way out to me. Selfish even."

Mitch rose up from his knees, ready to fight.

"You're just proving to them that you are exactly who they think you are."

They met each other nose-to-nose and stared, chests heaving, shoulders locked in a ready position.

"What?" Ryker said. "What's this about? Really?"

"Fuck." Mitch scrubbed a hand through his hair. "You're such a pain in the ass."

Ryker swung an arm around his shoulders for a tight squeeze, then shoved him away. "Of course, I am. That's how we work. How else were we going to survive?"

They filled a bucket with sea water and splashed it along the deck, revealing the clean teak.

"You do good work. Obviously more work than the rest of us even realized."

Mitch dropped to one of the benches. "Remember when we got caught in the attic by your dad?"

Ryker's eyes grew dark. "Unfortunately. He hurt a lot of people."

Mitch braced himself. "He hurt you. Sometimes he hurt you because of me."

175

The shame of his ten-year-old self choked him. "Then my dad left my mom. You know what an amazingly sweet woman she is, and he just walked out as if she were nothing. He saw you and me that day. I know he did. And he did the same to us. He'd thrown out words and accusations about kids that don't listen, too much stress, and a bunch of other bullshit."

He paused, gripping his hands into fists at his sides. "My mom got hurt, and part of that was my fault. I can't take the risk of hurting someone like Claire. She's a special woman, Ryker. I know I used to joke about her being a pain in the ass, but part of that was because I was trying to resist this weird pull she had on me."

He waited for his buddy's usual slap about being too emotional, but instead, he just listened.

"She needs a good man. A *really* good man. I'm not the right one for her. That woman needs to be cherished."

Ryker grabbed a bucket and helped Mitch rinse off the deck. "Dude, if I've learned anything in this life, it's that we all have successes, we all have failures, we all have our gifts, and we all have our demons. The difference lies in how we handle these things in order to move forward. The simple fact that you question whether or not you're the right man for Claire means that you are the *only* man that will treat her right and take care of her and support her the way she truly deserves."

Could he be right?

Mitch studied his friend, but only saw an intense sincerity in his gaze.

A kernel of hope flared, easing some of the pain in his chest, but it was tangled up with threads of doubt.

"You might hurt Claire going forward, but it won't be for the reasons that my father did, or your father did. Both of us have learned enough never to repeat those kinds of mistakes. You're not your father. You're more Janice Brennan than that man any day of the week."

He clapped him on the shoulder, and they set the buckets upside down to air dry.

"It's too cold out here today for this shit. Let's go over to the Lobster House and grab a bite to eat."

Mitch fell into step as they made their way down the pier and across the walkway to the South Cove boardwalk. The savory aromas floating on the breeze from the Lobster House pulled them in like a life preserver.

Clint Fenwick was handing out brochures that looked to be advice on improving one's moral compass, and they purposefully went the long way to avoid that conversation.

Even though it was a cool September day, the South Cove was bustling. Picnics, hikers, fisherman, everybody was out and about enjoying the sunshine, bundled in their boots and jackets.

"Excuse me, Mr. Brennan?" Mitch and Ryker spun around to find a young mother standing with her hands on her young son's shoulders. "I tried to talk with you at the town hall meeting, but there was a disturbance."

Mitch grimaced.

"I just wanted to say, thank you. We have heat for the winter, and if you hadn't stepped in, I don't believe we would have." There were tears glistening in her eyes, making them appear to be larger than they were. Her little boy scuffed his boot, looking down the pier at the seagulls.

Mitch stooped down to eye level. He couldn't place the mom, but he knew this kid. "Do you remember me?"

The boy nodded. "Yeah, you're the man that had the argument with Mr. Taylor."

Mitch remembered that day. He'd gone to serve papers himself and force the landlord to meet housing requirements. The two of them got into a lively conversation. He needed to keep in mind that no matter where he was in town, there were ears, and some of those ears just didn't need the stress of adults making bad decisions.

He ruffled the kid's hair. "It's better at night now?"

The little boy smiled, showing a big gap where his two front teeth should be. "Sometimes it's so warm I have to kick my covers off at night."

Mitch rose back to standing, his heart swelling with compassion, hating that the boy spent even one night trying to stay warm. He turned to the mother. "Let me know if there's anything going on. It's his responsibility to make sure the utilities are working."

"I will. Anyway, I'm so glad we saw you because I really wanted to say thank you."

Ryker slapped him on the shoulder. "He's a regular Mother Teresa."

She laughed but shot Ryker a look. "It's easy to make fun, but the difference he's made for me and my boy will not be forgotten."

Ryker and Mitch watched the boy skip down the boardwalk with his mom following close behind. His buddy slowly turned his head. "You've been working a lot behind our backs, haven't you?"

Mitch pulled in a breath. "Let's go get something to eat."

The hostess seated them in a booth, and Ryker swore.

"What?"

"This is the booth I met Judge Carter at when my grandmother came in and threw me under the bus. I'll tell you that I love that woman, but sometimes she has a wicked mean streak."

"I'd call it passionate. I don't know anyone who cares about this town as much as your grandmother does. She knew exactly what she was doing that day."

Ryker winced. "Please don't ever admit that to her. And I think you're just like her." He leaned across the table, refusing to let Mitch look away. "Fight. Stay. Set up camp. Make Cape Van Buren see you as the asset you want to be. In whatever the fuck way that looks like."

Mitch eased back in his seat, considering his buddy's words.

"And one more thing. While you're at it, tell the woman you feel needs to be cherished so much that you're just the man to do it."

But it was easy for the person outside of a fight to yell the command to charge.

~

Stay, fight, set up camp.

Mitch pulled in the fragrant sea air as he took the steps of the courthouse one at a time. Ryker's words had been echoing in his head all night. His heart was in the Cape, or rather the Cape was in his heart, in more ways than one.

How many times had he preached to anyone who would listen to really live in each moment, to allow luxury and bliss to take part in even the most mundane activities? But here he was asshurt and heartsore, ready to leave the town he loved because they weren't quite ready for him yet?

Well, they'd better damn well get ready.

He entered the front door and made his way through security. He'd walked the halls of this building ever since he was a little boy. There was always something about the grand front pillars, architecture that promised it knew everyone's secrets. He used to tag along with a family friend who'd been an attorney at the Cape for so long no one was sure who'd come first. As a boy, he'd always in been awe of how much the man knew about the townspeople, about the law. He'd wanted to be that kind of man, too, for this town.

Not someone else's town.

He'd forgotten that fact somehow over the past few weeks.

Down the corridor to the right was a conference room, and as he approached, he gave himself one last pep talk, then shoved through the door. "Judge Carter, members of the council, good morning."

The Judge's bushy brows drew together. "Mr. Brennan this is quite inappropriate. We were just in the middle of a meeting."

"I'm well aware." Mitch pulled a few papers out of his briefcase, passing them out to each member. "I won't take up much of your time, but it occurred to me that you all have a picture of a teenage Mitch, green and wild, running around with Ryker Van Buren, kissing your daughters and throwing eggs at your mailboxes. I get it. It's hard to see the youth of the town grow up into a position where you now depend on them to take care of it. But it's a position I want to be in."

He paced slowly in front of them, making eye contact with each and every one. "You may not think I'm the man for the city attorney position, but you're wrong. I am exactly that man. I am not afraid to get my hands dirty, I take part in every event, and being a product of my past I have a better pulse on the needs of the youth in our town than anyone sitting at this table. So just as a reminder, I am giving you all my most updated resume. I want you to look at it and study it."

Approaching the long table, he placed his hands flat and leaned toward the members. "Because in four years, I'm putting my hat back in the ring for city attorney. I'm here to stay. Setting up camp is what one of my good friends suggested."

He stopped for a moment and took a breath, all the urgency for the plans he had for the town forcing adrenaline through his veins like too many cups of Death Wish coffee.

The board stared at him as if unsure of what to say.

"I'm setting up a private practice downtown. I'll have a pro bono segment that will help cover those of this community who are not able to afford it themselves. You may think the city attorney needs to be your traditional view of a family man. But you're wrong there, too. I may not have a wife..." An image of Claire teased the edges of his mind, but he clamped down on that yearning. "Cape Van Buren *is* my family. And I'd never walk out on what's mine."

As he traced his steps back out of the courthouse, he crossed over Garden Parkway SW, heading to the South Cove Garden pond.

There was something about the tranquil waters, the light rhythm of the small waves kissing the grass and stone of the shore. The grass was still brilliant, and the evergreens bight—it was one of his favorite things about the Northeast.

He followed the brick path through the garden but slowed when he came along the bench where he and Claire had enjoyed the—if you asked Claire—sinful bliss of pastries and hot cocoa.

He rubbed the back of his neck. There was nothing more in the world that he wanted than to see that look of surprise and pleasure from the smallest things shine brightly from her eyes again. He wanted to show her that the pain of loss was worth the risk when the reward was love.

He dropped to the iron bench, reliving the moments of that evening in his mind, solidifying the idea that formed there. She'd accused him of running. Well, they'd always loved the little fights between them, so he wouldn't run. He'd stay and fight...and love and enjoy and cherish the woman who stole his heart.

It might not be in the next month or six months or even a year, but with friendship came comfort and trust, and eventually, she would realize he was the one for her.

As long as she realized she couldn't love anyone else.

Because if that look in her eye at the town hall meeting had told him anything, it was that she was already in love with him.

CHAPTER 20

*C*laire was hard pressed to find another time or event in Cape Van Buren that she loved more than the Fall Art Festival.

The smell of pine and cinnamon in the air, the warm glow of seasonal fire pits, all mixed with the light, salty breeze off the Atlantic, set the stage for something magnificent, something particularly special that she once only imagined could be found in a storybook.

The festival was underway and the smiles on the children's faces, the happy and possibly tipsy glow on the parents', warmed her heart and filled her with a satisfaction she hadn't experienced in a long time. The end results of her strategically planned blueprints for the festival were perfect.

Vendors and food and entertainment alternated as visitors made their way through the Cape trees, moving from one decadent experience to the next. Mitch would be proud of the lesson he'd taught her. She was a great student, if she did say so herself.

Every citizen would leave the festival with a multitude of amazing memories.

"With that dreamy smile on your face, I'd almost think you were thinking of a boy." Maxine's voice broke through her musings.

Janice chuckled. "You mean even though we've been told time and again there's no chance of any such thing? Very sad if you ask me. I was really hoping for an awesome daughter-in-law."

Claire's mother joined the crew. Claire secretly suspected that Tessa might have been brought in as an honorary North Cove Madam as well. "I don't blame you for being disappointed. As daughters go, she's one of the very best."

The pride in her mother's eyes was something she'd always seek, regardless of her age. "Thanks, Mom. You all really are having a good time?"

Maxine's smile shone as brightly as the rings dripping from her fingers. "You've really outdone yourself," she said with a serious tone. And then with a glint in her eye, she waved her hand toward her own table bedecked in a water-fall of blue jars filled with her secret recipe moonshine. "Judge even said I could sell my moonshine."

Claire's mother laughed. "Yes, but you can't profit from any of it. All of the money has to go to the children's fund."

Maxine tapped her chin. "That is true, but I do see it as one more step toward victory. I'll win him over, you'll see."

"The law is the law, Maxine, even you can't work around that." Janice's red curls were tucked under a cap. "How many times have you seen the inside of the Cape Van Buren jail cell?"

Claire giggled. Maxine's antics were infamous and told town-wide. Maxine waved her hand in dismissal. "Well, can't say I'm not having fun. Since I don't know how many days I have left on this good earth, fun is my middle name."

The ladies laughed and continued on down the path. Claire appreciated the love and support they had found in the friendship they'd grown. Blayne and Larkin ducked their heads through the path from the Cape lawn, and her heart expanded once again. She'd found the same.

Though the event was a success, her heart was heavy. She'd hoped Mitch would show, but it was a fool's wish. "I think I screwed up, you guys. I've been so afraid of losing that I pushed away a future that could have been really beautiful."

Blayne made a gagging noise. "Mitch Brennan? Really? That's who you fell in love with?"

Claire shot her an eat shit and die look, placing her hands on her hips as she pulled herself up to take advantage of every inch of height she possessed. "Mitch Brennan is much deeper than any of you know. And I seriously wonder if anyone has ever made an effort to see past his good looks and charm and antics to the kind of man he really is. Do you know that he fights for the rights of the low-income housing on the north side of town? Do you know that all the work he's done for the conservation center has been completely pro bono, or that he's put himself through extensive continued education in order to make sure that he implemented and protected the appropriate policies to ensure the Cape's health and future?"

She fisted her hands against her hips. "He cares about this town as much as any of us, and more than most."

She hadn't meant for her voice to raise as high as it did, catching herself when she noticed one too many heads turning her way. Blayne grinned. "Oh, we know. We were just waiting to see how long it would take you to notice."

Claire sucked in a breath and let it out in a rush. "I'm glad you know because of apparently the stupid city council doesn't. It was their actions—or reactions—to his submission for the city attorney seat that had him running and into the arms of another city."

Larkin laughed. "You make it sound like another woman."

Her shoulders sagged in defeat. "It might as well be. He'll keep that seat at least four years, and in that time, there's no doubt in my mind that some unique, artistic Portlandite with legs up to her armpits will have wrapped her talented fingers around his heart and keep him there for good."

She happened to catch Judge Teddy watching her with a serious expression. She loved the man, but she couldn't help pointing at him. "You all should be ashamed of yourselves, Judge."

He had the decency to shift restlessly and clear his throat. "Well, it's high praise for the man coming from you Claire Adams. You're one of the very best in this town."

She wasn't expecting that response, and a tinge of guilt replaced some of her frustration. "I'm sorry. It's just that I've really gotten to know Mitch recently, and I've been really impressed with what he has to offer."

People walked between them, too interested in the next booth or the smell of the coffee waiting at the end of the trail to bother paying attention to them.

The judge nodded, then sipped his moonshine. With a whistle, he raised it in a toast. "Here's to good people taking care of our town."

The band took that moment to strike up their next song. For the next hour, it would be rock and roll classics, and the energetic tunes got the kids screaming in their excitement. Claire approached the table she had set up, wondering if her head would make it.

Or her heart, with the heavy weight in her chest taking up too much room. She wasn't going to be able to do her coping skills classes after all, and the man her heart gave her no choice in loving was probably halfway to Portland. Plastering a smile on her face, she joined the kids, taking comfort in the pleasure of them wrapping their arms around her legs. "Miss Claire, Miss Claire!"

She called them all over to the table, explaining how their project would go. When they left, they would each have a canvas with their silhouette and five words of strength that described them. They all grinned, some with gaps, some still sporting the straight pearls of baby teeth, but each raising their hands with a "me, me, me" trying to score the position of going first.

Someone cleared their throat, and the familiar rumble skittered up her spine. She found Mitch sitting at the end of the table with a canvas in his hands. He waved at her with a sweet grin of his own, one that turned her heart inside out. "Miss Adams, I already have mine done. Would you like to see it?"

Blayne and Larkin approached, standing by the tree line with Maxine, Janice, Evette, and Tess linked arm-in-arm with eager expressions on their faces.

Her heart thumped in her chest with both panic and hope as she turned to take in the sight of the man she loved. His broad shoulders blocked out the band behind him, a look of earnest anticipation on his handsome face.

She bit her lip, trying to hide the smile that stretched her lips wide. And then made her best attempt at being aloof. "Well, I don't know, Mr. Brennan. Technically, I haven't set up the order in which the students can go yet."

One of the children yelled out, "That's okay, Miss Adams, we want to see what he has." All the other kids joined in their cries of agreement.

"It seems you have some fans, Mr. Brennan, so I guess it is only fair to see the work you've done."

She wasn't sure what he had in mind or what was going through that head of his. She had a hard time reconciling that he was sitting in front of her, though her eyes devoured him like Maxine's leftover moonshine.

He turned the canvas around, and she studied it, pulling in a shaky breath. It was the silhouettes of a woman with a crop of shoulder-length wavy hair. Underneath were the words *dedicated, generous, intelligent, loving, brave.*

She shook her head. She'd been far from brave; in fact, she could clearly see now what a coward she'd really been. It was humbling how much fear could steal from you if you let it.

"What are you doing here?" she whispered.

"Learning how to cope with my fears from a really talented woman."

Choosing her words carefully, she said, "Unfortunately, I can't help you. This is just an art class." Learning she wasn't going to be able to put her coping skills program forward had been crushing, but she wasn't about to give up so easily. Her activity today was an artistic endeavor, but it made the kids reflect on their strengths and not only verbalize them but put them on canvas for everyone to see. That kind of action was powerful and resonated within the brain in more than one way.

She was determined to find her path, even with its limitations. She had channeled her inner Mitch and decided not to care so much about what people thought and really focus on what she needed. And what she needed was to help the children of her town.

"Actually," he said, running a finger along the silhouette of her nose on the canvas, making her rub her own. He caught her in the act and smiled. "You'll be able to implement your Coping through Art program at the Cape center after all. However, there is a condition."

A whole different kind of hope, one that was found in a different area of her heart she didn't know existed, fluttered with the possibility of his words. "I don't understand."

"A colleague of mine from a past case agreed to supervise you, absorbing any liability risk that the Center would take on."

She opened her mouth to speak, her heart racing so fast she was afraid she'd pass out, but he put up a finger. "But only if you agree to go back and finish your degree like you've always wanted so that you can eventually take over the program and expand it as you see fit."

Fear and joy, self-doubts and determination, all swirled in her chest.

"I don't think—a"

He stood. "What do you want, Claire? Do you want to help the children, do you really want to serve this town in the way that you told me you did? Because if you really do, then you'll grab this opportunity."

"But there is no room in the budget to support a supervising psychiatrist."

"That has already been taken care of. The psychiatrist will be sponsored by a private practice law office that recently established itself in town."

Questions and confusion muddled her thinking, and she rubbed her forehead. Afraid to hope, afraid to dream, afraid to speak and make it all disappear.

"I'm staying, Claire. I passed up the opportunity in Portland, and I've opened a private law office here in town. I'm staying to fight for what I want. I am opening myself up to this town, and I am going to prove to you that risking the pain of losing for a love like ours is worth every bit of the risk."

Emotion lodged in her throat, and she worked to swallow around it. She wanted to throw her arms around him, but she was terrified of taking that step.

So he took it for her.

He walked around the table, removing the physical obstacle between them, but she didn't know how to make it better. So completely overcome with emotion, she simply stared.

Grabbing her hands, he pulled her close, settling her hips against his and sending a frisson of excitement through her body. "You're it for me, sweetheart. I'm terrified of hurting you, but that just means that I will work every day to make sure that doesn't happen."

His gaze roamed her face with an intensity that filled her heart. "But when I do, because it will happen, I promise to be there to make it better. I'll choose you and our life together in whatever form it takes every day." He released a breath. "I love you."

She was dizzy with emotion as she absorbed his words. "I know. And I'll do the same for you. I love you, too, Mitch. I kept telling myself not to, but here we are." She tried to swallow past the lump in her throat. "I was such a fool to think that loving you wasn't worth the risk or that I could possibly control it."

"You're stuck with me now. No turning back." His smile was full of satisfaction.

She squeezed his bicep to drive home the point and returned, "Never. You're mine."

"I don't deserve someone like you..."

She shook her head, but he placed a finger on her lips.

"I don't, but I want to. As a man who knows how to make a small moment special, you taught me the desire to cherish and embrace the big ones."

She pressed her lips against his with an urgent need to show him just how much she loved, admired, and wanted him. Her heart rejoiced. It was unlike anything she'd ever known before. Desperate and powerful, needy and generous.

As his lips slid along hers, she trailed her fingers along his shoulders to the back of his neck to keep him right where she wanted him.

In her arms.

He eased back just enough to smile down at her. "Claire, you are my big moment."

"And you're mine," she whispered.

EPILOGUE

*F*our months later...

"You have truly outdone yourself, my dear."

Emotion clogged Claire's throat at Maxine's praise. "I'm so glad you like it." She squeezed Mitch's hand tighter in her own. He returned the action, and her heart mirrored the love shining from his eyes.

She didn't know how much more love she could take.

"Like it? It's everything I never knew to dream for a winter wonderland wedding."

The judge and Maxine said their vows in an intimate ceremony at the courthouse, toasting the momentous occasion with a special brew of Maxine's moonshine. But the reception that followed was a city-wide affair at the town hall across from Van Buren square.

Maxine would have loved to have had her wedding at the new gazebo built by Ryker and Jay, but January was a bitterly cold month in Maine and waist-deep in snow. And there was no making that woman wait even one more month to unite with her Teddy bear.

The town hall was draped in white silks with large crystal snowflakes hanging from the beams. A pure white replica of the Cape house sculpted by the town's very own artist, Max Stanton, adorned the center of each bistro table, surrounded by deep purple gumdrops on velvets tablecloths.

Twinkle lights hung throughout the rafters and combined with the crystal snowflakes to cause a shimmering effect, almost as if snow was falling inside the Hall. Deliziosos catered the meal, North Cove Confectionery provided the amazing wedding cake that matched the party's motif, and the Flat Iron coffee-house kept the coffee pouring and the night going while Dine on the Vine filled wine glasses to the brim.

But of course, Maxine's own moonshine took center stage as party favors in mini cobalt blue canning jars.

Pride swelled in Claire's chest as she thought over the past four months. Judge Carter pulled some strings and got her a late acceptance into the local university's psych program to complete the remaining credits of her degree. She still had supervised hours that would need to be met before operating under her own license, but Mitch's contact, Dr. Warner, was overseeing her at the Center with her full-blown art therapy program.

She'd been so focused on the children that it hadn't occurred to her that many local adults needed the service as well until she took a hard look at herself and Mitch and what they had been through. And on top of that, she planned her greatest event yet.

The celebration of Judge Theodore Carter and Maxine Van Buren.

The Van Buren Tribune was covering the event, and the late founder's granddaughter, Sage Mathews was tucked in a corner, snapping photos.

Claire wanted to throw her arms out wide and do a little spin like a six-year-old in a candy store, but she kept her hand clasped tightly in Mitch's warm grip and pressed a kiss to his cheek instead.

"What's that for?"

"For teaching me how to make any moment a special one."

One of the Dawson triplets sighed with her fingers stacked in a hashtag. "Relationship goals right there."

Mitch laughed. "When are you and your sisters walking down the aisle?"

She guffawed, and the abrupt noise surprised Claire, coming from such a petite thing. "Not any time in this decade. It'll be all I can do in every twenty-four hours of a day to keep The Hide Away Inn afloat."

Ahhhh, Amber Dawson. Claire clasped the young woman's hand. "So, the rumors are true? Are you facing a buyout?"

The look of determination that crossed the young woman's face was admirable. "Some big luxury giant, Huntington Hotels...but not if I can help it. I have a plan, and no arrogant big city exec is going to come in and ruin our little secret paradise."

"If there's any way I can help, let me know." Mitch handed her a Brennan Law business card.

Amber directed her attention back to Jade. "My sister loves what you did with the wedding. I think she'd really like to team up on some projects at some point if you're willing. Your event skills with her eye for design would inspire more than one North Cove romance, that's for sure."

Pleasure tickled Claire to the point of bursting. "Tell her to call me anytime."

Amber raised a mini jar of moonshine. "You'll have to make sure you save up some great ideas for your wedding day."

Claire giggled, waving her hand in the air in dismissal as Amber Dawson made her way through the crowd.

"She's right you know."

She flashed him a teasing grin. "What makes you think I'd say yes?"

He pulled her tight against him, and her body immediately answered with a flash of *hell yes* that ran across the tips of her nerves like spider webbing.

"Because I'm going to cherish you in a way that will ruin the chances for any other man who tries." He gently slid a wisp of hair from her forehead. "But first I'm going to keep showing you just how important you are to me. There's no rush. We get to savor every phase of our relationship. Dating, fighting, make-up sex." He wiggled his brows. "Our engagement and marriage." He ran his lips across her jaw, sending a wash of goosebumps down her neck. "Our family."

She swallowed hard. "I'm afraid of getting pregnant. I don't want to hurt or disappoint you, but I'm afraid."

"Our family doesn't have to be like anyone else's. Maybe we'll have children when you feel strong enough."

She opened her mouth to speak, but he placed a soft finger on her lips.

He rested his forehead on hers. "Maybe we'll adopt. All you've ever wanted is to help children. Who needs our help more than those who don't have a family to love them? And if you're not ready for that, we have the children of Cape Van Buren. This whole town is our family. I love you, Claire."

Her heart expanded in her chest with so much emotion it was difficult to speak. "I'll never tire of hearing you say it. I love you. More than I ever thought possible."

She laid her head against his chest and swayed to the music, lulled by the warmth of his arms and the rhythm of his heart. She'd had love before, but this love was made of something different, something borne out of friendship first, out of despair, out of a need to serve.

She and Mitch would leave their mark on this town in a way that had her more excited than anything ever before.

"Sorry to interrupt you lovebirds, but are you ready to give your toast?" Maxine took her hand and led her to the front table, tapping a knife against the rim of a jar to get everyone's attention. "It's time for a toast!" She handed the mic to Claire.

Wrapping her fingers around the mic, she scanned the familiar, sweet faces of the crowd. "I've learned a lot over the past months. How to be brave, how to love in the face of fear...something I know we all struggle with." She glanced at the judge. "How to forgive with honor." And then to Maxine. "To love with an undeterred passion." And finally, to Mitch. "And how to make each moment matter. We don't know how long we have, who will stay in our lives or who will have to leave, so make each moment, no matter how simple...make it count."

She looked into the eyes of the man whose face she'd never tire of. "Cherish the loves of your life."

"And Maxine, one more thing..." With a wink at Larkin and Blayne, they doused their regal and sassy friend with a bucket of glittering male genital confetti, and Claire yelled, "Penis!"

Taking Mitch by the hand, she giggled at Maxine's squeal of delight and the laughter of the crowd.

She had a family to love, after all.

Did you love *Cherish on the Cape*? Reviews make a huge difference to an author's career. I would be extremely grateful if you are able to take a few seconds and leave a review on your favorite retailer!

Don't forget to join my mailing list for your **FREE** copy of *Honor on the Cape*, and for new release alerts, a monthly self-exam reminder, and NO spam! Visit my website to sign-up!

ALSO AVAILABLE IN THE ON THE CAPE SERIES

Love on the Cape
Honor on the Cape
Cherish on the Cape
Draw You In
One Jingle or Two
Love, Honor & Cherish: The On the Cape Trilogy

CONNECT WITH MK MEREDITH

Website
Twitter
Facebook
Instagram

ACKNOWLEDGMENTS

To my children and husband, otherwise known as my heart and soul, thank you for believing in me and always knowing I could do this even when I didn't. I love you. To my big brothers, Tommy, Todd, and Billy—as goofy as I am, you've always held me up. To Paula, my sister of the heart, I'm forever in awe of you. And to my mom, who's continued to mother me from the other side, I hope I have a fraction of your grace. Thank you.

Thank you to my editor KR Nadelson. Your insight and ability to really understand my story is truly a gift. Thank you. To my copy editor Jessica Snyder, you go above and beyond and are forever in my heart. Dawn Yacovetta, your eagle eye is priceless. Thank you all for being such an incredible team! Errors are inevitable but with your help my readers will be distracted by a lot less.

Thank you to the Romantics, your love lifts me up, and to my fan group, MK & CO, for your friendship and for believing in me. I love everyone in this family, from the very first to the still-to-come.

One more exuberant thank you to the readers of Cape Van Buren. I truly love this town. Experiencing life with you in this way is magical. I hope that at least one scene, one line, or simply one word resonates with each of you.

And to my sisters and brothers in the fight against breast and all types of cancer. I know both sides, having lost my mom to breast cancer at a young age, and having survived breast cancer myself…twice. My writing is one of the things that carries me through. I have many more books to write.

Thank you. Hugs, loves, and peanut butter,

MK

ABOUT THE AUTHOR

MK Meredith writes contemporary romance promising an emotional ride on heated sheets. She believes the best route to success is to never stop learning. Her lifelong love affair with peanut butter continues, and only two things come close in the battle for her affections: gorgeous heels and maybe Gerard Butler...or was it David Gandy? Who is she kidding? Her true loves are her husband and two children who have survived her SEAs (spontaneous explosions of affection) and lived to tell the tale. The Merediths live in the DC area with their large fur baby...until the next adventure calls.

www.mkmeredith.com

mk@mkmeredith.com

facebook.com/mkmkmeredith

twitter.com/mkmkmeredith

instagram.com/mkmkmeredith

bookbub.com/authors/mk-meredith

amazon.com/author/mk-meredith

ALSO BY MK MEREDITH

THE ON THE CAPE SERIES

Love on the Cape

Honor on the Cape

Cherish on the Cape

Draw You In

One Jingle or Two

Love, Honor & Cherish: The On the Cape Trilogy

THE SCRIPTED FOR LOVE SERIES

There's no place like paradise and the happy ever afters found in the film industry of Malibu, CA.

Love Under the Hot Lights

Just a Little Camera Shy

A Heated Touch of Action

THE INTERNATIONAL TEMPTATION SERIES

A strong dose of decadence along with a side of tall, dark, and sexy in your favorite travel destinations.

Playing the Spanish Billionaire

Seducing the Italian Tycoon

THE SEATTLE CRUSH SERIES

Seducing Seven

❧

STANDALONE TITLES

Not Your Usual Boob: The Good, Bad, and Wonky of Breast Cancer